Sourdough Creek

Caroline Fyffe

DEDICATION

For my dear nephew, Bryce Curtis Turner, who was taken from us too soon.

You are forever in our hearts.

.

ACKNOWLEDGMENTS

I'm grateful to so many incredible people for their help in creating Sam and Cassie's story. Theresa Ragan and Kayla Westra for brainstorming and plotting. Jenny Meyer, Faith Williams, Matt Fyffe and Emily Turner for editing and proofing. My wonderful critique partners, Sandy Loyd and Leslie Lynch, who give so generously of their time each week. My beta readers, Jennie Armento, Mariellen Lillard and Michael Fyffe for spotting plot holes and typos. Prospect Jewelers for schooling me about gold. My support team, all of whom mean the world to me, Mary Turner, Sherry Harm and Lauren Roe. Thank you to all of you! Your help and enthusiasm have made this journey from Broken Branch to Coloma and beyond, a pure joy.

As always, thank you to my treasured readers. You're the ultimate prize.

BOOKS BY CAROLINE FYFFE

Where the Wind Blows

Montana Dawn
Book One of The McCutcheon Family Series

Texas Twilight
Book Two of The McCutcheon Family Series

Sourdough Creek

Chapter One

Broken Branch, Nevada Territory, June 1851

"**I** don't want to call you Cassidy," Josephine announced boldly. Her eyes filled and her bottom lip wobbled. "You're Cassie. My *sister*."

Cassie almost winced at the distressed expression on her little sister's face. But there was no changing what had to be done. Time had run out. "From now on, and until I say different," she responded, looking into her sister's eyes to make her point known, "I'm Cassidy, your brother. Remember that."

Cassie smeared some dirt down Josephine's cheek and a tad more across her forehead for good measure. She rubbed a little on her own neck, too, just enough to seem as if she hadn't bathed in a good while.

Picking up shears, she lifted a handful of sun-colored locks from her sister's head and, with a sound akin to cutting wool, wacked it off one inch from the roots, leaving only thick stubble behind. A cry tore from her sister's throat as she pulled back.

"Sit still, Josephine. I've told you a hundred times this is only for a while." She sectioned off another portion and cut, unmindful of the tears running down Josephine's cheeks. "It'll grow back, when this is all over." The younger girl wiped her face with the back of her hand and nodded compliantly.

Forcing a smile, Cassie continued to cut. "I'll call you Joey. That's short for Joseph. It won't be so bad. Think of it— as a boy you can get away with all sorts of shenanigans. Remember Clarence? How he'd tell his ma lies and make rude noises? Well, I don't expect you to be fibbing, but being a boy does have some advantages."

Her little sister chewed on her bottom lip, considering her sister's words. "Can I spit and holler?"

"Sometimes."

Love lifted Cassie's chest. Josephine, only five, was strong and resilient. She was a survivor, a true testament to their ma's goodness. How Cassie wished her ma was here with them now. Every fiber of her being ached with the unbearable sadness of the loss.

Prickly heat burned behind Cassie's eyes but she willed the emotion away. She'd even appreciate the help of her Uncle Arvid, if he were around. Provided that he was sober. Despite being almost twenty years old, she wasn't used to being the sole decision maker of the family.

Finished, she helped Josephine, who now resembled a moth-eaten little muskrat, off the pine cupboard and set her on the floor. She held her by the shoulders and looked into her face. "Go put on the dungarees I altered for you. Use the cord for a belt."

Josephine's face was resolute, her beautiful hair already forgotten. Her gaze held all the trust in the world. *I wish she wouldn't do that.* A whirl of dread cramped Cassie's insides and she looked away from her sister's innocent blue eyes. "Go on now. Be quick. Make sure everything is in your satchel. There's not much time to cut my own hair before those good-for-nothing Sherman brothers show up."

She rubbed the top of Josephine's fluffy head. "And don't you go thinkin' you're the only special one, now, you hear?" Ignoring her request, Josephine stood rooted in place.

Cassie had no time to push her along. She propped the cracked mirror against the wall, angling it back and forth until she found her reflection. Gathering her waist length chestnut hair behind the nape of her neck, and before she could think twice, she cut it off just under her ears. The blunt remains swung loosely around her face. She swallowed, looking at her reflection. "There."

Josephine's eyes narrowed. "It ain't as short as mine."

Cassie picked up the mirror to get a closer look. "That's because I'm older. I'm tying it with a cord, like the older boys do." Replacing the mirror she took a thin strip of leather from her pocket and raked her hair back with her fingers, tying it in a knot, taut against her scalp.

Josephine scrunched her face. "It don't look too good."

"It's not supposed to. Question is, do I look like a boy?"

"Sorta."

Cassie plunked a tattered old hat on her head. "Now?"

Josephine nodded, wide-eyed.

"That's good enough, then. Run, put your clothes on. Time's short."

Cassie was just finished binding her smallish breasts and pulling her chemise over her head when a loud pounding sounded on the front door. Josephine came dashing into the room and threw her arms around her waist with the strength of Samson. "They're here!"

She peeled Josephine's arms from her body and quickly threaded her own arms into the bulky, green plaid shirt of her boy costume. "Go into Miss Hawthorn's bedroom and lock the door. Scoot under the bed and cover yourself with the quilt I put there, just like I showed you. Make sure nothing is sticking out. I'll call when the coast is clear."

"I don't want to leave you."

The doorknob rattled violently, jiggling back and forth. Josephine's eyes grew large and frightened.

Cassie wished she believed the words she was about to say. "Don't you worry a smidge," she whispered hurriedly. "We'll be eating cherry pie before you know it. Bristol Sherman isn't worth a barrel of monkeys. And neither is Klem. I'm way smarter than the two of 'em put together. Once I tell them Arvid Angel has moved on and took his nieces with him, they'll go away."

"What if they don't believe you?" Josephine asked quietly. "I wish Uncle hadn't made 'em mad by stealing Klem's watch."

"We're not even sure he did," Cassie replied, not wanting her sister to think their uncle was a thief. "You just stay put under the bed." She gave Josephine a little shove. "Go on, now."

When her sister's bottom lip wobbled, Cassie knelt down and pulled her into a comforting hug. Her little body was shaking uncontrollably. In a moment of painful clarity it occurred to Cassie that this could be it. *This could be goodbye*!

Cassie put her face just inches from Josephine's. "You know Psalm 23. I want you to say it to yourself over and over." When Josephine didn't move Cassie began, "'The Lord is my shep—'"

A pounding on the door rattled the room. Trying to ignore it, Cassie took Josephine's hands into her own and gave them a little shake. "Come on, sweetie, say it with me. 'there is nothing I lack.'" As Josephine's raspy little voice melded with her own, Cassie turned her sister's body toward Miss Hawthorn's room and gave an encouraging push. "Go on now and do as I say. Hurry."

Josephine moved away, her whispered words scarcely audible.

"And remember, be quiet as a mouse."

"I will, Cassie. I promise," she called in a small voice over her shoulder.

Cassie snatched her ivory cameo off the dresser, and with fumbling fingers pinned it to the bodice of her chemise, hiding it beneath the heavy shirt. She heard her mother's words as if she were standing here before her. "Take my guardian angel cameo. I pass it on to you."

Boot steps moved across the porch toward the parlor window. She cinched up the rope around her waist, making sure the knot was securely tightened. The pounding sounded again, but this time on glass with a force so great Cassie was sure it would break the pane.

Cassie hefted her pa's Colt 45 from the mantle and hooked it inside her pants on the rope belt, making sure her shirt concealed the bulge. "Hold your britches on," she shouted back crossly, forcing the deepest voice she could muster. "*I'm comin'!*"

Chapter Two

The sign read: Broken Branch, population 432.

Sam Ridgeway dismounted and stretched his legs. Turning to his horse, he flipped the stirrup over the saddle horn and gave a firm tug to loosen the cinch. A gentle breeze ruffled the gray mare's long black mane and stirred the leaves on the ground.

Sam ran his hand down her right foreleg and lifted it up. With his thumbs, he felt around the spongy frog at the center of her sole. Finding nothing suspicious, he covered her pastern with his palm and felt for warmth. Her shoe looked fine. On several occasions he'd felt Blu favor that foot, but nothing seemed amiss now, at least nothing he could discern. He'd have the blacksmith take a look as soon as he got a room and settled for the evening.

With the sun behind him, Sam tipped his hat back and took his first good look at Broken Branch. The town at the bottom of the hill was undistinguished. Consisting of several dusty streets with the usual commerce buildings and houses, it could be any of the half dozen places he'd ridden through of late. There wasn't a soul in sight.

6

"Hope there's a smithy," Sam said to his horse. His stomach let out a loud growl. "Not to mention a thick, juicy steak."

Unbuckling his chaps, he pulled them off and slung them over the saddle, and then ambled ahead.

Just then loud voices erupted, drawing his attention to a house a block off the main street. Two figures skittered around the large front porch in some kind of scuffle.

It didn't look life-threatening to Sam, so he decided to stick with his rule of keeping to himself. Appeared to be two kids, anyway. *Probably arguing over who had to clean out the chicken coop*, he thought with a lopsided smirk. The skinny one was fast as a jackrabbit, and all over the place. The taller of the two was cumbersome and slow, and would never in this life catch his quarry. What Skinny lacked in bulk he made up for in speed. Despite the fact it was actually quite entertaining, Sam looked away.

***

Cassie ducked under Klem's fist and darted behind a rocking chair, thankful the scoundrel had shown up alone. She'd already taken several painful punches to her body and didn't know how many more he'd land before bringing her down. She gasped for breath. This couldn't go on much longer. She was spent, hurting. It took every ounce of her energy just to lift her arms in defense. The tinny taste of blood inside her mouth made her want to retch. Things had gone from bad to worse and she needed to draw Klem away from the house, away from Josephine hiding under the bed, before giving up the fight. The gun, hooked inside her pants, was cumbersome, but she was glad she had it for a last resort. Maybe he'd listen to reason if he were looking down its barrel.

Reaching for her shirt, Klem tripped over the spittoon Miss Hawthorn had out for her boarders' convenience. His boot caught and he fell to his knees, knocking his head against the porch railing with a crash.

Without thinking, Cassie leaped over him, trying to reach the porch stairs. In mid-air his hand shot up and gripped her ankle. *Too late*! He'd been playing possum. They rolled together towards the stairs and bumped down into the dirt.

Adrenalin kept her scratching, punching, and squirming to get free. With his overpowering weight, Klem rolled her to her back and sat on top of her, forcing the air out of her lungs. He pinned her arms up over her head as sweat from his face dripped onto her own, running down her neck.

If only the gun would go off!

It would splatter his family jewels from here to kingdom come. Didn't matter if it killed her too; it'd be worth it.

Klem reared back, raising a doubled fist, his eyes filled with rage. "Tell me where Cassie is, you little skunk!"

Gunshots rang out and bullets kicked up dirt all around. Clasping her eyes closed, Cassie prepared to meet her maker. Klem's brother Bristol must have shown up for the party.

"Fun's over," a deep voice called out. "Get off him."

At the sound of the shots, Klem had collapsed onto her in a shocking show of cowardice. A moan gurgled from his throat. "I'm hit," he shrieked, looking at his hands in disbelief. "I'm bleeding, I'm bleeding."

Cassie tried to extract herself from under his heavy body, but was pinned. "Stop your sniveling." She gasped for air. "That's my blood on your hands, not yours."

Klem crawled to his knees and stood, wiping dirt and debris from his clothes. He eyed the stranger as he approached.

"What the devil is going on here?" the man asked through clenched teeth. He dropped his reins and left his horse standing as he approached. Offering Cassie his hand, he pulled her to her feet.

Klem was backing away when the man turned on him. Grasping him by the front of his shirt, he yanked Klem up close to his face.

"Never could abide bullies like you." He motioned with his head toward Cassie. "That boy weighs less than a bantam."

Suddenly, Klem took an awkward swing at the cowboy, who easily caught his arm and twisted it around his back, shoving it upward. Then the man pushed Klem away with such force he fell to his knees in a puff of dust, pitching forward and landing flat on his face. He came up spitting dirt from his mouth.

"You ought to mind your own business, mister," Klem mumbled. He climbed to his feet.

"Really?"

The one word, delivered with such controlled fury, sent shivers down Cassie's spine and she took a tiny step back, giving him space. Time stood still as he enforced his own patience. Then, with measured movement, he rolled up the sleeves of his white broadcloth shirt and stood with his fists tensed at his sides.

"What I *ought* to do," the stranger replied, "is give you a taste of what you were about to give this young boy. How would you like to take on somebody *my* size?"

Cassie couldn't help but hope this tall newcomer would make good on his offer. *Yes, beat Klem to a pulp! Make him beg for mercy!* The warm blood flowing from her nose went forgotten. Inwardly she cheered. Finally, someone strong enough to stand up to Klem!

Her nemesis shrank before her eyes. His shoulders drooped and he looked everywhere but at the man. He was a whipped dog getting ready to slink away from his master.

"Well?"

"Nah." Klem shook his head.

"Then apologize."

Klem's face flamed.

"Do it or take the consequences." The stranger took off his hat and handed it to her.

"I apologize."

As soon as the words were out the coward turned and stormed down the boardwalk, around the corner and out of sight.

Now Cassie was the object of the stranger's intense brown eyes. By the way he was looking at her she thought for sure he'd ask why a girl was masquerading around as a boy. Earlier, when she'd confronted Klem on the porch of the boarding house, she'd been shocked that he'd fallen for her ruse. He and his brother, Bristol, knew her and Josephine as they all lived in the same town. Just went to show how stupid he was.

He didn't ask, though. Instead, he retrieved his hat from her hands and refastened his shirt cuffs. He looked embarrassed.

"This happen a lot?"

Stung, Cassie squared her shoulders. "No." She swiped at her bloody nose with the back of her hand.

"You should get cleaned up. Where do you live?"

Cassie hitched her head toward the boarding house and made her way to the steps. When she lifted her foot a sharp pain sliced through her side and she gasped.

Instantly, the cowboy was there, gingerly placing her right arm over his shoulder and snaking his left carefully around her middle. When their bodies connected, confusion marked his face for a moment. She turned away quickly as she felt her face go hot. Still, he held her steady as they climbed the stairs and she fumbled with the key in the lock.

Chapter Three

Josephine met Cassie at the door, tears running down her cheeks. She shook her fist in the air. "I'll beat Klem Sherman to a pulp! He's a *no* good, lily-livered—"

"Joey!" Cassie scolded. "Be quiet. I'm not hurt much." She wiped her nose again. "It looks worse than it is."

"Why, if he came back right now I'd..." Josephine was circling around Cassie, punching and kicking as if she were fighting Klem at that very moment. Her dungarees nearly tripped her, and she tottered for balance. "Break his nose and tar and feather his mangy, ugly, smelly hide. He's no good! No good, ya hear!"

Cassie glanced at the stranger standing silently in the doorway. His brows were raised and his lips tipped up in amusement. Josephine, with arms still flailing dramatically, jabbed at their cat, Ashes, who was crouched on an overstuffed parlor chair. She missed the startled animal's nose by a half inch. The cat leaped from her perch, scrabbled on the hardwood floor, and disappeared into the other room.

Cassie bristled at the stranger's amusement. Josephine's passionate show of love and protection was sweet. Poor thing must've snuck from under the bed and watched Klem's vicious attack from the window. She wished she could comfort her little sister, understanding that fear was her motivation, not bravado. But she didn't dare; it might give them away.

"Just settle down," she said, her voice harsh from pain and apprehension. "It's barely even a bloody nose."

Josephine froze at the curt, unfamiliar command. Her confused expression said it all. She backed away, perplexed.

Cassie didn't have time at the moment to worry about Josephine's hurt feelings. She'd promised their mama just moments before she'd died that she'd watch over Josephine, take good care of her, never leave her. She had to be smart and strict.

She limped into the kitchen and over to the sink, working the pump handle until water gushed forth. Catching some with her trembling hands, she held it to her face, turning the water red. Oh, it felt wonderfully good. And cool.

The cowboy stepped forward, reaffirming his presence. "Where is everybody?" he asked, glancing out the kitchen door into the parlor where the hall led to several guest rooms. "Seems pretty deserted around here."

"Most everyone's gone." Cassie held a dishtowel to her face gingerly, not caring if it stained. She applied light pressure under her nose as she hobbled to a chair and sat. "Just a few people left besides us and the Shermans."

"Klem Sherman was the one doing the fightin'. His big brother Bristol is bad too," Josephine said, standing close beside her chair.

He smiled at Josephine, this time a real smile, bringing lightness to his face. His eyes narrowed with pleasure and his face took on a whole different look. Inviting.

Even at her tender age, Josephine, turning shy, ducked her head at his attention, an obviously feminine response to a handsome man.

"Who is this young lad?" he asked Cassie with a nod toward her little sister.

Was he blind?

Even with short, ragged hair, her diminutive form encased in well-worn dungarees and grime smeared on her face, Josephine was the epitome of little-girl sweetness.

"My brother, Joey," came her dumbfounded reply. "And I'm Cassidy. Cassidy Angel."

At the name, the man straightened. It was obvious to Cassie he was pondering his next move, as sure as Ashes mused which end of a mole hole to watch.

He extended his hand to her. "Nice to make your acquaintance, Cassidy," he said, as she took his hand firmly in her own. "And you too, Joe." He looked from one to the other, his face softening even more as he shook his head in astonished disbelief. "I'm Sam Ridgeway. Any chance you're related to Arvid Angel?"

Cassie's instincts flashed on high alert. Was Uncle Arvid is some sort of trouble? He'd been here week before last, but she hadn't seen him since. That didn't mean he wouldn't show up tomorrow.

Still dazed from the fight, Cassie couldn't decide if it would be better to acknowledge their relationship or keep quiet.

"Arvid's our uncle," Josephine announced in her gravelly little girl's voice. Now that she wasn't shadowboxing the cat, her speech was back to normal, the likeness to stones rolling around on sand paper. Brightness flashed back into her blue eyes at being able to help. She blushed.

"Your uncle?" A single-minded grin spread across his face. "I've been looking for him. He around?"

Cassie gave Josephine a no-nonsense glare, promising swift punishment if she said another word. "No, mister, he's gone. We haven't seen him for some time."

Sam Ridgeway came forward and pulled out a chair, making himself comfortable. Resting his elbows on his thighs, he leaned forward and looked at Cassie intently, his hat dangling in his fingertips. "I've been trying to hook back up with him for a few weeks now. You sure he didn't say where he was headed?"

Cassie shrugged. "Can't help you."

He regarded her closely for a moment. "Town's quiet. Where did everyone go?"

He was giving up too easy, making her more suspicious than ever. She dabbed at her nose with the cotton cloth in her hand, thinking.

"The Lucky North, that's the mine that kept this town alive, closed up three months ago," she mumbled through a sore jaw. With trembling fingers, she felt around her puffy nose. "Since the vein went dry, people have been leaving here, thirty to forty a week. For the past two days I've only seen a handful of townsfolk. No more stagecoach either." She stood and went back to the sink, rinsing out the towel.

"What about your ma and pa?"

"Our ma died a few months back," she replied, shoving the memories aside. "The doctor thought it was typhoid fever. Our pa has been gone over a year."

He studied her a moment longer. "How do you make your way?"

"Odd jobs. Most for Miss Hawthorne, the owner of this boarding house, before she packed up and left."

"She let us live here, too," Josephine added.

"If the town is all but dead, as you say, what're you planning to do? Stay here alone?"

Josephine had quietly inched closer to Mr. Ridgeway, obviously curious about him. Cassie was fearful of what might pop out of her sister's mouth next. Until she figured out their next move she couldn't chance Josephine giving away too much information.

"Joey, go find Ashes. It wasn't nice how badly you scared her."

A cloud swept across Josephine's face. She hurried out of the room calling the cat's name.

"Didn't want to talk in front of my little brother," Cassie said. "Don't want to worry him."

Sam looked interested.

"We're leaving, too. Tomorrow. To California. It's a state now, you know."

He nodded.

"We're headed to the abundance of gold in the American River." Cassie was surprised when Sam Ridgeway remained silent. His eyes narrowed infinitesimally.

"Won't take but six months to make what a grown man does in a lifetime," she added, a niggle of anxious energy sprouting within her as he continued to stare. "Then we'll have enough funds to do anything we want." Her voice caught. Her mother's dream was to start a bakery and stay in one place forever. Irked with herself for getting emotional, she covered her face with the cloth and sat back, closing her eyes.

She wanted a reaction from him. A question. Something! "Me and Joey will start a bakery."

Sam's chuckle went straight to her heart. She tried to stay her temper.

"Everyone's got to eat, don't they, Mr. Ridgeway? Just cause we're boys doesn't mean we can't cook! Our family recipe will make us famous and we won't ever have to depend on anyone," she said through the cloth. "All this from the nuggets we find."

Usually any talk of gold made men crazy with excitement. They'd get wound up and while away the hours, night and day, drinking and carrying on about how they would be the next one to strike it rich, hit a bonanza, discover the mother of all veins. Certainly, the men in Broken Branch did.

The reality was quite the opposite: backbreaking, life-wrecking work that seldom paid off. Still, she and Josephine had little choice but to try, even if it was a dangerous idea. Especially for a little girl. Without family and with little money, their only option was to go forward and hope.

An inexplicable urge to chatter on gripped her. *Why the heck didn't he say something?* Just like the dim-witted men she'd just been thinking about, she blurted, "Coloma. Ever heard of it?"

She removed the rag from her face and stared back at him, refusing to say another word until he responded.

For several heartbeats he sat quietly, dropping his gaze down to the hat dangling in his hands. Then, with a slow, deliberate movement, he set it crown side down on the tabletop and nodded.

"Sure I have. As a matter of fact, I'm headed there myself."

Chapter Four

At last! Sam couldn't believe it. Cassidy and Joey had to have the deed to his claim on Sourdough Creek. There could be no other explanation why Arvid's relatives would be headed to Coloma. Somehow they'd gotten it from the fraud. But—his conscience gave him pause as he looked into Cassidy's surprised face. Could he live with himself afterward? Retrieving the claim back from Arvid—lying, thieving skunk that he was—was one thing, but now that he'd met his two nephews, who were so young and innocent, that was another thing entirely.

What the heck was he thinking? Of course he could! The claim was his. It wasn't stealing to take back what rightfully belonged to him. Arvid Angel had lifted the claim from his saddlebag as he'd slept: stolen it outright after he'd won it from the Swede in a hand of seven-card stud. It was going to provide the money needed to start his ranch. Taking it back wasn't going to bother his conscience one iota.

Besides, a claim on a river was no place for children, especially two as young as Cassidy and Joey. They wouldn't last a fortnight out there alone. It was for their own good to spare them that danger.

At Sam's pronouncement, Cassidy looked as if he'd just bitten into a lemon. His eyes bulged and his face turned crimson. Sam almost laughed.

"I'm not surprised you're headed to California with all the gold being scooped out of the cold waters of the American these days," he said. "Everyone's doing it. But what a coincidence that I should meet up with the two of you the day before you set out upon your way. My dear friend's nephews. What a twist of fate. We'll go together. It's safer traveling in a group."

Before the boy could respond, his little brother was back, carrying the dark gray cat they called Ashes. He set the feline on a chair and stroked her fur from head to tail.

Once again doubt darkened Sam's thoughts. Did he really want to be responsible for this boy's life? Cassidy must be around fifteen or so, but little Joe was really young—and would be a huge responsibility. Any number of things could happen.

Joey turned his immense blue eyes on Sam. "Cassie...*dee* is going to make a cherry pie today. Miss Hawthorn left behind her last bag of dried cherries, just for us. Do you want to stay and have some? She—" Joey stopped hard and shook his head, "*he* makes really good pie."

Sam couldn't stop the laughter that burst out. Cassidy's incensed expression fueled his amusement. The little one sheepishly ducked his face at calling his brother a girl, even though it was highly understandable. The small, sinuous young man with his slim hips and chiseled face was probably taken for a girl more often than not. And heck, the little one was talking about baking a pie, after all.

"Cherry pie?" he choked out, biting the inside of his cheek to quell his laughter. He coughed into his hand, but not before humiliation flickered across Cassidy's face.

Darn! He'd hurt the boy's feelings—again. He hadn't intended to. "Cherry pie, why, that's my favorite. I have a few things I need to take care of first. When I get back maybe the pie will be baking. Can't say that I'd enjoy anything more. Thank you. That's a hospitable offer."

He stood. "But, only if it's good with you, Cassidy. Then we can discuss our plans and route to California. By my calculations it won't take us more than a week, give or take a couple of days, to get there."

Joey's mouth dropped open at this pronouncement.

"That's right, son," Sam declared with enthusiasm, chucking Joey under the chin. "We're going to Coloma together. California, here we come!"

He went to the door and put his hat on. Cassidy and Joey followed. "Since almost everyone's left town, I guess you don't have a blacksmith anymore."

Cassidy found his voice. "We do. Bristol Sherman is a smithy of sorts. You'll find his shop on the corner of the next street over. He might be able to help you, but be warned. The Shermans are capable of just about anything. I wouldn't trust either of them at all."

"Appreciate the warning. You sure you're up to it? The pie I mean," Sam added, his hand on the doorknob.

Cassidy's chin tipped up in defiance.

"I promised Joey I'd make him a pie before we left Broken Branch."

Sam felt another stab of guilt about the whole situation, but it wasn't enough to prompt him to ride off and leave them with his rightful claim. "Well, I'll be looking forward to it, for certain."

The second the door closed Josephine threw her arms around Cassie's middle. "I'm sorry I invited him to pie. I'm sorry I called you a girl. I'm so stupid!"

"Hush now. You're not stupid. You're a very smart girl. We've just been put into, I don't know, a dreadfully bizarre situation." Ashes, winding her way through the legs of her mistresses, meowed her support. Josephine let go of her sister to pick the cat up.

"What about poor Ashes after we're gone?" Josephine asked, scratching the cat under the chin. The cat purred, closing her eyes. "What will become of her?" Josephine frowned in worry as she rubbed her cheek against the cat's warm coat.

"I've already told you she can't go. Cats are afraid of horses." Looking at Ashes in Josephine's arms almost broke Cassie's heart. If there was a way to keep the cat safe she'd take her along. Their ma had brought her home as a kitten after their father's passing, to make them feel better, and she was a dear friend to both of them. But, a long trip in the wilderness would be a death sentence to her. Cassie had more than enough to worry about now. No, Ashes would be safer here in town. "She'd most likely get scared off and lose her way. You don't want her to be supper for some hungry coyote, do you?"

Cassie limped back to the kitchen with Josephine tagging behind. Baking was the last thing she felt like doing right now. She'd much rather lie down in a dark room with a cool rag on her face.

"Ashes will be much better off staying here where she knows her way about and can feed on mice," she added, trying to make the betrayal sound better in her own mind.

"I wonder how that fella knows Uncle?" Josephine asked, still holding the cat.

"That's a good question," Cassie responded, assembling her baking tools. She used two knives to deftly cut lard for the crust. This was the secret recipe her grandmother had passed down to her mother years ago, the one that would be the foundation of their bakery. "But until we know the answer or exactly what he's up to, I don't want you talking to him about anything. Especially stuff to do with our family or the gold claim. Or Uncle Arvid. Do you understand, Josephine? He could be trouble."

At Josephine's look of distress Cassie quickly added, "But I don't think he is. We just have to be cautious. He seems like a good man. He's clean. Has all his teeth. He's good looking and has a nice smile." At the reality of how handsome he really was, butterflies fluttered in Cassie's chest. She glanced at her sister who was nodding her agreement.

"And he *did* help when Klem was lightin' into you," Josephine added in Sam's defense. "He was actually rolling up his sleeves to fight him. He didn't have to do that."

Cassie scooped a cup of flour into the bowl and added a little water. "You're exactly right: he sure didn't. But then, looks *can* be deceiving. A wolf in sheep's clothing, as ma used to say."

Josephine pulled out a chair and climbed up, standing on the seat of it so she was eye to eye with her sister. "Sort of like us?" she asked innocently. "Are we like wolves in sheep's clothing, pretending to be boys?"

Josephine had her there. They were being about as truthful with Sam Ridgeway as she suspected Sam Ridgeway was being with them.

"You make a good point. But I'm not sure it's quite the same. Time will tell." Cassie took a moment to smile, even if drawing her lips up into what felt like a grotesque grin sent hot slivers of pain radiating about her face. "I think you might be a politician when you grow up."

Josephine smiled back. "A politician or a showgirl. I haven't decided." Josephine curtsied and twirled around, careful not to fall off the chair. It was a silly sight given her boy get-up.

Cassie raised her eyebrows, surprised. "A showgirl?"

"I like their shiny dresses with all the pretty feathers. And their ruby red lips."

Good Lord, no! I promised Ma I'd take care of her! "How in the world do you know about all that?"

"Fannie at the Paper Doll."

Cassie's face warmed. "Well—fine. Let's concentrate now on getting to California. There's plenty of time later to think about that."

Chapter Five

Sam found the smithy deserted. He tied Blu to the hitching rail and ventured around back, where he found a rundown shanty that listed to one side.

"Hello—anyone home?" he called, feeling uneasy. It was less than an hour since he'd sent Klem packing. It wasn't hard to believe the boy would still be nursing a grudge.

"What the devil *you* want?" came a whiny reply from inside. "We're closed to vermin like you."

The sounds of a scuffle penetrated the paper-thin walls. Moments later a medium-sized man dressed in overalls appeared at the door. His messy hair and bloodshot eyes shouted hangover.

This must be Bristol, Klem's older brother, thought Sam, who'd already decided he'd look after his mare himself before allowing either Sherman to lay a finger on her. Instead, he was looking to see if the blacksmith had a horse for sale.

"Name's Bristol Sherman." He slurred his words between his teeth. "What can I do ya for?"

"I'm looking to buy a horse."

At the prospect of making a buck, Bristol's eyes lit with interest. He stumbled down the step and toward the barn. "Anything special?"

"Just something to get me down the trail."

Sam followed the man into the dark interior of the barn. Urine vapors, wafting from stalls long overdue for a mucking, burned his eyes.

A horse snorted. Sam glanced into the closest stall. A tall bay munched on hay and eyed him sleepily. He had a nice head and straight legs. A darn fine looking animal, in fact.

"How much you want for this horse?"

"He ain't for sale. The gelding in the next stall over."

Bristol picked up a broken stool leg leaning against the wall and proceeded to the stall door. As if on cue, the horse inside lunged at him, snorting and shaking his head. Bristol lifted the weapon in a threatening manner. "Get on back!"

"This horse? He's not only nasty but the ugliest animal I've ever seen."

"Take him or leave him."

Sam didn't have much choice. For Blu's foot to heal she needed time without him on her back. The only way for that to happen was if he could secure a second mount.

"How much?"

"Thirty."

Obviously Bristol was starting high so he'd have room to haggle. When the man turned away the horse lunged again, baring his big teeth. Sam jumped back and Bristol fell over a bucket into the straw.

"Damn! You should pay *me* to take him off your hands."

Bristol climbed to his feet and began brushing the straw from his overalls. "He ain't as bad as he seems. Once he's caught up he's gentle as a lamb."

Sam could see in the horse's eyes that he'd been mishandled and abused. Hatred for Bristol burned in them, too.

Bristol must have sensed his sale slipping away and added, "He rides real nice. Twenty and your horse in trade."

Sam gazed out the door, thinking. What were his choices? If he waited for Blu's foot to heal, Cassidy and the gold claim would be long gone. He needed that gelding to carry him, not win a beauty contest.

"I'll give you ten and not a nickel more."

"Ten, plus your horse."

"Ten."

Bristol hacked up some sputum. "I'll take your horse in trade. No extra money."

"It'd be a cold day in hell before I sold her to the likes of you," Sam said, looking one more time into the stall. The deadly click of a gun being cocked resounded. Anger with himself burst through Sam's mind. He turned to find Bristol Sherman's weapon leveled at his chest. Cassidy had been right! He'd walked right into their snake pit, even after the boy's clear words of warning.

Bristol laughed. "That mare of yours will bring me a pretty dollar, yes indeed. Haven't seen horseflesh so fine in a long, long time."

A shot rang out. Dirt kicked up between Bristol's boots. Both men reacted and Sam had his gun drawn before he hit the ground.

"I *know* for a *fact* you gave Miss Hawthorn three dollars for that horse not more than two weeks ago!"

Sam recognized Cassidy's voice calling from some hidden spot in the livery yard where he'd gotten a clear shot through the barn door. The boy must have anticipated trouble and followed him.

"That Cassie Angel can take a hike!" Bristol growled nastily. "That girl is a thorn in my side." His face turned a dark burgundy. "*Hawthorn owed me money!*" he shouted back. "Gave him to me for a good deal in payment for something else. Ain't none of your business, anyway!"

For a moment Sam was confused. Then realization dawned. A tidal wave of embarrassment washed over him and his face tingled with warmth. Now the large green eyes and slim body made perfect sense! Something hadn't rung true about that boy, but Sam hadn't figured it out. Today when he'd offered his help at the steps of the boarding house and their bodies had touched, he'd felt a surge of something, scaring the heck out of him. Relief flooded now and he stifled a laugh.

Sam stood and motioned with his gun for Bristol to throw his to the side. Bristol complied and climbed to his feet.

"I'll still give you ten," he said to Bristol. "And a couple more for a bridle. You know that's more than fair. And I'll forget you drew on me, too."

"Deal."

Sam took a leather pouch from his pocket and fished out the money. "You catch him up and saddle him. I want to see you ride him down the street." He wasn't going to get his neck broken when he was so close to getting the claim back.

Bristol shrugged and went into the stall, rope in hand while Sam retrieved his saddle off Blu. After a loud commotion, Bristol emerged leading the horse. It was true. The gelding seemed quite docile.

27

Bristol smiled revealing a row of stained and broken teeth. "Jist like a little lamb."

Now, out in the open, Sam could hardly bear to look. The gelding was the ugliest, ewe-necked animal he'd ever laid eyes on. His sizable Roman nose went unpleasantly well with little pig eyes. When Bristol threw the blanket and saddle on the gelding's back, the animal pinned his ears. The left ear, split down its middle, was his brand. Sam had seen brandings of the like before, but didn't agree with them. No need to mutilate a horse to mark him. The horse sucked in air as Bristol tightened the cinch, using the old trick in an attempt to keep the saddle from being properly secured. His one redeeming quality was his color—a nice liver chestnut—and his white markings—wide white blaze, and four white socks. It didn't matter what he looked like, Sam thought, as long as he was broke to ride.

Sam wondered if Cassidy—Cassie, he corrected himself, was still around, hiding. Bristol must not know that she was masquerading as a boy. She'd fooled his brother Klem a short time ago. Was she doing it to avoid the two men?

Bristol mounted. He thunked the horse's side and loped down the deserted street and back. Then, dismounting, he handed the reins to Sam. "Pleasure doing business."

"He have a name?"

Bristol pointed to the animal's head. "Split Ear."

Taking the gelding's reins and gathering up Blu, Sam walked down the street toward the boarding house. So, his skinny little friend was really a girl. What a surprise. Sam felt stupid for not seeing through the deception on his own. He had to admit it was good thinking on her part to follow him over. No telling what might have happened if she hadn't.

At Hawthorn's Boarding House, Sam turned Blu out into a corral. He unsaddled Split Ear, and for the moment set his rig on the top of the fence rail. The horse cast a disgruntled look his way and pinned his ears. With a chuckle, Sam gave him a rub on the neck, and then turned him out, too. The gelding cautiously made his way toward the mare that was cropping away at the green grass.

Leaning against the weathered boards of the corral, Sam removed his hat to feel the cool breeze in his hair and on his face. He glanced at the quiet house. He'd play along with Cassie for a while—until he could figure out what she was up to. One thing troubled him, though. Taking the claim back into his possession didn't feel quite as simple now as it had an hour ago.

Chapter Six

Cassie peeked out the kitchen window as Sam turned his mare out, noticing that he took extra time with the new gelding. He seemed gentle with his animals, a good sign for any man. Then, when the gelding laid his ears back in warning, Sam's lips tipped up into a lopsided grin, as if he understood the horse's edginess in a new place. Surprisingly, like a perceptive father might do, Sam stroked the cranky horse's neck anyway.

Cassie's cover gave her time and the proximity to finally get a good look at Sam Ridgeway without seeming curious. He was tall and muscular. His profile was distinctive, with a strong jaw, high forehead and ample eyebrows. His expression, when not threatening to thrash a body, was contemplative and calm and seemed more than a little intelligent. A mild breeze played with the fringes of his brown hair, and when he looked up at the house, it tousled over his forehead in a boyish manner.

"Should I go feed the horses?" Josephine asked from the other side of the room. Cassie, embarrassed at being caught looking, felt her cheeks tingle with warmth. "Good idea. Pepper and Meadowlark will be sorely put out if you don't hurry. Supper will be ready when you get back."

"Is it biscuits and gravy again? I'm tired of them. That's all we ever eat."

"Have you forgotten so quickly? There's cherry pie for dessert. And, I'll open the last can of corn syrup for the biscuits. You always like that, right?" Josephine's eyes lit with pleasure as she ran from the room.

As she watched her sister go, a longing so deep swept over Cassie, almost stealing her breath. "I'm trying my best, Ma. I am. But, things have gotten a bit complicated. I hope I'm doing the right thing going to California. It's hard to know."

Taking this opportunity of quiet, she went into the bedroom and shut the door. From her satchel she took out the Bible that had belonged to her mother and her mother's mother before that. Opening it, she withdrew the deed to the claim Uncle Arvid had left in her dresser drawer, and set it aside. She thumbed through the pages until she reached a yellow, dog-eared page. In the dim light, a tingle slipped down her spine knowing her mother and grandmother had read the exact same verse at some trying time in their lives. That thought alone bolstered her confidence. "For I am convinced," she read quietly, "that neither death, nor life, nor angels, nor principalities, nor present things, nor future things, nor powers, nor height, nor depth, nor any other creatures will be able to separate us from—" She stopped reading as voices were heard in the kitchen. Sam and Josephine must be back.

She finished the sentence and replaced the deed into the Bible and closed it. A moment passed. "Ma," she said into the stillness of the room. "I'm relying on my own smarts, just like you told me. I won't forget what you said about men, no matter how good intentioned they seem, that they will only let me down, and—" she stumbled to a stop. She hated to remember that her mother had told her that her father was a liar. What a horrible thing. But she knew her mother had felt a need to warn her and Josephine when she was dying and they were going to be on their own. "I'll remember your words, Ma, I will. I know they were hard for you to say. I'll do my best for Josephine, I promise."

Cassie returned to the kitchen to find Sam and Josephine setting the table for supper. The pot of thin gravy she'd put on the stove earlier was bubbling gently. "You don't have to set the table, Mr. Ridgeway. Joey is capable."

"Call me Sam," he said, setting a napkin and fork beside each plate Josephine placed on the tablecloth. "We're going to be traveling together so there's no need to be so formal. Since you're kind enough to feed me, I'm going to help."

"That's just it. We're not going to California with you. We want to take our time and I'm sure you're in a hurry." That was the only fib she could think of to get him off their backs. When Sam stopped what he was doing and looked her way, she avoided his gaze by grasping the long wooden spoon and stirring the pot.

"That's nonsense. I'd never hear the end of it if I didn't extend a helping hand to Arvid's kin. And besides, you just saved my hide from Bristol Sherman. He was in a mind to kill me for my horse. I owe you and won't take no for an answer. I'll be your guide and guardian."

She placed the bowl filled with biscuits on the table, next to the can of sweet corn syrup and pitcher of milk. Miss Hawthorn had sold her cow for traveling expenses just days before, but the leftover milk and a crock of butter she'd kindly given to the girls. They'd been using them sparingly. The milk, kept in the root cellar, was on the verge of spoiling.

Cassie searched her mind for another reason not to travel with Sam but knew it would sound contrived if she made a bigger fuss about the arrangement. It made more sense for them to go together than for her to argue. She and Josephine needed to get out of Broken Branch. Maybe trusting him for a few days wouldn't be all that bad.

"Well, sit yourself down. It's ready."

Sam and Josephine sat and Cassie passed the bowl of biscuits. She poured a little milk into Josephine's glass, but Sam declined.

Sam took a bite of biscuit and chewed, prompting Cassie to pass him the pot of gravy. "They're dry without this, Sam. Have some."

"Or you can put corn syrup on 'em," Joey added. "I like that the best."

Silence fell around the table as the three ate hungrily, not slowing down until every biscuit and all the gravy was gone.

"What do you do?" Cassie asked finally, looking at Sam.

Sam glanced up from his plate. He scooted his chair back and stretched out his legs.

"I'm a rancher."

"Cattle?"

"No. Horses. That is, in the future when I buy the land I need and get my breeding stock. My mare is bred for working cattle. A horse many men would pay good money for."

A sizzling sound came from the oven.

"The pie!" Josephine shouted.

Sam lunged for two dishtowels lying on the drain board. He opened the oven door and stuck his hands inside as bubbly syrup overflowed the crust and spilled onto the hot cast iron. Steam hit him in the face but he held onto the pie tin, unwilling to give up the prize without a fight.

"Careful. Careful! Don't get burned," Cassie cautioned. He felt her hovering behind him, looking over his shoulder. He was amazed at himself for ever having believed she was a boy, even for a second.

Heat seared through the dishtowels and the pie bobbled in his hands. He straightened quickly and swung around, looking for a spot to drop it.

"Here," screamed Joey, pointing to an open spot on the counter. "Here. Here. Put it here."

He did. With a shove. It came to a halt with half the pie teetering over the edge of the counter.

Cassie's face flushed with surprise. Her eyes glowed with astonished pleasure that he'd saved the pie. When she laughed, happiness filled Sam's chest. He had to drag his gaze away from her face before he gave himself away. This was going to be one long trip to California, no doubt about it. And he was looking forward to every step of the way.

Chapter Seven

"You saved the pie!"

Cassie fussed over the sweet pastry as a mama cat does over her kittens. She'd forgotten her manly Cassidy façade entirely for the moment, her eyes sparkling with delight and her laughter filling the room. She moved the bubbling-hot dessert from the edge of the drain board and put it on the sill of the open window to cool.

Sam was waiting for realization to hit her as she brushed some tendrils from her forehead. "I was just so sure you were going to drop it," she said on a breath, looking over at him. "I can't imagine how hot that was." She gazed at the pie and fanned it with her napkin. "It would have been just dreadful if it'd been smashed to bits on the floor."

"I can't argue with that," Sam replied, captivated by her pretty face.

"Cassie...*dee*," Joey spoke up for the first time since the hullabaloo had settled down. "It looks yummy even if the edges are burnt some." The boy poked at the blackened crust with a small finger.

When Joey fumbled her name again, Cassie turned from Sam's gaze to compose herself. Her boy façade slid down over her lovely features as she remembered her masculine pretense.

"Is it cool enough? Can we have a slice?" Joey asked eagerly.

"Not for a while yet, little brother," she replied, this time with the deeper voice. "Help me get the kitchen cleaned up first and by the time we're done, it'll be ready."

Both Sam and Joey cleared the dishes from the table as Cassie pumped water into the dishpan.

"Sam," she said over her shoulder, "why don't you pick a room down the hall. They're all empty except the last. That's Joey's and mine."

The clock over the parlor mantel chimed seven times. "All right, if you're sure you don't mind."

She nodded.

Sam went to the front door and retrieved the bedroll and saddlebags he'd left there earlier before heading down the hall. As Cassie had said, all the rooms were unoccupied, a condition unusual for a boarding house. He entered one and looked around. The cat was curled in the middle of the bed.

Unpacking for him consisted of draping his saddlebags across a chair. That took all of two seconds. He sat on the bed, testing the firmness. The cat opened her eyes and looked at him. She yawned once and laid her head back between her paws.

Before returning to the kitchen, Sam veered down the dimly-lit hall and stopped at the door of Cassie's room, which was cracked open a few inviting inches. Temptation was strong. He stilled, listening to make sure no one was coming his way.

Where was the deed? Directly in his line of vision a satchel leaned against the wall and a few garments covered a rocking chair in the corner. He listened again for any sound of footsteps. Nothing but some clattering of dishes from the kitchen. He pushed the door gently with the toe of his boot. Regardless of it squeaking, he took one step in before his conscience stopped him short. He just couldn't do it this way. It felt wrong for so many reasons. He turned to leave.

"Sam?"

Joey was standing in the hall. The trust shining in the boy's eyes filled him with remorse.

"What are you doing in there?"

Sam hunkered down to his level. A moment passed. "Thought I heard something coming from inside this room. After I took a look I realized it was yours." He shrugged. "Must have been the cat."

As soon as the words were out Sam regretted them. Lying straight to Joey's face reminded him all too much of the times his own father had done the same to him and his younger brother Seth. And even worse, to his mother before her death. The memory made his stomach burn bitterly. Trying to retrieve the claim was one thing, but lying like this was another. His father's deceit had ripped his family apart. It had heaped mounds of shame on his mother as she tried to scratch out a living for her and her little sons. Brewster Ridgeway was now paying the price for those lies, and his other nefarious deeds, rotting away in prison.

"Ashes is sleeping on *your* bed. Didn't you see her when you put your saddlebag away?"

He reached out and put his hand on the boy's tiny shoulders. "Why, come to think of it now, I suppose I did," he mumbled, thinking how one lie always led to another. He ruffled the fuzzy golden head before him and then stood, shouldering the heavy burden of guilt. "The pie cooled off yet?"

Joey preceded him out the door and up the hallway. "Almost."

He entered the kitchen right behind Joey and ambled over to his seat. Nonchalantly leaning his palms on the back of his chair, he watched Cassie as she dried the last blue dinner plate and put it in the cupboard.

He glanced at Joey, fearful the boy might mention his nosing around their room. If Cassie's suspicions were raised now he might never see the deed to his claim. He decided to ask Joey a question to distract him. "Son, do you know anything about Split Ear, the horse I just bought?"

Cassie was in the process of wiping the drain board with a dishtowel. What an odd question for him to ask Josephine. A child wouldn't know anything about a horse she didn't own.

"All I know is he's ugly as mud," her sister replied, screwing up her face in a grimace.

Turning, Cassie folded the dampened dishtowel and set it aside, all the while avoiding looking at the man who was too handsome for his own good. "Joey doesn't know anything about the horse, but I do." She took three small plates from the cupboard and placed them on the table.

Sam brought the pie over. "Go on."

"Miss Hawthorn bought him six months past from a traveling salesmen who arrived in Broken Branch. She needed a horse to pull her buggy because she'd taken to making noonday meals and delivering them to the miners at the Lucky North."

Cassie cut the pie and gave generous slices to all. Sam took a bite. He closed his eyes as he chewed. "I understand now why you want to open a bake shop."

Josephine wolfed down her pie in a matter of minutes and hopped up from her chair. "I'm getting Ashes. She's asleep on Sam's bed." She turned to Cassie with a matter-of-fact look on her face and pointed to Sam. "He's staying in the garden room."

Josephine was almost out the door when she stopped and turned around. "Cassie...deem," she began, making Cassie doubt she'd ever get the name right. "Sam heard something in our room. A noise. He tried to see what it was, but couldn't find nothing. What do you think it was?"

Chapter Eight

Dang! Unless the last vestiges of evening light were playing tricks on him, he was certain the unusual emerald shade of Cassie's eyes, a hue he'd never seen before, had just transformed instantaneously into the suspicious color of dark moss.

She was weighing the words her brother had just said as sure as he felt the unease growing in his gut. Emotions crossed her pretty face. He put the last bite of pie into his mouth and its sweet flavor turned to straw.

"What were you doing in our room, Sam?" she asked after a moment. "Nosing around for something interesting?"

Sam chuckled and scraped his plate with the bottom of his fork, finishing the last crumb as she waited for an answer. "Could have been a woodpecker on the roof, I suppose. That's the only thing I can think of."

"Woodpecker? That's not likely. I haven't seen a woodpecker around here—ever."

"There's always a first." He pushed his plate forward, satisfied. A moment before he'd felt she might actually be warming to him. Trusting him. Not so now. "I'm turning in."

"It's not even eight."

He stood and placed his plate in the sink. "That's true, but tomorrow we'll want to start at sun-up and I've been on the trail for days. I'm looking forward to that nice soft bed. I suggest you two do the same." She was watching him closely. "You have everything packed?"

She stood. "We'll be ready to ride when you are."

He fought the smile he felt within. A porcupine wasn't as prickly as this one. No doubt she was trying to figure out what he was up to. Would the truth really be impossible to tell her? Would she believe him about her uncle and peacefully hand over what was rightfully his? He needed that claim. Seth was depending on him. If he had to wrestle a porcupine and ride the ugliest nag this side of Nevada to get it back, then so be it.

***

The next morning, cold air nipped Cassie's ears and cooled her sore face as she walked in from the barn. Sleeping had been difficult. No matter which way she laid, she hurt. She'd finally dozed off a little around dawn. She'd get through this day, and then tonight she'd get a real night's sleep. All she had to do now was stay upright in the saddle.

The horses were saddled and ready to ride. She needed to wake Josephine and get her fed and dressed. The morning frost crunched beneath her boots as she headed toward the back kitchen door. Anticipation swirled within her chest. What if they really did find a gold nugget? Hope blossomed in her heart, put a smile on her face and lightness in her step.

She stopped for a moment in the yard. Drawing a long, measured breath, she looked at the town that had been her family's home for the past three years. The old market, where

Mrs. Gifford used to give her and Josephine black licorice, stood dark and quiet. Something tied to the balcony of the Paper Doll Saloon flapped in the breeze as if to say goodbye. What would become of this place?

She hadn't seen Sam yet but he was up and around somewhere. A man of few belongings, he could be ready to go in a heartbeat. When she'd gone out to feed her animals, she'd been surprised to find her horses already eating, fed by Sam when he'd fed his own.

She hurried through the back door into the kitchen, which was warmly illuminated by a single lamp.

"All set?"

His deep voice crossed the room, making her turn toward the stove. He leaned against the warmer side, a cup between his palms. His expression was guarded but the rest of him looked inviting and clean, his hair damp and combed back from his freshly-shaven face.

"Yes. Well, just about. I still have to wake Joey and help him dress. That will only take a moment."

"I had some coffee with me in my saddlebag. Want some?" he asked, holding out a second cup to her. He must have seen her coming through the window.

Sam's expression fell when she stepped into the lamplight and he actually got a look at her face. He set the cups down and closed the distance between them. She pulled back when he reached out to her cheek. His hand dropped to his side.

His gaze moved from her swollen nose to her eyes. "How do you feel?"

Cassie forced herself to look away. The gentleness in his voice was something she had never experienced from a man before. "Looks worse than it is." She explored the bridge of her nose with her fingertips. "But, I'll admit, it hurts worse now than it did yesterday."

"It *looks* painful," Sam replied. "How's the rest of you? Sure you're able to ride this morning?"

Although staying was tempting, it was chancy too. How she'd love to crawl back into bed and pull the covers up over her head--and sleep for a week. But sooner or later Klem would be back. In his search for his watch he might find the deed. Once he had it, there would be no way of getting it back. Or proving it was hers in the first place. As much as she hated to admit it, she needed Sam, and she needed to get out of Broken Branch.

"Yes. We're leaving today. I'm not letting a few sore muscles or a puffy nose hold us up."

"Your ribs? As I recall, they were pretty tender yesterday."

"Better."

"If your mind is set then." Again he handed Cassie the hot cup of brew. She took it thoughtfully and sipped.

"I'm not changing course now," she replied, keeping her gaze glued to her cup of coffee. Sam was a *very* likeable sort. *Very likeable.* But there was just that little something that told her to stay on guard.

***

Sam was surprised how fast Cassie was able to get her little brother up, dressed and fed. They gathered the last of their belongings while he waited out with the horses. Split Ear, saddled with his rig, saddlebags, bedroll, rifle, and rope, would be his mount for however long it took Blu to recuperate. He'd lead Blu alongside for the next few days or until he felt sure she was sound.

Joey ran out of the house, hefting his duffle bag. His baggy clothes engulfed his small body. A black felt hat tipped back on his head, secured with a rodeo strap under his chin. He groaned from the weight he bore, which nearly tipped him over.

Sam met him halfway. "That looks heavy. Let me help you."

"Naw, that's okay," he responded, shaking his head, "I got it. My brother told me I'm supposed to pull my own weight."

The boy went directly to the opposite side of his small black pony and worked at getting his duffle stuffed into his left saddlebag. It was taking some doing and he glanced at Sam several times around his saddled mount as he tried to hurry.

"Sure you don't need some help?"

Joey shook his head. He finally succeeded and snapped the buckle. Finished, he ran back up to the house. "I'll be back in a jiffy."

Sam kept an eye out for the smithy. He didn't want either of those brothers to show up, causing trouble for Cassie. If they did, they'd have more than a slip of a girl to contend with this time. Part of him wished they *would* come back looking for a fight.

The sound of the door slamming brought his attention back to the walk. Cassie made her way to the horses, her arms laden with provisions.

"Here, give me those," Sam said as he strode to her side.

"I've got 'em."

Determined, he wrestled the pack, a book, and several folded garments from her arms, but not before he felt her bristle. He smiled inwardly. "Go find that brother of yours and we'll be on our way."

"I don't need your help," she answered as he walked toward her horses. "Just because I took a few punches yesterday doesn't mean I can't do for myself today."

"I know. I know. You're as capable as the next man."

Beside Meadowlark, Cassie's chestnut mare, Sam reached for the saddlebag.

Suddenly Cassie was by his side. "I'll do that."

Astonished that he'd so quickly forgotten the real reason he was here, he unhooked the flap of her saddlebag and looked down into the dark leather pouch before she could stop him.

Chapter Nine

Did Sam have corncobs stuck in his ears? Why was he being so, so…what was he being, anyway? Cassie shoved Sam's hands off her saddlebag and faced him, plunking her hands on her hips. Irritation bubbled inside. "What do you think you're doing? You can't go looking through my things anytime you want. Didn't your ma teach you any manners?" She took her things from his arms.

A muscle in Sam's jaw tensed. "It's pretty obvious, isn't it?" The pleasant feeling when he'd so sweetly handed her a cup of coffee this morning was gone. "I'm trying to help. But I can see that wasn't the right thing to do." He crossed his now empty arms across his chest and glared back. "I've put you off again, right? I can't seem to win you over."

Cassie jerked her gaze away as she felt her face heat. It was true. He was only being helpful and she was being as sensitive as a sore toe wedged in a boot two sizes too small. She needed to focus on Josephine and keeping her safe. If Sam could help her do that, then so be it. She'd made sure the deed to the claim was safely hidden away where no one would stumble across it easily. She needed him, and she couldn't be such a sour puss all the time that he'd want to up and leave them on the trail.

"Sam, I'm sorry." She forced herself to look into his guarded face. "I appreciate all you're doing for Joey and me. Really, I do." And she did. Last night as she lay in her bed, she discovered in reality she was relieved that Sam was riding with them. And, maybe even more. She was excited to be starting this new chapter of their life with him. "I can do things for myself, though. Just because I'm small doesn't mean I'm incapable."

A moment passed before a smile inched up his face.

"Of course you're not. I never meant to imply anything by my helping. I'll be more careful in the future."

She straightened. "I'd appreciate that."

Sam walked over to his two horses and tightened Split Ear's cinch. The horse pinned his ears in protest and rolled his eyes. Ignoring him, Sam untied both horses' reins from the hitching rail. Then, sliding his boot into the stirrup, he mounted the gelding in one smooth motion.

"Joey," Cassie called out, looking to the house before he caught her gawking. Her reaction to his close contact had her senses humming. Sam was the kind of man any woman would fall for. A handsome face, winsome smile, kind and considerate. "Come on," she blurted, wanting to change the direction of her thoughts. "We're ready to ride out." Finished with her saddlebags, she gathered her reins and mounted up. Their new home was calling from the west.

***

Morning passed quickly. To Sam's relief, the Sherman brothers hadn't shown up for a sendoff. Cassie seemed deep in thought, so Sam left her to her musing. She moved easily in the saddle but he'd caught a grimace of pain every so often. Joey rode a few pony lengths behind, humming and chatting to himself. Sam had little experience with children, but even his lack of familiarity couldn't stop him from recognizing that this youngster seemed more than a little strange. He blushed an awful lot for a boy. And he seemed to have the habit of batting his eyelashes. Could be that this little guy would turn out to be light in the stirrups, so to speak. Sam glanced back. Joey's body was twisted in his saddle, his hand stuck deep into his saddlebag. When he saw Sam looking, he jerked his hand away and tried to whistle, but couldn't through his face-splitting smile.

Sam turned back to the road ahead. That boy was up to something. As sure as he was strange, he was up to no good. Hadn't he been that age once, too? He'd better keep a close eye on him. Sam checked the thick cotton rope draped loosely around his saddle horn; the other end of it was attached to Blu's halter. The mare walked steadily by his side, enjoying her hiatus. After several miles the two horses had lost their curiosity with each other and settled in as if they had been stable mates for years. Amazingly, as crooked-legged as he was, Split Ear had a nice stride, and riding him felt much like sitting in a rocking chair.

"Hungry?" Sam glanced at Cassie. She hadn't complained once during the hours since leaving this morning, but he was sure she must be sore and uncomfortable.

"I could use a stretch," she replied, turning to look at her brother. "And I'm sure Joey must be hungry by now."

"Fine. We'll stop up there by the alders and give the horses a break." He patted his stomach. "I could use a bite myself. I have some jerky."

"And I have some bread."

She smiled at him, causing a capricious lightness to fill his head. He returned the gesture before forcing himself to look away. She was more often than not forgetting to use her deep-voiced charade. He should have told her immediately that Bristol had given her away. As time passed it became more and more difficult to fess up about it, and he felt certain she'd be spitting mad when she found out he'd known about her secret from the get-go.

"Whoa." He dismounted and hobbled the animals, then released them in the meadow so they could eat while they rested. They'd passed a stream earlier, where all four horses had quenched their thirst. He rustled around his saddlebag, looking for his bag of jerky, watching Cassie and Joey out of the corner of his eye. If she weren't so proud he'd tell her to sit in the grass and rest while he took care of her horses himself—but he knew where that would take him.

The meadow was small and just off the narrow road they traveled on. A tall stand of alders rimmed the edge of the grassy opening, their leaves rustling in the cool breeze. The only other sound was the twittering of a few birds and the chomping of the horses' teeth.

Cassie sank to her knees in the sweet-smelling grass, a sigh escaping her lips. She folded her legs beneath her and untied the napkin encircling a loaf of bread. Sam followed suit, stretching his legs out in front of himself and resting back on an elbow. Joey was still fumbling with his saddlebag, chattering away to no one in particular.

Sam chuckled. "I don't know much about kids." He motioned with his head toward Joey as he handed Cassie a strip of jerky.

She took the dried meat and ripped off a portion with her teeth. "He's always been good at pretending," she said between chews. "I'm glad he's taking all this so well."

"All this?"

"The move. Ma dying. Just everything."

Sam accepted the hunk of bread she offered and took a bite. The crunchy crust was nutty and the doughy soft middle melted in his mouth. It was good.

"I see," he answered, after swallowing.

"Joey, come and eat some lunch," Cassie called. "We won't be staying long."

Joey seemed reluctant to leave his pony's side.

"Come on now, son. Do as your sis…," Sam caught himself mid-sentence, "your seniors tell you," he finished awkwardly." He threw a chastising look in the boy's direction. "Time's short."

Joey ran over and plopped down beside Cassie and wolfed down his food. "I'm thirsty."

Cassie handed him her canteen. "Not too much. We aren't sure when we'll reach another stream."

Cassie finished up the crust she was eating and brushed her dungarees. "Should I pack things up?" She glanced up at him, her skin looking softer than a flower petal.

"Not just yet. We can rest for a few more minutes." He laced his fingers together behind his head and laid back. Huge white clouds drifted overhead without obscuring the warm rays of the sun.

Joey ran off again and Cassie lay back too. For a moment all of nature was completely silent, and time seemed to stand still. The crisp mountain air felt good. Scents of freshly sprouted grass mixed with cedar and pine teased his senses. He closed his eyes as the warm sunshine slowed his mind.

"Hmmm, a baker. That's what you're planning to be?" he asked, mainly in an effort to stay awake.

"Yes." Her tone was a bit defensive. "Men can cook too, you know."

"True enough. My favorite person on a cattle drive is usually the cook. If he's any good, that is." He laughed softly.

A moment passed before she went on. "Just so you know, our grandmother worked in an eatery when she was young. She fell in love with the owner and they married. The restaurant flourished under her management. Our ma grew up there and passed on the recipes that made the business successful. I'd like to follow in their footsteps."

"What about your ma? Did she follow her mother's dream, too?"

"She always wanted to, but we moved around a lot. She was able to make a little money by baking bread and pies and sold them from our home. But it always seemed that just when she was getting well known, and started doing a good business, we up and moved."

Sam glanced over. Cassie's brow was crinkled and he couldn't miss the longing in her expression. "That's an ambitious dream, Cassidy. Takes a lot of capital to start a business from scratch."

"I agree. But we'll get it going, I know, and it'll be a success. My grandma Cookie was known far and wide for her creations. All I need is a small shop to lease in a town somewhere. Sweat and knowledge don't cost a thing."

"And that's where the gold comes in?"

She nodded.

"Your family moved around often?"

"Yes. My ma never wanted to be left behind. Love demands a presence, she'd always say. She said we'd stay together and take care of each other. Even when…"

She paused. "They died," she said, finishing her sentence.

Moments slipped by in silence.

"Love demands a presence," Sam mumbled to himself. Thoughts of all the years pining for his father, not knowing where he was, if he was dead or alive, flitted through his mind. With a conscious effort, he shoved the hurtful feeling away, not wanting to spoil this newfound closeness with Cassie.

"It's true, Sam. Think about it." She pushed up on her elbow and gazed down at him, her eyes now as emerald as the grass they laid upon. "People always claim they love something, but in reality don't give it a second thought. If you love something you desire to be around it and spend time there."

He grunted, not having a reply, but enjoying her nearness immensely.

She lay back down. "Look."

"What?"

"Don't you see it? A steamboat. Just like the boats going up and down the Mississippi. That big fluffy cloud right over there. There's the waterwheel. And the smokestack. Let your imagination go."

Sam looked. He didn't see anything but a vast sky filled with clouds.

Cassie scooted closer until her head was almost touching his. She pointed, and then her finger swirled around as if she were drawing something in the air. "That extra puffy spot is the waterwheel."

He could feel her disappointment, hear it in her voice. But, dad-blast it, he couldn't see any boat in the clouds.

Slowly she dropped her hand. "Sam Ridgeway, don't look with your eyes. Look with your heart. Relax. It's turning," she said, pointing again.

He laughed out loudly in surprise. "Yes! It's bigger than I was looking for, is all. Now it's as clear as the nose on my face."

He felt her looking his way and turned to catch her velvety soft gaze.

"Didn't your ma ever teach you that your heart has eyes too?" she murmured, her look reaching deep inside him.

Sam cleared his throat and looked away. "Has anyone ever told you you're a different kind of lad?" He couldn't help it. He hoped she'd offer to tell him on her own that she was, in fact, a girl. Couldn't she feel it herself? This cloud-watching and whatnot was an odd activity for two men.

Before she could answer, a piercing scream shattered the moment. They both leapt to their feet.

Chapter Ten

Cassie ran through the open meadow up to the forest's edge, one stride behind Sam. "Where are you?" she shouted.

"Here!" came the reply from deep within the woods.

Sam pushed past some low branches.

Scrambling through the trees, the two burst out of the thicket together, emerging into an open area. Josephine still wasn't in sight and dread scorched Cassie's heart. Turning a complete circle, Cassie scanned the area. Panic pushed her forward, and she ran for the other side of the field, where a steep incline threatened to block them.

Side by side they climbed. At the top of the rock face, they bolted forward.

"Where are—" Before Cassie could finish calling, Sam skidded to a halt and grabbed the back of her shirt, saving her from falling into a deep crevasse directly in front of them. Eight feet across, perched on a narrow ledge, was Josephine, her back pressed up tight to the red earth wall. Ashes was clutched tightly to her chest with her left arm and her right hand, in a white knuckled grasp, held the root of a tree to keep her balance.

A low moan came from the child's lips as dirt and a few pebbles under her boot gave way and fell in a clatter against the rocks below. Ashes squirmed. The frightened cat looked as if she was on the verge of panic. If that happened, Josephine was sure to fall to her death.

"Drop the cat," Sam demanded.

The shake of Josephine's head was almost imperceptible. She held tightly to her beloved pet, her eyes never wavering from those of her sister.

Sam changed tactics and his voice became pleading.

"Joey, you need to let her go. She'll be okay. You've seen cats jump from very high places, haven't you? Please, son, let her go."

Still Josephine refused. "He's in shock," Sam said to Cassie. "I'll get my rope.

With Sam gone, all Cassie could do was pray. "Just stay still, Josephine. Don't move a muscle. Sam will be back soon. Stay still, honey."

Josephine moaned as the cat scrambled up around her neck, trying to find some sort of security. Her little legs shook violently, and her smooth leather sole slipped off the edge. She cried out.

Cassie gasped. She couldn't bear to lose her sister. "Hold on!" she choked out. She reached out her hand, wanting desperately to touch her, stroke her velvety soft cheek. Every moment felt like an hour. "Sam will be back. He'll get you out of there. Just stay very, very still."

Right then, Sam came bursting through the trees on Split Ear and slid to a halt. He slung his leg over the saddle and dismounted his rope already in his hands. He tossed his reins to Cassie.

"Joey, there's another branch a few inches above your head. It's bigger than the one you're holding. I'm going to toss this rope and lasso it. If I miss and the rope lands on you, don't let it knock you off. Just keep holding tight to that root, okay? Keep your eyes focused on your sister."

Cassie jerked up straighter and heat rushed to her face. He'd known!

"Here it comes." He hesitated. "You sure you won't drop that cat first?" When Josephine didn't respond, he slowly swung the rope over his head.

Cassie gripped Split Ear's reins tightly in sweaty palms.

Sam let his loop fly. Gracefully, as if in slow motion, it went up and then began to descend towards Josephine. Cassie sucked in a breath when it stopped short, snagged by another root above its intended target. It dangled for a second and Sam gave a gentle tug. It dropped onto the branch above Josephine's head, teetering precariously.

"Okay, Joey, now you have to let the cat go and reach up for the rope with your left hand. Don't worry; the cat's not going to let go of you. Just try not to react if it moves. When you get the rope, slip the loop over your body. This might be difficult. Be very careful. Go on now. Take your time."

Josephine didn't move.

"You must," Cassie said softly. "Sam's not going to let you fall."

Josephine's small body turned slightly once her hand found the rocky cliff wall. As Sam had predicted, Ashes gripped tightly to her mistress. Bit by bit, Josephine's hand edged higher until her fingers touched the branch. The rope was only inches away.

"Very good," Sam encouraged. "Now, take hold of the rope and bring it down over your body."

It was so hard to watch. Minutes crawled by. The rope was now around Josephine's body, looped under her arms. She had a white-knuckled grip on the root in her right hand and the rope with her left. She wobbled, unbalanced, her face ashen. Sam ran to a tree near the cliff's edge and tossed his end of the rope over a thick branch a few feet over his head. Striding to Split Ear, he secured the end of the line to his saddle horn.

"You're going to have to swing across, Joey. Try to take the impact with your legs. They're strong. Sam turned to Cassie. "Hold tight," he whispered hoarsely, motioning to the gelding. The apprehension in his eyes gave him away. "If there happens to be a jolt on the rope I don't know how he'll react to the pull on the saddle."

She nodded.

"I'll pull you up, son. It's not far between us. It won't hurt much."

"What about Ashes?"

Sam shrugged. "She'll just have to hold onto you. When you go, take hold with both hands."

Gripping the rope he braced his foot against a large rock. "Back the horse up until the rope is taut," he called out to Cassie, and then waited as she did what he'd asked.

"Okay, Joey—now!"

Cassie was astounded that her sister had the courage to drop off the ledge. A muted thud prompted Sam to pull hand over hand, until Josephine's scruffy head appeared over the edge of the ravine. Cassie wanted to run to her but forced herself to hold fast to Split Ear, reins in hand. Once Josephine was lying safely on the ground Sam rushed over, dropping to his knees. Ashes jumped to the side, scampering a few feet before stopping. She sat down, as if nothing out of the ordinary had just happened, and began licking her paw.

"Are you hurt?" Sam asked, brushing dirt from Josephine's body and picking sticks from her hair.

Josephine opened her eyes and looked around. She seemed surprised to have made it. "Am I alive?" she asked, her childish voice awash in disbelief.

A cry of anguish tore from Cassie's throat as she hurried over. She engulfed Josephine in her arms, holding her tightly to her breast and rocking back and forth.

"Sam, you saved her! You saved my little sister." Her voice was hoarse as tears began to flow. "I can never thank you enough!"

Several moments of complete silence made Cassie look at Sam, who was staring at her wide eyed. He sat back on his heels; a shocked expression marked his face. With his thumb, he tipped his hat up and then pointed an accusing finger at the scraggly little person snuggled next to her chest. Finally, he opened his mouth, "Not you, too?"

Chapter Eleven

"**I**'m sorry for not being truthful with you from the beginning," Cassie said, her voice was still hollow with fear as she clung to Josephine. "It was just too risky. We didn't know anything about you."

He was surprised by the magnitude of the relief flooding through him now that Joey—what was her real name, he wondered fleetingly?—was sitting safely on the ground. His own secret prickled his conscience, telling him this was the perfect time to reveal what he in turn was keeping from her. If he'd been waiting for the ideal time to speak up, this was it.

"I didn't like fooling you," Josephine said, laying her small hand on his arm. "My *real* name is Josephine Elizabeth."

"Well, that's a real pretty name, Josephine Elizabeth," he responded, again amazed at his own stupidity. He'd thought the little brother was extremely different, actually a bit strange. He should have put two and two together after learning about Cassie. "Why the pretense?" he asked, looking at Cassie.

"When everyone started leaving town, our being alone didn't seem like such a big deal at first. Then, when there were only a few people left, I suddenly realized that living in

Broken Branch with Klem and Bristol Sherman was not a safe place for either of us." She didn't want to share the fact that Uncle Arvid was accused of stealing Klem's personal property.

Josephine looked up at him with her big blue eyes from the safety and warmth of her sister's bosom. "They're not nice! Klem watches everything I do," she said innocently, not understanding the implications. "He always smiled with his stinky breath and tried to give me candy. Cassie said I could never take it—ever."

Sam and Cassie exchanged knowing glances.

"I really didn't think our boy costumes would trick them, but I guess we weren't around long enough for them to figure it out."

"Did Bristol ever see you? He recognized your voice right away."

"So that's how you found out." She cocked an eyebrow. "You could have enlightened me, you know. Instead, you let me make a fool out of myself. I'll bet you were laughing the whole time."

Cassie released Josephine and stood up, pulling her sister to her feet. She turned her in a circle as she inspected for injuries. Finding nothing broken, she brushed at the dirt clinging to her back.

Sam shrugged. "At times." He took his handkerchief from his pocket and went over to Split Ear for his canteen. Returning, he dabbed at a few abrasions on Josephine's face.

"Ouch."

"Don't be a baby," Cassie said gently.

Sam winked at Josephine. "I think you and your sister make darn fine-looking men. I can't picture the two of you as girls."

Josephine puffed out her chest proudly and patted her trousers, but Cassie blushed and looked away.

"You ride a horse better than most men I know," he added, giving Josephine a friendly man-to-man pat on the back, but looked at Cassie. "I'll bet you can drink 'em under the table, too."

She turned on him, angry, shaking her finger in his face. "I never drink. We all saw how it affected our fa...uncle. He was..." she shut her mouth, leaving the sentence unfinished.

He winked again and gave her a nod.

Her expression softened when she realized he was jesting. "Sam Ridgeway?"

"Yes?" he answered innocently.

"Don't go treating me like some girl," she shot back. "I *am* capable. I probably shoot better than you, too."

He burst into laughter. "That's just it. I'm agreeing with you!" He struggled to get the words out. "You put that bullet square between Bristol's boots. I didn't know what was happening." All the nervous tension over the near tragedy with Josephine escaped, and he laughed until his side hurt and eyes watered. Josephine looked back and forth, clearly confused by the exchange, and began laughing with him.

Cassie was having none of it. "I don't see what's so darn funny."

"Well," he answered, and once again took out his handkerchief and dried his eyes. "I guess you wouldn't. But, I have to say, between that event and now this—I think we make a darn fine team, Cassie Angel. How about you?"

She ignored his question and looked at Josephine. "Now, I'd like to know how in the world you ended up on the other side of that cliff?"

"It wasn't my fault." Josephine's expression darkened and tears pooled in her wide eyes, most likely going for sympathy so she wouldn't be punished. "Ashes ran off into the woods and I went to find her. Farther up, the ravine isn't wide and I jumped across and then followed Ashes back to where you found me. When I went to pick her up, I slipped."

"I thought we'd agreed to leave Ashes in Broken Branch. Where she'd be safe and have plenty of food. What happened to that?"

Ashes, sitting on a log nearby, mewed, as if trying to plead her own case.

"I just *couldn't* leave her, Cassie. Look how sweet she is." Josephine cast a glance at the cat. "I love her. Please don't be mad."

Cassie wrapped her in her arms again. "Actually I'm relieved that Ashes is coming along. I've felt horrible all day leaving her behind. Promise you won't go looking for her without telling me first."

Josephine pulled away and nodded, wiping her nose with her sleeve. "I promise."

Sam went over to his grazing horse and picked up his reins. "Time to move on. We need to make a few hours before stopping to camp." He chuckled. "That is—if you men are up to it…"

***

Darkness had fallen, making the forest seem even spookier as Cassie listened to the horses' hooves plodding along. Sam, now as grumpy as a bear, couldn't seem to find a place he felt comfortable making camp. Every time they found a clearing, he'd find some reason not to like it. Too close to the river. No

62

forage for the animals. An abundance of animal droppings. Too open. Too dense.

Exhaustion and irritation grated inside Cassie. She was starting to think he was the one that was too dense. Josephine had fallen silent two hours ago, and Cassie wouldn't be surprised if her sister was asleep on her pony's back.

"Sam," Cassie called out to him, one horse length in the lead.

"Whoa," she heard him say. He waited as she came up alongside.

"Sam, we're tired. Look, over there. That seems like as good a spot as any."

"How can you tell in the dark?"

The moon outlined his silhouette as it made its appearance above the hills behind him. His face was shadowed by darkness, but she could see the whites of his eyes as they regarded her.

"I don't like it. Too close to the rocks."

"*Sam!*"

"Okay, let me check it out first." He draped Blu's lead rope across the pommel of her saddle.

It took him a few minutes to make his way to the spot she'd pointed out. He dismounted and stood quietly. After a moment, he bent over and tossed a rock into the boulders nearby.

A chorus of deep rattling erupted from crevasses and cracks. Split Ear snorted and tossed his head nervously. Slowly, Sam and his horse backed away.

"Like I said, too close to the rocks." He mounted back up and took the lead rope from her shaking hands. "Rattlers," he said and continued up the road.

Rattlesnakes! Lord above. If she and Josephine had been alone she would have stopped there, most assuredly. Or one and all of the prior places he had found unacceptable.

Thank heavens for Sam. It was becoming more and more evident how much his wisdom counted.

***

A man's voice rumbled her name, and someone shook Cassie's leg. She opened her eyes, pulling herself from the remnants of a dream. Raising her chin, she blinked. She was…she was on a horse, Meadowlark…and the man… Oh! It was Sam. She must have dozed off.

"Here," he whispered. "Dismount."

He took her hand and she was too tired to fight him. She would show him tomorrow how capable she was. Groggily, she swung her leg over Meadowlark's back but her boot heel caught the back of the saddle. She fumbled. A small cry of alarm escaped her lips. If not for Sam, she'd have landed in a heap on the ground.

As it was, her arms looped around his neck and she slid down the length of his body. When her boots touched the ground, she gripped his shoulders, not enough space between them for a piece of paper. She gazed up into his face and a burst of tingles lit up her senses. The stars, glittering in the sky, were like a halo around his head.

"You okay?" His breath was warm on her cheek as he leaned in close.

Her voice deserted her. She'd been dreaming about a prince from some faraway land, who'd come to marry her and take her away. Now, she realized with a resounding shock, that prince had been Sam! Sam's eyes. Sam's hair. *Sam's lips*!

"Cassie?" He took her arms from about him and gave her a little shake. "Are you sleepwalking or what? Wake up."

She stepped back and nodded. "Yes. I'm awake now."

Sam went over to Pepper, untied Josephine's bedroll and then lifted her from her saddle. He carried her over to a level spot. When Cassie followed he handed her the blanket. "Spread this out." When she did, he laid the littlest Angel down without waking her. "You two bed down and I'll take care of your horses and start a small fire."

When she started to protest he put a finger to her lips and her dream returned in a flash. She was glad he wouldn't see the warmth in her face.

"Just for tonight. Tomorrow I'll welcome all the work you want to do. Go grab your blanket. Josephine is cold."

Without another word she did as he'd asked. She sank down by her sister's side, welcoming the warmth. She listened as Sam went back and forth unsaddling the animals and putting them out into the meadow. When he returned he made a campfire and laid down too.

The ground was hard. Although time had passed, Cassie now found herself wide-awake. She reached under her blanket, feeling around for the pebble that was digging into her hip. She tossed it away.

Sam sat up.

"Sorry, that was just me."

He lay back down and she gazed up at the stars glittering in the black sky, remembering how Sam had looked when he'd caught her, and held her close. She glanced at the fire. An owl hooted somewhere off in the distance.

"Sam?" Cassie whispered.

It took a moment for him to answer.

"Hmmm?"

"Thank you for everything."

She heard him roll to his back.

"I didn't do anything."

"Yes, you did." The sounds of the night were the only response.

"Sam…"

"Cassie." His voice held a note that she couldn't discern.

"You saved me from Klem. You kept Josephine from falling to her death. You're helping us get to California alive."

"If it will make you stop talking and go to sleep—you're welcome."

"I'm really glad you're with us. I…" A moment passed. "We do make a good team, Sam…"

"Cassie, *please*"

"Well, good night, then."

"Good night."

***

Cassie opened her eyes a narrow slit, her head just inches out of the blanket. What time was it? It was still very dark. The dead of night. There was no sound, not even the crackling of the fire. Something had awakened her. She had the unnerving feeling of being watched from behind. She glanced across her sister's head to the dim bed of coals that had been the fire a few hours ago, and let her eyes adjust to the thick, intimidating darkness.

Five feet farther would be Sam, curled in his blanket. Fifteen feet more would be the horses.

She listened. Everything seemed fine. She closed her eyes and willed herself to relax. Again, the hair prickled on the back of her neck. With a deep breath, she tried to fall back asleep.

One of the horses snorted.

No use. She was going to have to turn over and look. If she didn't, her childish fears would keep her up until it was time to get up and ride. Gathering her courage, she scooted forward, nearer to Josephine, then rolled quietly to her back. She slowly turned her head.

Chapter Twelve

Relief flooded Cassie. There was nothing but trees in the distance. And darkness. The stars far above. Releasing a sigh she smiled to herself for letting her fears startle up like a spooky horse. Her eyes drooped.

"*Stay awake.*"

It was as if someone had whispered into her ear. But then, that wasn't possible. Josephine and Sam still slept soundly. Very slowly, she once again opened her eyes.

From the outer edges of the clearing she thought she saw *something*. Yes! Two golden orbs pierced the blackness. Cassie squeezed her eyelids together several times, straining to focus. Her breath caught.

She needed to call to Sam but her voice had left her.

The eyes blinked. Cassie released the air locked in her lungs. *Ashes*! Not some horrible monster waiting to pounce. That darn cat was going to be the death of her yet.

Cassie rose to her elbow. "Here kitty, kitty, kitty," she softly called to their pet.

Right before her eyes the golden orbs seemed to take flight into the sky. A heart-stopping snarl shattered the stillness, causing all the horses to snort and squeal in unison.

Cassie's scream ripped through the darkness. In turn, Josephine shrieked hysterically and reached for her. Scooping her up, she dashed over to Sam's side of the fire and fell down beside him on his bedroll.

"Mountain lion," he yelled over the roar of his gun. He shot another round into the air.

Cassie was a shivering ball of fright. Josephine was crying and holding tight. She couldn't stop herself and took hold of Sam's trousers as he stood. The thick stench of gun powder burned her lungs. He tried to take a step but was stopped by her grip around his leg.

He knelt. "It's long gone." The horses snorted again nervously, milling around.

"I need to check the horses," he said. "We'll be sore put out if they get loose and run off. I'll be right back."

"We'll go with you."

"Cassie, the mountain lion is clear over the other side of the Sierra Nevadas by now."

Her teeth wouldn't stop chattering. Josephine was silent, but her grip on Cassie's arm was fierce.

He took one step and stopped. "I'll be back before you know it."

A swirl of thankfulness for Sam's protection moved through her as he walked away. He was *such* a good man. Nothing like the men her mother had warned her about. She was safe with him, and so was Josephine.

Returning, Sam found Cassie and Josephine's blanket moved from the other side of the fire. Placed neatly between his bedroll and the now crackling flames, their blankets touched his, and looked like one big bed. Josephine was already curled up in it, fast asleep. Cassie added wood to the fire and now it was blazing.

"The horses are all right, then?" Cassie sat atop her side of the blanket, with the fire to her back.

"Yes. Just a bit spooked. I'm grateful for the hobbles."

Moments passed. Sam stood, wondering what to do.

"This isn't necessary, you know," he offered, gesturing to the new sleeping arrangements.

Cassie held her finger to her lips, looking at her little sister. "Do you mind? Josephine insisted on it. She's frightened to tears."

Josephine, Sam thought, looked pretty darn relaxed.

"Uh…I see." He fidgeted and repositioned his saddle next to his bed. Once settled on his bedroll, he stretched out on his side, facing Cassie, with only Josephine between them. He cupped his head in the palm of his hand and smiled. "You should get back to sleep."

"I will."

"Be careful your blanket doesn't catch."

"I made sure it was far enough away." She glanced back, checking the distance. "Plenty of room. I wonder where Ashes is. I hope the mountain lion didn't eat her."

"I hope it did."

"*Sam*! Josephine would be heartbroken if something happened to her. Ever since our ma died, she and that cat have been inseparable."

"Well, I guess I'm just teasing, or maybe not," he murmured. "But be warned. There is a good chance the mountain lion has scared her off. We may not find her in the morning."

Cassie bit her bottom lip. She looked very young in the firelight, her chiseled cheekbones and angelic profile enchanting. Her nose had almost returned to what Sam thought must be its normal size. Her hair glistened.

"I didn't think of that." Her brow furrowed.

She reached down and fingered the downy hair on her sister's sleeping head. "I want to protect her, Sam. She's already suffered so much for someone so young."

For an instant he wondered what it would feel like to kiss her, hold her tight in his arms. More than a few thoughts had gone through his mind when he'd rescued her from falling. She'd smelled sweet, and her eyes were twinkling so much he hadn't a clue to what she was thinking as she had gazed up into his face. Even with her short hair and baggy clothes she was a real beauty. She was on his mind now more often than not. He didn't know what to make of it. "I understand," he said quietly. "But, the world is a hard place. I hope you know that. It's easy to get battered by it."

She was lying on her back now, after climbing under the covers with Josephine. Still, he rested on his elbow, looking at the two girls. The campfire, a few feet away, picked up the golden highlights in her mahogany hair.

"I want to spare her all that pain. Give her a good life. An education."

"That's a tall order, Cassie."

"But worthwhile. With God's help it will happen."

Out of the darkness stepped the cat. Without invitation she walked onto the blanket and curled up between Josephine and Sam.

"Well, I guess that answers that question," Sam said. "Please, make yourself comfortable." Ashes closed her eyes. Within moments she was purring loud enough for both to hear.

Cassie laughed softly. "Maybe she'll be sticking closer from now on. I can't believe Josephine had her stuffed in that saddlebag all day. Just getting her in without a fight must have taken some doing. And we didn't even know it. That's pretty amazing."

Sam pulled his blanket around his shoulders. "No worries tonight. That mountain lion is long gone. Unless sick or hurt, they usually steer clear of humans as much as possible. Now, get some sleep. The sun will be up before you know it."

A coyote howled in the distance, and was answered by a few more. Within moments a whole chorus erupted, sounding like hundreds.

"That's pretty," Cassie whispered. "Nothing like that cougar."

The coyote song over the crackling flames was the only response. "Sam, you still awake?"

"Hmmm."

"I know I said this already—but—thank you for helping me and Josephine. I'm glad we're traveling together."

Sam opened his eyes and looked out into the darkness. *How will she feel when I ask her to hand over the deed to my claim?* he thought slowly. *How thankful will she be then?*

Chapter Thirteen

*"**I** didn't take it, Pa. I didn't!" Fear sliced through Sam as his father advanced and grasped him roughly by the arm.*

"Don't you lie to me, boy! You stole the knife from my drawer. Now you don't even have the guts to own up to your actions." They started for the woodshed—

Sam sat up with a jolt. Terror thickened his tongue and he thought he'd choke. Gasping, he blinked away his sleep. He'd never tell on Seth—no matter what. The whipping he got that day was one of many he'd taken shielding his little brother from their father's anger. What galled him more than anything, and hurt deeply, was his father's uncompromising disbelief in anything he said. Why wouldn't he listen?

He breathed in a lungful of crisp morning air, trying to rid himself of the nightmare and the feeling of doom they always seemed to leave behind. What about the claim? His claim. The claim that was going to buy the acreage needed to get his and Seth's ranch going. Seth had left two summers ago to push cattle for a spread in Texas, and except for the bare minimum, was saving everything he made for their land purchase. Sam worked as a saddle tramp too, until the night he'd won the claim.

Even now, that battered piece of paper called to him from Cassie's saddle pack, so close at hand. What was he to do when they reached Sourdough Creek, the inlet off the American River? Cassie wasn't going to just hand it over to him, easy as pie—that was for sure. And even more troubling, what would happen to her and Josephine if she did?

Josephine slept under the blanket, completely covered. Cassie was on her side, her arm wrapped protectively over her sister. Her bobbed hair fell over her eyes and her mouth was pursed into a little smile, making him wonder what she was dreaming about.

When his horse neighed, Cassie opened her eyes. For a moment, she looked confused, but as realization dawned, her eyes took on the smile that was still on her soft-looking lips.

"Good morning." She pushed the hair from her face and sat up on her elbow.

"Did you sleep at all last night?" he asked, completely thrown off by her dazzling green eyes. What a dim-witted question. How could she be waking up if she hadn't fallen asleep?

"Yes. It took me a while to settle down though." She sighed and pulled the blanket up under her chin, warding off the morning chill.

"You?"

"Sure. But, I never get used to sleeping on the ground."

She stretched her legs, a soft groan escaping her lips. "Oh, I know what you mean. It *is* hard. And bumpy. I think I was dreaming about a goose-feather stuffed mattress as tall as a barn." She lifted up the blanket and peeked at her little sister. "Josephine doesn't seem to mind."

He'd never met anyone like Cassie Angel before. So open and honest. Well, that is, aside from her ruse to protect her sister and herself from the Sherman brothers.

"Sam?"

She was gazing at him now with her heart in her eyes. "You never said why you were going to Coloma. Why you're traveling there. Is it family?"

Now! His mind screamed. *Tell her!* Now was the time to speak up. Even if it tore them apart, and she hated him for it, he should disclose the truth and have it out. He opened his mouth to speak, and then closed it.

"Sam?"

"No. Not family."

That statement gave her pause.

"Do you have any family?"

He rolled to his back so he didn't have to look at her anymore. "I do. A brother. He's working punching cattle and I'm not sure where he is exactly."

"What about parents?

"My mother has passed on and I haven't seen my father for years."

"Why not?"

"You ask a lot of questions, you know that?"

"You don't have to tell me if you don't want to."

"Good. Because I don't. Give a man a chance to wake up." He rolled out of his blanket and stood. "We best get moving. I hope we can make it all the way to the next town before nightfall. If you'll get something out for breakfast, I'll saddle the horses."

The horses walked along briskly, single file, following the deserted road. Every once in a while Sam, with Blu ponied by his side, would break into a trot, slowing only when the horses were slightly winded. Josephine had awakened cranky and Cassie had a hard time getting her up and fed. Now the younger girl rode behind on Pepper, with Ashes buckled in her saddlebag.

When they stopped for a quick bite to eat at noontime, Josephine mainly kept to herself and her animals. They ate quickly and continued on, agreeing to give the horses a longer rest in the afternoon.

Sam pulled up and waited for Cassie to catch up. He pointed to the ground. "Look." He ran his hand over the growing beard on his square jaw as he glanced back at Josephine. "Get on up here. Stay up with us."

"What is it?"

"Our friend from last night."

He dismounted and squatted, looking intently at the tracks in the dirt. He followed them a short way before returning to Cassie. "His right paw has been mangled. Could have got it caught in a trap."

"How can you tell?"

"He only uses it every other stride. And when he does, he doesn't put much weight on it." He glanced about. "After seeing this I'm really glad you woke up last night."

Josephine had stopped ten paces back. She sat listlessly in the saddle. "Come on," Cassie called to her. "That mountain lion is still around. We have to stay close together."

When Josephine didn't respond, Cassie rode back. One look at her sister's flushed face and uncharacteristically drowsy eyes and Cassie knew something was wrong. She placed the back of her hand on her moist forehead.

"Sam!"

In the time it took to dismounted, Sam was by her side. He reached for Josephine, laying her in the grass. Cassie unbuttoned her coat and threw it to the side. In an attempt to cool her, Cassie stripped her to her chemise, finding two red scratches on the inside of Josephine's wrist.

Cassie sucked in her breath. "Ashes must have scratched her when they were on the cliff."

Sam stood. "We need to get her to the next town quickly in hopes they have a doctor, and some medicine." He grabbed the canteen from Pepper's saddle and poured a good amount onto the child, covering her hair and clothing.

He gathered up the reins to all the horses. "I'll take her with me and carry her in front. You'll have to pony Blu and we'll let Pepper follow on his own. He'll not want to be left behind."

She nodded.

"You think you can keep up?"

"Just get Josephine to a doctor as fast as you can. Don't worry about me."

Sam looked doubtful. "Leading another horse is not as easy as it looks. Takes some getting used to. Especially at the lope." He went from one horse to another, checking their cinches. When he got to Pepper, he removed the pony's bridle and stuffed it in his saddlebag. "You're a good rider, so you shouldn't have a problem. Just pay attention to your surroundings and you'll do fine."

Sam picked the child up, careful not to jostle her too much. Her head rolled over and lay against his shoulder. She never opened her eyes. He handed her to Cassie so he could mount, then took her back in his arms.

Chapter Fourteen

Cassie watched as Sam guided his mount a few feet down the road and then stop. Josephine was cuddled to his chest, small and vulnerable. "Don't let the rope get too long. Keep Blu snubbed short. Actually, the closer she is to you, the safer it is. And, don't tie the rope off. Just wind it around the saddle horn twice, and hold the end, so you can let it slide easily."

He looked worried.

"Be careful of your fingers."

"I'll be fine! Just get Josephine to town."

Cassie mounted, feeling a lot more tentative than she'd indicated. She took the lead rope and did as Sam had instructed. She nudged her horse forward. As the rope tightened it lay taut against her leg, and pulled on Blu too, bringing the mare along. Meadowlark pinned her ears at having the gray drawn so near.

"Let Meadowlark know right now you mean business," Sam called from twenty feet up the road. "They'll get used to each other quick enough."

Cassie waved him on, her heart in her throat. It was unnerving having another horse so close. There were a lot of hooves down there to fall under. "Don't worry about us," she called back. "Just get moving and I'll catch up."

He waved. "Stay on *this* road. It can't be that much farther to Rosenthal."

"*Go!*"

Sam turned his horse and eased into a lope, quickly pulling away. Meadowlark jumped forward when Cassie squeezed with her legs, asking the mare for a trot. There was a moment of panic when Blu passed Meadowlark and the rope tightened. Her mare tugged the reins aggressively and again pinned her ears, wanting to be in the lead. Secure in her seat, she pulled Blu's head back next to her knee and snubbed up the rope, and kept riding.

Pepper, who had been grazing by the side of the road, raised his head at the sound of his companions leaving. He nickered once before taking off after them, eventually settling into his spot behind Blu.

***

Josephine lay on the doctor's table limp as a rag doll, while Miss Annabelle Hershey, daughter of the town's doctor, hovered close. Dr. Hershey was out, but she had expected him back hours ago. She assured Sam he'd be walking through the door any moment.

"How long can she stay so hot?" Sam asked gruffly, feeling completely useless. They'd reached Rosenthal ten minutes ago after riding hard for several hours. As soon as he'd brought Josephine in Miss Hershey washed her wound and applied sulfur to the red, parallel lines. She now bathed her in tepid water from head to toe, being careful to keep the child discreetly covered. Keyed up, he went over to the window and pulled back the yellow eyelet curtain, looking down the street. All was dark, and quiet.

No sign of Cassie.

"I need some ice," Miss Hershey said, interrupting his thoughts.

"Where can I get some?"

"You'll find the icehouse down the street on the left hand side. Behind the jail." The girl's long black hair, tied back with a ribbon, swayed when she dumped the water she'd been using and handed the white basin to Sam. "You'll need this."

"Please," he began, feeling a lump rising in his throat. "Take good care of her." Sam closed the door with a soft click and started down the street. Josephine was burning up. If they didn't get her fever down soon, she may start to convulse, or even worse. He'd seen it happen once when he was a boy and his ma had been nursing a sick friend. Nothing she did had seemed to help.

To make the whole nightmare worse, he'd come upon a split in the road a few miles before reaching Rosenthal. With nightfall coming on, Cassie could easily miss the small sign indicating the right direction to go, especially if she was fighting with the horses.

Leaving her had been a bad idea. He thought she'd be able to keep pace, at least for a while, but with Pepper running free to complicate matters, any number of things could have happened. Every possible scenario was playing itself out in his mind like a ghoulish stage play.

First he'd get the ice for Josephine. On the way back, he'd stop at the sheriff's office and see if there was anyone to help go out and search for Cassie. It was dark and she must be frightened. The street was quiet. There were a few lights in windows, but he hadn't seen another face except Miss Hershey's.

He found the icehouse and descended the thirty or so steps by the light of a lantern he'd found on the porch and helped himself to a pick leaning against the wall. He chipped enough ice to fill the bowl.

That done, he proceeded to the jail, where a lantern burned dimly from within. The door banged as he entered, waking a man sleeping in the jail cell.

"Where's the sheriff?" Sam barked.

"Who's asking?" The prisoner looked groggily through the bars.

Stench permeated the room, telling Sam the prisoner had been incarcerated for some time. The captive got up slowly and approached the cell door. Wrapping his hands around two of the steel bars, he positioned his face so he could get a good look at the newcomer, regarding Sam through rheumy eyes.

Sam's patience was worn thin. He didn't have time for games. But, he hadn't seen anyone else on the street so far. He began sifting through the things atop the desk.

The inmate snickered.

Just then footsteps sounded on the boardwalk and the door opened. A man in his early twenties bounded through the door, holding a gun. "Who're you?" He wasn't wearing a badge.

"Sam Ridgeway. I'm looking for the sheriff."

The man kept his gun aimed at Sam's chest.

"I never saw you ride in." His eyes narrowed as he looked Sam up and down. "Where you say you're from?"

"I just arrived with a sick little girl. She's at the doctor's office." Sam pointed at the pan of ice sitting on the bench next to the door. "She has a fever."

The young man's shoulders relaxed as he holstered his gun. "That's a relief. I'd thought someone had come in here to bust him out," he jerked his head in the direction of the prisoner. "The sheriff's dead. Killed by this one two months ago. We're waiting on a new sheriff and the judge so we can hang him."

The murderer let go a string of obscenities. "You ain't gonna hang me."

"Shut-up, Spencer! You'll get yours, and this whole town will turn out to watch."

"Not before my men break me out of this stink hole."

The young man's face turned ugly. "They haven't tried yet, have they?"

"They're coming and every last person in this rotten town will pay with—"

Sam picked up the ice and was several steps out of the jail building before the prisoner finished his sentence. The young man ran to catch up.

"Wait up, Mr. Ridgeway. I'm headed to the doctor's office myself."

Chapter Fifteen

"Whoa," Cassie said, pulling on Meadowlark's reins. The tired horse stopped abruptly, causing Blu's head to bump into her leg. Cassie reached out and stroked the gray mare's neck. Pepper trotted up behind and stopped, completely hidden by darkness.

"We're lost." She glanced in Pepper's direction, and toward the cat crying softly from the back of the pony's saddle, buckled inside.

"But don't panic, because we'll keep going and sooner or later, we'll have to come to something. We have to."

Ashes let out a dreadful howl from her long captivity in the saddlebag, probably needing to relieve herself. Cassie had to relieve herself in the worst way, too. She'd been putting it off for a good hour, stopped by the thought of coming eye to eye with the mountain lion that, she was sure, was still out there somewhere.

She didn't know what to do. She was worried sick about Josephine. Had Sam found the town he'd been talking about? She surely hadn't. Was there a doctor there to minister to Josephine? Oh, how she wished she'd kept up with him, even if it meant galloping the whole way.

The cat's cries were pitifully loud now. "Hush up, Ashes. You're going to bring that big cat down on our heads for sure. I know you have needs, but if I let you out you'll run off, never to be seen again."

Still, she decided, there was no help for it. She'd have to let the cat out of the saddlebag and just hope for the best. But first she had to dismount alongside these two horses in the dark. Cassie unwrapped Blu's rope from the saddle horn and held it in her hands. Grasping the saddle, she swung her leg over her horse's back and slowly let herself down until she felt the ground with her toe. By now the animals were comfortable with each other and tired. They stood quietly side by side.

With reins in hand, she turned and approached the worn-out pony, standing with his head hung low.

"Whoa, Pepper. Whoa now, boy." She stroked his neck as she felt her way slowly, inch-by-inch, down his body to the noisy cargo he was carrying.

She'd hardly gotten the buckle unfastened when the angry cat burst out and bounded off into the night. "Well, that's one problem I won't have to be dealing with anymore." Though saying that made her feel a little better, she still regretted losing a good friend.

"Now, I have to take care of my own business. Hmmm..." In the dark she couldn't see any place to tie the horses. "Well, I'll just make do."

Cassie stepped carefully to the side of the road and pulled down her britches. "This place is as good as any."

Just then she heard a voice. Far off, but definitely a voice. It was followed by a deep rumble of unpleasant-sounding laughter. For a brief moment Cassie had hoped it might be Sam. The fear in her heart told her otherwise. Shivers coursed through her.

Hide!

It was the same inner voice that had awoken her last night.

Hurry!

Cassie scrambled to pull up her pants. Losing her balance, she fell, landing palms down on a jagged rock and she dropped Meadowlark's reins as pain shot up her arm.

The laughter came again, closer this time.

On hands and knees she swiped back and forth frantically until she found one strip of leather. Turning, unmindful of the noise she was creating or what might be in front of her in the dark, she ran as best she could, pulling the two horses along like a pack train, stumbling in panic until she was off the side of the road and into some bushes. She couldn't tell if the foliage they were in covered the gray mare completely, for her coat seemed to shimmer slightly, even in the darkness. Pepper hadn't followed.

"Pepper! Pepper! Here, boy," Cassie called out in a panicked whisper.

Any moment, whoever it was would be around that bend in the road and find the black pony. If they did, it would only be a matter of minutes until her horses gave her away. Her hands shook so violently she could hardly keep them together as she rubbed them back and forth, creating the same swishing noise she'd used at feeding time to attract his attention.

"Pepper. *Oh, please, Pepper...*" she called out to him again in an urgent whisper, all the while continuing the rubbing with her hands. "Come on, boy, come here, come here, come here." Unshed tears burned behind her eyes. "Please come here, Pepper."

After a moment she heard his hoof beats coming through the grass as the pony trotted down the slope looking for his companions and whatever Cassie had to offer.

"Come on, that's right, come on."

He was by her side now, snuffling her hands and body. In a frenzy, Cassie jerked her rope belt from the loops on her pants and used it to encircle the pony's neck.

With the pony haphazardly secured, Cassie had hold of all three horses, and crouched close to their heads. Meadowlark and Blu stood silently side-by-side, but Pepper was still nosing around, looking for his treat.

"Stop." Cassie held his muzzle in an effort to settle him down. "I lied. I don't have anything for you. I'm sorry." He put his head down into the grass and pulled on the makeshift rope, grazing. "Get up here and be still!" Cassie yanked on the rope and circled the end of it around his muzzle, as she now heard the approaching horses. It sounded like there were several riders.

"Oh, dear God…"

Blu's head lifted and her ears pricked as she looked in their direction. Cassie quickly reached out and rubbed her muzzle, pulling on her to bring her head back down to where she could hold onto it. Now, Meadowlark's head came up, and she nickered softly.

"Shhhh. Quiet," Cassie whispered. She rubbed their muzzles, and blew in their nostrils in an effort to keep the oncoming horses' scents from them.

Cassie couldn't see the group, but she could hear their foul language well enough. Close to the spot where Ashes had leapt to her freedom, they stopped. She thought about her gun tucked away in her saddle bag. Should she try for it? Even if she were able to get it, the odds wouldn't be good.

"You hear somethin', Bart?"

"No."

"Coulda sworn I heard a horse nicker."

One man hawked and spit. "You're *always* hearin' something, Billy. You're skeert of your own shadow. There ain't no one this far from town."

"*We're* out here, ain't we?"

At that moment, the moon came out from behind a cloud and lit the area in a dim glow. Cassie ducked farther down, praying the horses would keep still. Her hand went from one muzzle to the next, as she stared between the branches. There were three men in all.

"I'll feel better when we bust my brother out of that rotten jail."

"We all will. By this time tomorrow we'll be long gone—that is after I kill some people. Now, let's get moving."

The skinny one suddenly sat up straight. "There!" He pointed in Cassie's direction.

Chapter Sixteen

"*Listen*!"

"Criminysake, Bill you—"

All three men stopped and looked directly at the bushes where Cassie was hiding. Sheer fright surged through her. Even in the coolness of the night, a sheen of moisture broke out on her skin and slicked her palms. *Where can I run? There are too many for me to escape*!

he fat man rode forward a step, and then lashed out, hitting the skinny one in the face and knocking him off his horse. "It's a cat, you idiot." He pointed ten feet up the road.

Ashes sat in the middle of the dirt lane, her tail curled around her feet, gazing at the men. After a melancholy mew, she started toward the side of the road. She slipped off into the tall grass, but lifted her head and looked at the men again, as if uncertain.

The skinny man stood up and brushed off his clothes. "Well, damn. How the hell would I know it was only a cat? At least *I* heard it."

He remounted as he wiped the blood trickling from his nose on the back of his hand.

"Don't get mouthy with me, or the next time you won't have nothin' to pick up."

The third man, on a big black-and-white horse, drew his revolver and shot off several rounds at Ashes. He laughed. "That takes care of that."

Cassie's three horses startled with the shots, but under the cover of the gun blasts their brief movements went unnoticed. She sucked in a horrified breath, brokenhearted at the thought of their beloved pet being blown to pieces. *Poor Ashes!*

"Why'd you go and do that, Seamus?" the young man yelled, as he pulled off his hat and hit it across his leg in a show of frustrated anger. "That cat *never* done nothin' to you. *Nothin'*! He was just a poor little kitty."

Seamus continued laughing. "When did I ever need a reason for killin', Billy? Now be a smart fellow and listen to Bart and you'll stay out of trouble. If not..." He shrugged ominously. "Let's get back to the others."

He kicked his horse and galloped down the road. The other two followed behind.

Cassie stayed in her hideout for a good twenty minutes, huddled with the horses as she tried to calm her shaking nerves. Oh, Ashes! What a horrible way to die. What if those men decided to come back this way? What kind of a person shoots a cat for no reason whatsoever?

What should she do now? Turn around? Yes, at least until daybreak. That was better than going in the same direction as those frightful men.

Totally exhausted from her expenditure of energy and the awful fright, she sat down on a rock, letting her shoulders slump forward and closed her eyes. In the quietness of the night Pepper nudged her shoulder, perhaps still looking for the treat he thought she had. His muzzle came up to her ear and his warm breath tickled her face and brought a rush of hope.

She reached over and scratched under his cheek. "You almost gave us away, you bad boy. But I still love you." Disappointed again at finding nothing, Pepper dropped his muzzle into the grass and started grazing.

***

Sam handed the bowl of ice to Miss Hershey and went directly to Josephine's side. "Any change?" He ran his hand over her hair, taking in the small scrap on her face with a heavy heart. She looked so sweet. Like a little angel. But the heat radiating up into his hand was more than he could handle. He turned to face the nurse.

"No," she replied, holding the pan. "She hasn't woken up. But this ice should help."

Miss Hershey's eyes lit with pleasure when the young man Sam had met in the jail followed him through the door. He took off his hat and held it in his hands.

"Jonathan, what brings you out tonight?" she asked, her voice softening.

"I ran into this fellow down at the jail," he said, nodding at Sam. "He needs our help."

"No word from your father?" Sam asked.

"No. And I'm extremely worried. He's never done this before, gone off without letting me know where he is or when he'd be returning. I have no idea what could be keeping him away so long."

Sam rolled up his sleeves. "Let's get this ice placed around Josephine before it melts. We'll need some towels."

Miss Hershey left and returned within minutes with several towels. Sam lifted Josephine in his arms as she laid one out underneath her.

"Okay, set her back down," Jonathan said.

Annabelle and Sam quickly rolled the remaining towels up and put them around Josephine, forming barriers to hold the ice. That done, they laid the ice all around her small body.

Jonathan stepped forward and stuck out his hand. "Now that the important things are done, I'd like to introduce myself. We never got a chance to meet proper in the jail. The name's Jonathan Pearson." They shook.

Sam's mind was anywhere but here. He had to get out there and look for Cassie. Any number of things could have happened to her.

Sam looked at Josephine and was filled with warmth. He took her hands in his. "She feels cooler," he said as his thumb caressed the back of her hands. "Feel."

Miss Hershey placed her cheek on Josephine's forehead. "I don't know. She seems the same to me. I think it's a little too soon yet to expect the ice to be working."

"What else can we do?" Sam asked, frustrated. "You must have some medicine here."

"Nothing for a fever, Mr. Ridgeway. It's up to Josephine now to fight off the infection from within. The fever helps her do that. All we can do is try to keep it from going too high. The rest is up to her."

Sam was torn. He didn't want to leave Josephine, not for a second, but he needed to find Cassie. Making a split-second decision, he grabbed his hat from the wall and put it on.

Both Jonathan and Miss Hershey looked surprised.

"The right fork before town. Where does it lead?"

"Clayton. But it's a rough road. And long. A good three days' ride."

"Do you have a fresh horse I could use?" Sam asked.

Jonathan's eyes narrowed.

"In order to get Josephine here as fast as I could I had to leave her sister behind. I think she must have gotten lost."

"And taken the road to Clayton?"

"Exactly. It's the only thing I can think of." That wasn't quite the truth, but Sam didn't want to go into all the other possibilities that could be holding her up.

He grabbed the doorknob. "Take good care of her."

Annabelle nodded.

Jonathan put his hat on also.

"I won't leave Josephine's side for one moment, Mr. Ridgeway," Annabelle called as the men hurried out the door. "I'll care for her as if she were my own."

Chapter Seventeen

The horse Sam was riding pricked his ears as if sensing something ahead in the dark, something Sam couldn't yet see or hear.

"Cassie," he called out. "That you?"

"*Sam!*"

The answering call was loud and clear. It was Cassie all right, but it also sounded as if the whole United States Cavalry was descending on him. Pepper reached him first, circling the new horse with great interest. Sam dismounted and tied his horse to a tree, hurrying out to meet her. Without a word, he swept Cassie from the saddle and held her close to his chest, thankful she was alive.

"I never thought I'd see you again," she said, huddled in the safety of his arms. "It's been a wild night. How's Josephine? Did you find a doctor? Is she better?" Her voice was wary, as if expecting the worst.

"She's at the doctor's now," he whispered close to her ear. "They're doing all they can." He didn't want to tell her about the doctor being missing. Not now, with so much time and distance between her and her sister. That could wait. He rubbed her back.

Cassie leaned back, looking up into his face. "Thanks for coming for me."

He tucked her chin-length hair behind one ear, stroking down her curved jaw line with his thumb. "I'd never forgive myself if anything happened to you," he replied softly, wondering at the surge of emotion he was feeling. "How are *you*? I was worried."

Cassie's face crumpled and she tucked her head back into his shoulder. "They killed Ashes," she whispered against his chest. "Just shot her for no reason." She trembled and Sam pulled her closer.

"Who?" His cheek pressed softly to the top of her head and he felt a pang of sadness for the pesky ol' cat.

"Some men. I hid in the bushes when I heard them coming. Then, Ashes showed up and got their attention right when they were about to find me."

"It sounds like you think the cat's actions were deliberate."

"I know it sounds crazy, Sam, but that's what it seemed like. One man, he…he pulled out his gun and shot her. It was horrifying."

Sam held her away from him so he could see in her face, but didn't let go of her completely.

"How many were there?" These must be the friends of the prisoner in jail. The man named Spencer.

She took a step back and he instantly felt the void. "Three. But they said they were going to meet some more."

"Where did they go?"

She pointed in the opposite direction. "Up the road. That way."

Sam surveyed his surroundings in the dark. "That way leads to Clayton. Maybe they have a hideout somewhere up there."

"You know who they are?"

"I think so. Rosenthal has a killer in their jail waiting for the territorial judge to show up. He claims to have a gang just waiting to break him out before the town can hang him. Maybe he's telling the truth."

She gasped. "Are you saying they could be headed back to Rosenthal right now?"

"Josephine's safe. They were going to the jail, not the doctor's office."

"They were talking about something like that. About one of their brothers being in jail and wanting him out. They said they'd be gone by this time tomorrow, but not before they killed a lot of people."

Cassie ran to Meadowlark's side and mounted. "Come on—we've got to get back!"

Sam mounted. "I'm thinking the exact same thing. You up to riding some more?"

Her weary expression was gone, replaced with determination. "Just try to stop me!"

***

It was near daybreak when they finally rode up to the hitching rail in front of the doctor's office and dismounted. Unable to wait, Cassie tried the door while Sam tied all four of the animals and collected the saddlebags.

"Give her a second, Cassie," Sam called. "She'll open up."

Cassie knocked on the door a second time. "The doctor is a woman?"

"No. It's the doctor's daughter who's watching over Josephine at the moment. Unless her father has returned."

Cassie turned as Sam joined her in front of the locked door. "You never told me that. Does she know what she's doing?"

"Keep your voice down. You're going to wake the whole town." Sam put his ear to the door, listening. He knocked gently with one knuckle.

"Here she comes. I can hear her footsteps."

The curtain in the window was pulled back and a young woman peeked out. The door opened. "Thank goodness it's you. Come in, Mr. Ridgeway. Hurry."

With Sam and Cassie inside, the black haired young woman locked the door and leaned against it. Cassie rushed over to Josephine's side, placing her hand on her forehead. "I'm here now, sweetie. I'm here." She ran her hand back and forth over Josephine's soft hair, remembering the day she cut it. A sob lodged in her throat. *Why, she doesn't look better at all!*

"This is Annabelle Hershey, the doctor's daughter and assistant," Sam said, as the woman walked over to the other side of the table where Josephine slept. She put her hand on Josephine's forehead, too. "This is Cassie, Josephine's sister."

Miss Hershey brows drew down in confusion. "Sister?" She glanced over her shoulder at Sam. "Then—she's your daughter, also?"

Sam shrugged. "No. We're all just traveling together."

"Please, how is Josephine? Has her fever come down at all?" asked Cassie.

Miss Hershey's brows drew down in worry. "Exactly the same as when Mr. Ridgeway left. She hasn't woken up, either."

Cassie tried to hide her crushing disappointment. All this time she'd been picturing her sister better, and now this. It was too much to accept.

"Has something else happened, Miss Hershey? You look upset," Sam asked. Her eyes had filled with unshed tears.

"Yes. They found my father. He's been beaten half to death and is unconscious. Jonathan thinks it was the outlaws the prisoner keeps bragging about. Rosenthal is in great danger keeping him locked up." She looked away. "I think my father may die."

"Where is Jonathan now?"

"He's trying to round up some men. Unfortunately, there aren't many in this little town. Well, not many who are able bodied and know how to shoot well. Until the day that atrocious man killed the sheriff, this was a peaceful place. So much has changed so quickly."

Sam's gaze sought Cassie's as she held Josephine's hand. It spoke volumes, and she shuddered inwardly. He squeezed her shoulder in passing as he went into the other room, followed by Miss Hershey. Cassie glanced in as Sam looked the doctor over.

"He's not good, not good at all," Miss Hershey choked back. She pulled the sheet up closer to his chin and tucked it around him gently. "I don't think he'll make it more than a few more hours."

The gray-haired man was deathly white. His face, heavy with wrinkles, was so still Cassie thought he looked dead now. On the bedside table were his glasses, lying on a book.

This must be Annabelle's room because it was decorated in greens and pinks, with a big stuffed teddy bear sitting close to the bed in a whitewashed rocking chair. Several pretty dresses hung in a small closet and an array of perfume and toiletries mingled on a highboy.

So much had changed so quickly with her, also. She'd been so relieved when she'd heard Sam's voice calling in the darkness of the night. She'd just expected things to be different here...Josephine was supposed to be safe, with a doctor. Recovering.

Chapter Eighteen

There was a knock on the door. "Open up. It's Jonathan," a deep voice called through the weathered wooden panels.

Annabelle dashed past Cassie and unlocked the door. A tall young man slipped inside the room, closing the door behind him. The doctor's daughter fell into his embrace. His hands pulled her closer, unmindful of their visitors.

"How's he doing?" he asked softly, his gaze finding Cassie as he spoke.

"I fear the worst. How could anyone treat an old man so? I don't understand."

The newcomer set Miss Hershey aside gently. "I can only tell you that they're more animal than human. Not the kind of men you're used to."

Sam stepped forward. "What have you found out?"

"There's going to be a town meeting over in the saloon in a few minutes. Most of the men who live in the township will be there."

"Across the street?"

Jonathan nodded, his eyes troubled.

Sam turned to Cassie. "Get your gun out and make sure it's loaded. I'm going to go to the meeting to find out what this is all about. If you need anything at all just call out. I'll hear you."

She went over to her saddlebags lying in the corner and took the pistol out. Placing a box of extra cartridges on a ledge by the woodstove, she held the heavy gun, her eyes resting on Josephine. "I can take care of things here."

As the men turned to leave, Jonathan set Annabelle away. "Everything is going to be okay. You just stay put and keep this door locked." He nodded toward Cassie, whom he'd not yet been introduced to. "This boy looks plenty capable. He'll keep a close watch out for trouble."

Sam chuckled, then cleared his throat. "Ah, this boy's really a girl. Josephine's sister I was telling you about. Cassie Angel, that's Jonathan Pearson and Miss Annabelle Hershey. "

Cassie tried to smile. She should feel pleased that her getup had worked so well, even if she did feel shabby next to Annabelle. "Sam, be careful." She set her gun on the side table next to Josephine. He was so much older and experienced compared to the man named Jonathan. Even though she'd known Sam only a short time, she was confident he was as skilled with his gun. He could take care of himself, and them also, if need be.

The soft lamplight must be playing tricks with her vision. Sam's expression was different from anything she'd seen before. There was something soft there, sweet. Almost a boyish longing as his dark hair framed his face.

She glanced away, remembering his warm breath on her ear, his cheek caressing the top of her head. Could this be the same Sam Ridgeway who'd barged into their life only a few days before, offering protection and safe passage?

"Will do," he finally replied.

"We won't be letting anyone in," Miss Hershey assured Sam. "Will we…ah, Cassie?"

Cassie shoved her hands in her pockets and looked at the two lovebirds standing hand in hand. "No, we won't."

The door shut quietly behind the men and the two women stood looking at each other.

What must Annabelle be thinking? Cassie wondered as she nervously shoved her hair behind her ear and turned back to Josephine. Her clothes and ragged appearance were a far cry from the beautiful picture the nurse made, even in her disheveled state. "What can I do for her now?" She picked up Josephine's little, limp hand and kissed her fingertips.

"I think we should remove the damp towels and put dry bedding around her," Annabelle answered.

"Annie?" A soft plea came from the other room.

Annabelle sucked in her breath and ran to her father's side. Cassie followed.

"Water." He whispered the one word so softly Annabelle had to lean close.

"Here, Daddy." She lifted his head and held a cup of water to his lips.

His eyes widened briefly and his last breath came out on a sigh, his head rolling to the side. It knocked the cup from Annabelle's hand which clattered to the floor, spilling water everywhere.

"*Daddy?*"

Frantically, she patted his sallow cheek several times. "Daddy. Daddy!"

Annabelle's voice rose higher with each passing moment. She took him by the shoulders and gently shook him. When he didn't respond, she collapsed onto his motionless chest, crying uncontrollably.

Hurrying over, Cassie placed her fingers on the man's neck, feeling for a pulse. When she was sure that the poor doctor was indeed dead and nothing more could be done for him, she sat on the side of the bed and rubbed Annabelle's back, not knowing what else to do.

Annabelle was inconsolable, her sobs wracking her small frame so violently that they rocked the bed. Her fingers gripped the man's bedclothes in a tightfisted ball.

"Here, Annabelle," Cassie said. She pulled the girl's stiff body away from her father's, and turned her in her arms. She held Annabelle tightly, remembering the day her own mother had died. "Go ahead and cry," Cassie whispered.

Many minutes passed as Annabelle let her grief flow. Then she quieted and pulled away. Her eyes were vacant, lost. The clock on the mantel chimed softly. Cassie stood and pulled the sheet up over the departed doctor's head. It hadn't been that long since she'd done the same for her mother.

Chapter Nineteen

Sam stood just inside the swinging doors, taking in the barroom. It was dingy and dark. It reeked of stale, dirty bodies.

"Quiet!" the bartender shouted. His wooden gavel banged down several times on the bar top, rattling whiskey stained glasses and dishes soiled with leftover food from the night before. His eyes shone brightly with excitement above his long, gray handlebar mustache. "I will have *order* here!"

Jonathan, his elbow dangerously close to the banging gavel, was talking with a farmer. A skinny little man with a wooden leg stood nearby, listening. Two boys, who looked a lot like Jonathan, sat at the other end of the bar, rolling dice. Neither one looked a day over fifteen.

Bang, bang, bang!

Jonathan's face pinched in annoyance and he covered his ear with his hand. "Walter, do you have to pound that thing so hard? We're all right here."

"Yer darn tootin' I do. This here's important business. Y'all need t' shut yer traps."

One man, draped across the top of a scuffed-up table in a pile of disheveled playing cards, snored loudly. His partner threw back another shot glass filled with whiskey and belched. Sam counted that as his third since he'd pushed through the doors and joined the group.

Walter pointed the gavel at him. "We'll have civility here, Chester! Now, wake Larry up. Ever' man counts."

The drunkard shook the shoulder of his sleeping friend. "Larry," he slurred into his ear. "Wake up! All hell's breaking loose."

Sam glanced back through the open doors of the saloon, between the horses tied in front, and across the street one more time to make sure everything was okay over at the doctor's office. The boardwalk in front of the tiny building was empty. Satisfied nothing was amiss, he made his way to the bar and got comfortable, leaning against the shiny wood. He propped his boot on the brass footrest that ran its length.

These were the men that were going to defend their town against a band of cold-blooded killers? Miss Hershey had been dead right. They were a motley group to say the least. He couldn't have imagined any worse for a gun battle if he'd tried.

Walter held up his hand. "As we know, this here town is in danger of bein' set upon by gunmen," the bartender said. "Spencer's been sayin' it fer some time and now Jonathan says a newcomer to town not only saw them, but heard it directly from their own mouths. If that's indeed the case, what do you men want t' do about it?"

"I say we hang Spencer right now! Today," the one-legged man called out. He limped over to the spittoon, his irregular stride tip-tapping all the way to the end of the bar, and let go a stream of brown tobacco. "Then his men won't have no interest in Rosenthal no more."

The farmer shook his head. "Can't do that. It's against the law. Besides, that would make his men madder than they are now. Then where would we be? No telling what they would do if they took it upon themselves to get back at us, even though I agree Spencer deserves it."

"Let him go," the drunkard said to no one in particular. He stood and approached the bar, weaving and bumping into chairs and tables. He pushed up against the bar next to Sam, regaining his balance. "One less problem for us."

Now it was Jonathan who held up his hand, waiting to speak. One by one the men quieted and silence filled the room. "The way I see it, the gang out there thinks we're as good as sitting ducks now that our sheriff is dead. They won't be expecting a fight when they ride in to town to bust their leader out."

"Jist let 'em try, let 'em try," Chester shouted from the side of his mouth. He poured whiskey into his already-full glass, emptying the bottle and spilling liquor onto the bar.

Sam could guess where this was leading. Jonathan would volunteer to take on the duty of sheriff even though he was barely out of short pants. A nice young man, but Sam doubted he'd ever gone up against others before, especially outlaws.

"Let me finish," Jonathan said heatedly. "We need an authority figure here, someone who can make a plan and organize the few men we have. At least until the law from Carson City shows up. We can't just sit here doing nothing but twiddling our thumbs until they come calling."

Chester looked around as if searching for another bottle. His hands shook violently as he picked up his shot glass, but stopped half way when he spotted Sam. "Who're you?"

"My own thoughts exactly," Walter the bartender added. "No telling what you're doing here! Maybe yer one o' *them*. A spy?"

Sam opened his mouth to reply, but Jonathan beat him to the punch.

"His name's Sam Ridgeway," he said, giving Sam a nod.

"I never seen him around town before. Could be he's part of the gang." The farmer stepped closer so he could get a better look at Sam.

"I'm not with the outlaw gang. I'm just a passerby; be moving on as soon as I can."

"That's easy 'nough said. Then why're you here listenin' in on privite business?" The bartender's hand slid to his side arm.

Oh, for Pete's sake. Why *was* he here, anyway? Everything had gone so haywire lately. If only Arvid Angel hadn't stolen his claim, he'd be off at *his* mine right now, minding *his own* business without a thought of Cassie and her little sister. But his if-onlys weren't doing him any good now, as the men crowded around.

Sam slipped his boot off the footrest and straightened. "Like I said before, I'm just passing through. Jonathan invited me along."

"Men," Jonathan said, interrupting the men's talk. "Sam's trustworthy. We need all the dependable men we can find. I'm going to take it upon myself to volunteer for the position of acting sheriff until a new one gets hired. Time is of the essence."

The men cheered, relieved to have someone taking the reins. Sam pushed a peanut shell around with the toe of his boot, thinking. Miss Hershey counted on this young man. Their future together wasn't hard to see. It would be a shame if anything were to happen to him now, especially with her father over there dying. And Josephine, she wasn't going anywhere for some time. Who knew how long it would be before she could sit her horse.

"I'll be your temporary sheriff if you want me," he said finally. "I'm going to be here for a while, and I've got more experience than Jonathan."

Jonathan looked at him gratefully, as if he'd been hoping he'd volunteer. "I think it's a good idea. I believe these men will be more apt to take orders from you, someone they don't know so well, than they would be from me. I vote yes."

The drunkard, head down on the bar, snored loudly. The farmer shrugged. His one-legged friend just looked suspiciously from one man to the other. Jonathan's younger brothers crowded up to Sam's side, in awe.

The bartender poured a glass full of whiskey and offered it to Sam. "I think you've just been elected our new sheriff. Drink up."

Sam took the proffered glass and poured the drink into the sawdust on the floor. "First rule. No more whiskey. At least until the crisis is over. We need our wits about us." He pointed at the farmer. "You, there, take these two men out to the trough and sober them up."

Chapter Twenty

There was a shout from outside. A horse galloped past the saloon doors, his hooves kicking up dirt and rocks, causing all the other horses tied at the hitching rail of the Happy Deuce Saloon to spook. One pulled loose and ran after the rider, his reins trailing behind him, flying this way and that.

Expecting danger, Sam hurried outside, along with every other body in the bar, to see if trouble had finally arrived.

At the end of the long street, next to the jail, a big black-and-white pinto slid to a stop, its rider firing shots into the air. The horse reared and the outlaw shot out two street lamps and the pane glass window of the dry goods store, opposite the jail.

"We're comin' for you, Spencer. You'll be outta that stink hole 'fore you can count to three."

"What're y' waitin' for? Christmas?" Spencer bellowed back from the jail.

Crowded between Brox, the farmer, and one of the wobbly drunks who'd latched onto his arm for support, Sam was unable to take a decent shot. The bartender, standing alone, pulled up his gun, leveling it on the outlaw and squeezing off a shot before Sam could stop him. Halfway down the block the window in the Blue Bell Café shattered, and inside a woman screamed.

"Hold your fire!" Sam yelled. He glanced across to the doctor's office. Cassie was standing within the doorframe, her Colt 45 in her hand. Fatigue etched her face, but her back was ramrod straight as she watched the scene unfolding at the end of the street.

The rider laughed brusquely. He spun his horse in a tight circle, shooting wherever his gun pointed, breaking glass, kicking up dirt and spooking horses. Cassie darted inside and slammed the door. The crowd outside the Happy Deuce hit the boardwalk as shots flew down the street in their direction. Suddenly, the rider spurred his horse viciously and galloped away up a side street, whooping and hollering all the way until he was gone.

The men slowly climbed to their feet, brushing dirt and debris from their clothes. The faces of the two boys were ashen, all pretense of bravery gone.

Chester gawked at Sam. "Ain't y' going after 'im? If you're the new sheriff, do somethin'!"

"Could be he's trying to lure us into a trap. We'll move in our time, not theirs," Sam said, just before sprinting across the street.

"Was that one of the men you saw last night?" he asked Cassie, now inside the doctor's office.

"The hideous man who shot Ashes was riding a horse just like that. I'm certain it was him."

"No doubt. That animal is quite distinct."

"When do you think they'll make a move on the jail?" Cassie asked. "Soon?"

He nodded, even though he didn't want to add to her worry. "I'd think within a day or two. Spencer's a caged dog wanting out."

As expected, a frown furrowed Cassie's brow. "Annabelle's daddy passed on."

A rush of sadness took Sam by surprise. "That's too bad. How's she taking it?"

"Not well. She's still in there with him. I can't get her to leave the room."

Sam went into the bedroom to find the doctor's body covered with a sheet and Annabelle curled up on the bed staring at the wall. Leaving quietly, he closed the door with a muted click.

"As soon as Jonathan gets here, I'll have him go to the undertaker to get a coffin. We'll take care of the body. You and Annabelle shouldn't have to. For now, you need some rest."

"I can't sleep now," Cassie said. "Just look at her, Sam. She's so small and defenseless." Josephine's cheeks were two splotches of red on her little face. "I just got here. I need to do something."

"No arguing. You can't do Josephine any good if you pass out from exhaustion. Your eyelids are dropping half-mast right now. We'll look after her while you take a nap. Come on," he said, taking her hand. "There must be a bed up here somewhere."

She *was* too tired to dissent further. His big hand felt warm, wrapped around hers as he led her to the stairs.

The passage to the second floor was narrow. Sam had to duck his head to avoid smacking it on a low-hanging beam. At the top, the landing opened up to a tall ceiling and a hallway with three doors. Still holding her hand and pulling her along behind him, Sam glanced into the first room. "A study."

He guided her into the second room; it must have been the doctor's. It was clean and neat, with a bright red-and-blue overstuffed quilt on the four-poster bed. There was a highboy, cluttered with all sorts of interesting looking items that any man would probably love to have, and hanging on the wall was a tintype of the doctor in his younger days, next to a woman holding a baby. The window was open a few inches, and sweet, clean air filled the room.

"I don't want to stay up here, Sam," Cassie said as they neared the bed. She felt skittish being in such an intimate setting with Sam. She was getting used to his calm presence, and knew she was depending on him much more than she should.

He gently pushed her to a sitting position on the side of the bed and reached for her boot. She drew it back abruptly out of his hands. "I can do that."

The corners of his mouth tilted up as he rocked back on his heels. "Still as prickly as ever, huh? It's just a boot the last time I checked."

"Oh, really? And to think I thought it was a turnip," she retorted, trying to put some emotional space between them. "I can take it off by myself."

Sam stood, shaking his head, but his grin remained. "Sometimes I think the fairies dropped you in my path just so you could aggravate me and torture my every waking moment." His eyebrows arched, making him devilishly handsome.

Cassie looked away and mentally chastised herself. She liked Sam Ridgeway way too much. *Certainly* more than she ever expected to. She felt flustered with his nearness.

"Well, suit yourself, then," he said when she didn't respond. "Leave your boots on if it'll make you feel better."

At the door, he turned back. "But, don't you dare show your face downstairs until you've slept at least—" he looked to the window where the early morning light filtered in, "—at least two hours. We'll be watching over Josephine. She's fighting the infection, so don't worry. Get some sleep." He closed the door quietly behind him.

Cassie sat for a moment, and then slowly removed her boots. She was stiff and sore, and her eyelids fairly drooped. She lay back onto the soft quilt and pulled a corner of the cover over her body, a weary sigh escaping her lips. She closed her eyes.

After three ticks from the clock on the nightstand, her eyes eased open and she glanced around. Was it just her imagination, or was the room more shadowy now that Sam had gone? Around the highboy and under a brown corduroy chair that sat sadly along the wall, darkness seemed to shift softly, as if to taunt her. When something moved in her peripheral vision, she jerked the quilt over her head. Moments passed. She peeked out. It was just the breeze waving the curtain. Still, the quiet *tick, tick, tick*, sent a tiny shiver up her spine. It felt odd to be in the doctor's room—and on his bed—with his passing away just moments ago. She took a deep breath, glancing at the tintype of him on the wall. Was his soul still lingering nearby?

She was too worn out to worry over anything. Her eyes drifted down, and she let the tension that had been building in her body fade from her thoughts. "The Lord is my shepherd," she whispered. "There is nothing I lack. In green pastures you let me graze..."

Sam stood patiently at the closed door, his ear pressed against it, making sure Cassie wasn't going to get up. She was mumbling something. So many responsibilities on her small shoulders. When the soft drone of her voice quieted, he tip-toed down the stairs.

With enough light now coming in the window, Sam turned down the wick in the lamp and put the flame out. People braving Main Street were out talking excitedly about the shooting that had jarred them from their beds. Sam opened the door, looking for Jonathan, but found the two boys from the saloon instead. They were sitting on the chairs outside the door.

"Howdy," one offered, jumping to his feet. His brown hair fell into his eyes and he quickly pushed it back.

"You're the boys from the saloon this morning."

They nodded. "I'm Frankie, and he's Bill. Jonathan is our brother."

Sam stepped out and shut the door, keeping his voice low. "I thought as much. I'm looking for Jonathan now. Do either of you know where he is?"

"Yes, sir," Bill answered. "He's down at the jail, guarding Spencer."

Jonathan was going to get himself killed yet.

"I'd like you," Sam said, gesturing to Bill, the taller of the two, "to run down there and tell Jonathan that the doctor is dead and we need to discuss what we're going to do about it."

Both boys' eyes opened wide.

"Also tell him to circulate the word that we're having another meeting at ten this morning, back in the bar. Is there an undertaker in town?"

Frankie shook his head. "He died. But there's still a few coffins left in the back of the mercantile."

"Good. Go tell whoever's in charge we'll need one this afternoon."

Frankie turned to go.

"Hold on," Sam said, handing the boy a silver dollar he pulled from his pocket. "When you're done with that, stop over to the café and get three plates of breakfast. That should cover the cost. If it's not enough, tell them the new sheriff will settle up a little later on today."

"Yes, sir," they answered in unison, and hurried off.

Chapter Twenty-One

Sam didn't have to wait long before he heard footsteps on the boardwalk and the door opened.

"Good morning, Sheriff Ridgeway. I'm Grace Hearthgrove. I've—" Unable to go on, she dabbed at her puffy, red eyes with a handkerchief that was twisted in her hand. "I'm sorry. I just got the news about David." She stopped and looked away for a moment. Her voice was smooth as honey, with a soft southern drawl.

Sam marveled at how fast the news had traveled. A warm, cinnamon scent followed her through the doorway. She was tall and slender and a few years older than he. Her chestnut hair was piled high on her head, with several locks falling down around her attractive face. "I just returned this morning to the heart-breaking news," she continued. "Where is his…"

Sam pointed to Annabelle's room. "In there, ma'am. But," he added quickly as she turned to go, "I'm sorry to be so tactless—but…" he began again. "As you know, the doctor is already dead, but this little girl here, isn't." He indicated

Josephine, lying on the examination table. "She has a high fever. Is there anything you might know of to help bring it down?"

Seeming to see Josephine for the first time since entering the room, a small sound escaped her mouth and she went over to the child's side. "Of course, Sheriff Ridgeway. There will be time for grieving later. I'll do whatever I can." She placed the back of her hand on Josephine's forehead, and then ran it down her cheek. "She's extremely hot. What happened?"

"She was scratched by an animal and it's gone into infection." In his mind he could see Josephine standing on the cliff's edge, her eyes as round as saucers as she firmly gripped her cat. He pointed to the marks on Josephine's small arm.

Grace Hearthgrove looked at Josephine for several moments. She lifted each eyelid. "We packed her in ice a few hours ago. I think it helped. And the doctor's daughter put sulfur on her wound."

"Both very good." She nodded in thought. "At this point, I'm afraid it's mostly up to her. Our efforts will be for our own peace of mind, with the outcome left to God." She smiled sadly at him again across Josephine's small, unconscious body. "But that won't stop us from trying, will it? Is she your daughter?"

Sam shook his head. He could see she had more questions, but kept them to herself.

She went back to the door and opened it, looking up and down the street until she saw someone. She waved, calling, "Mr. Fennimore, over here. Can you go over to my house and wake my father? Tell him I need some goldenseal, as much as we have, and bring it to me. Can you do that?"

Sam heard a mumbled response.

"And then go over to the ice house and get me a load of ice. I need it right away."

Sam looked around the woman to the door. The one-legged man stood there, his hat in his hands. "I'm sorry to hear about David," he said to her. "Such a sorrowful shame. And the two of you to be wed next week."

The woman straightened, as if gathering her courage. "That it is, Mr. Fennimore. Thank you for your kind words, but now time is of the essence. Can you hurry?"

He slapped the tattered, black hat back on his head and nodded. "Yes, ma'am. I'll do whatever I can to help."

She closed the door. "If you could get me some tepid water, Sheriff Ridgeway, I'll give her a little bath while we wait. That will help cool her."

***

Air caressed Cassie's face, causing her eyelids to flutter. She was so warm and comfortable, languishing in a sea of utter euphoria. Then a strange sound made her eyes pop open with a sense of urgency. Someone was lurking nearby. She lay still.

Where was she? Nothing looked familiar. Was this somebody's house? Fatigue, stronger than her fear, drifted over her like a heavy blanket, numbing her limbs and immobilizing her. Then another bump on the windowsill made her catch her breath.

"*Meoooow.*"

Cassie pushed up on her elbow and looked up. Ashes! Not only alive, but standing right there in the bedroom window. The cat jumped down effortlessly and started rubbing against the carved leg of the big mahogany bed, mewing her every complaint.

Cassie reached for the cat and held her close to her face, relishing her warm, soft-as-silk fur. "I thought you were dead! You aren't hurt, are you?" she asked, quickly turning her upside-down and rolling her back and forth, looking for any type of wound.

Ashes purred all the louder, obviously happy to be reunited. Cassie set her on the quilt and the cat flopped over instantly, her paws kneading the cover. She stared at her mistress in a long, shuttered gaze.

"I'm glad you woke me up," she said quietly to the cat. "I may have slept all day if not for you." She slipped her boots on and tied up the laces.

Halfway down the staircase Cassie stopped, an unfamiliar voice drifting up to her. It wasn't Annabelle. And it certainly wasn't Josephine. Cassie took a slow step, listening to the soft, silky, unhurried words, her hand tracing down the hallway railing as she went. She stopped in the doorway. A woman stroked her sister's forehead with a rag and then dipped it into a basin of water. Although she didn't think so, Cassie must have made some sort of sound because the woman turned around.

Chapter Twenty-Two

"Is everyone here?" Sam asked Jonathan in the back of the saloon, the morning well underway. They'd pulled some chairs into rows so they could have a meeting without the attendees thinking too much about drinking.

Sam had eaten a portion of the blackened bacon and plenteous flapjacks that Frank had gotten from the Blue Bell, leaving more than enough for the remaining people in the house, including Cassie.

The doctor's fiancée had prepared his plate, smothering the warm, doughy cakes in melted butter and syrup from the doctor's icebox, making Sam feel a wee bit uncomfortable at being helped to another man's provisions. He'd been hungry though, and had eaten his fill at her encouragement.

Jonathan looked around. "This is everyone." It was the same group as before, with two additional young men around the ages of Frankie and Bill. The two drunks slept on in the corner, never having left the saloon at all.

"Wake up those two," Sam directed.

Frankie went over and picked one of the men up off his face using a handful of hair and began firmly patting his cheek. When this failed the bartender handed the boy a bucket of water and the youth dumped it over their heads. They came up sputtering.

"What the heck," Larry cried, blinking and trying to figure out what just happened. When he saw Chester in the same condition he was in, he began to laugh.

Sam cleared his throat. "Men, thanks for coming back. As you know we have some planning to do. We don't know when the outlaws will make their next move, but I believe it will be sooner rather than later."

Walter had removed the white apron he'd had on the last time Sam had seen him banging the gavel on the bar top, and now had two six-guns strapped to his hips. In one hand he held a rifle and in the other a biscuit, crumbs from which dotted his mustache.

Sam looked at a stout farmer with his bulging legs and arms. "Your name?"

"Broxton Lee. But I go by Brox."

It will be easy to remember his name, Sam thought fighting a smile. It rhymed with ox, an animal he resembled.

"You?"

The one-legged man stood a little straighter in response, his suspenders taut on his shoulders.

"Jasper Fennimore." He sniffed and looked around the room importantly. "Friends call me Jasper."

A few men laughed and Sam held up a hand. "As of now we know we have three men outside of town and one in the jail. That's not a solid number—there could be more. Those are just the ones we're sure about."

As he looked from face to face, Sam felt as if he had a boulder in the pit of his stomach. What were their odds against a bunch of outlaws? He needed to keep Cassie and Josephine and the rest of these townsfolk safe.

"We all saw what kind of men we're dealing with by the one who rode in here this morning shooting at anything and anyone. Not to mention murdering the sheriff and brutally beating the doctor to death. They don't care who they kill in their quest to free their leader. Now, I'm not thinking we have many sharpshooters here. Am I right?"

Walter elevated his rifle.

"I saw this morning just how sharp *you* are. It's a wonder your wild shot didn't kill an innocent bystander," Sam said, leaning over and pressing the rifle back to the bartender's side. "What we have to remember is that this is a town filled with women and children, and these houses aren't made of rock. Every shot has to count. I don't want any unnecessary shooting on our part, sending bullets everywhere. That's why we're going to do things a little differently from the usual shoot-out. If it came to that, we'd be out-gunned. We wouldn't stand a chance."

"What exactly are you thinking?" Jonathan asked. His hat was tipped back, eyes earnest.

"Brox, you have a couple of strong horses you use for plowing?"

"Sure I do."

"I want you to go get them." Sam motioned to the group of boys sitting together. "Take one of these fellows to help you. On your way back find a couple of big logs and bring them along."

Broxton stood. "Come on, Danny." The boy jumped up importantly and took off after the farmer, who was already out the door.

Sam looked at the remaining town folks. "Who has some extra livestock, preferably young horses?"

Walter, Jonathan, and Jasper all nodded.

"From what I've gathered, there are two roads into Rosenthal, is that right?"

"You're correct," Jonathan replied.

"Okay, good. Walter, take the yearlings and tether them, one on each end of the town, as far out as you can, but where a lookout will still be able to see them from the rooftops. I believe that'll be about a half mile." He glanced to the boys. "You'll be the lookouts."

Jonathan nodded, a small smile playing at the corner of his mouth as he followed Sam's line of thinking.

Sam continued, "Bill," he gestured to the boys again, "you'll watch on the east end of town. Frankie on the west. We'll get a good five to ten minutes' warning, if it goes as it should."

Bill and Frankie stood up, all smiles.

"This isn't a game, boys," Sam said, fixing them with a powerful stare. "If anyone lets down, even for a moment, and doesn't fulfill his responsibilities, the whole plan could fail. That would mean a lot of bloodshed."

Their smiles faded and brows dropped, all traces of tomfoolery gone.

Larry stood up and, still a bit drunk, knocked his chair over in the process. "Hey, what about us? What's our job?"

"You sober?" Sam asked, sizing up the two men.

"Purt near."

Sam looked at Jonathan, who only shrugged.

"I need you to dig through the trash and collect all the empty bottles you can find, take them into the back room and break them in a barrel. When you're done, take the whole thing over to the back door of the jail house, but keep it covered. And take your friend with you."

Both men wobbled to the back door of the saloon and out into the alley.

That left Jonathan, Jasper, and a boy named Pug. And, ashamed of himself for thinking it, Sam knew how the boy had gotten that name. He had a face only a mother could love.

"Jasper. Pug. Make the rounds and quickly tell everyone what's going on. They need to take cover and stay inside if any shooting starts."

As they left, Sam started for the street. "Come on, Jonathan. We're going over to the jail to do a little carpentry." He chuckled at Jonathan's confused look. "Bring some hammers, nails, and a few blankets, enough to cover the front window and to make a partition between the cell and the office. I don't want Spencer to see what we're doing."

Chapter Twenty-Three

Cassie felt her face warming under the woman's sympathetic stare. "Who're you?" Cassie asked, when she finally found her voice. She felt shabby in comparison to this woman, whose spotless white eyelet apron was tied around her tiny waist and blossomed in a perfect bow at the small of her back. Expecting to find Sam or Annabelle caring for Josephine, this complete stranger had her mind whirling.

"I could ask the same question of you." Her voice was soft and compassionate.

At that moment, Annabelle came out of the bedroom. Her eyes were red and swollen and her hair a mess. When she saw the woman, she gave a cry of joy and fell into her arms.

"Oh, Grace!" Annabelle gasped, hugging herself to the woman. "Poor Daddy! They killed him." She gasped and she set into another bout of crying, holding her friend and sobbing inconsolably.

Cassie hurried past the two of them over to Josephine's side, where a fresh supply of ice had been administered. "How is she?" she asked, ignoring Annabelle's hysteria. It wasn't that she didn't feel bad for the poor girl, because she did. There were just other things to worry over.

"About the same since I've been here," the woman replied, looking at her over Annabelle's head. "But I'm just about to make up a goldenseal poultice and some tea. I've had good results with it in the past." She smiled. "Never lose hope."

Cassie shook her head. "No, I'm not." She was grateful that this woman seemed to know what she was talking about. "How can I help?"

"First things first. Sam, I mean, Sheriff Ridgeway gave me explicit orders that you were to eat as soon as you came down. Come on," she said, proceeding to the kitchen and pulling Annabelle along after her, "you must be famished. I'll put the herbs on to steep while you two have some breakfast."

Cassie *was* starved. It felt like an eternity since the meager little breakfast they'd eaten before packing up and hitting the trail yesterday morning.

"I'm Grace Hearthgrove, the school teacher here in Rosenthal," she said, putting water in a pot and stoking the fire. "You see, 'To teach is to learn twice,'" she added with great flamboyance. Her imitation French accent was stilted by her southern drawl. "My great uncle, Joseph Joubert from France, said that. After his death, his works were even published."

Cassie took a seat at the table next to Annabelle and put a flapjack on her plate. She helped herself to the butter and syrup in the center of the table, and to the bacon, too. She began eating, trying to keep some semblance of etiquette even though she longed to wolf it down.

"David and I," the woman continued, "Dr. Hershey—" At that her voice caught, and she paused, her hand shaking as she pulled some of the herb from a cloth bag and put it in the pot. "We...were to be married next week."

Cassie wiped her mouth quickly with her napkin. "I'm so sorry to hear that." She thought about the doctor. He looked as if he'd been a kindly man, and even with their difference in age, Cassie could picture the two of them together.

Finished with her task, Grace turned. "I guess we'll be having a funeral this afternoon." Her voice was filled with sadness. "But first we have a poultice to make for Josephine and hopefully get her to take some of the tea."

Annabelle just stared out the window, sniffing and wiping her eyes with shaky hands, between bites.

"Thank you..." Grace's expression was expectant and Cassie realized she hadn't yet told her her name.

"I'm Cassie Angel. And Josephine is my sister," she said, looking toward the examination room.

"And Sam?"

That was an excellent question. After last night in his arms, with moonlight all around, she wondered that herself. She must keep her head about her, though. "He's a friend. He offered to help us travel to Coloma."

It sounded strange even to Cassie's ears—a man, a stranger, really, being so inconvenienced for a couple of girls he didn't even know. "He knows our Uncle Arvid," she added quickly. "Arvid Angel."

"I see. Sam Ridgeway seems to have a big heart. That was kind of him. But why Coloma? Family?"

The pot jiggled on the stove top, the water obviously boiling. Grace took hold of the handle and stirred the contents.

"No. No more family except our uncle." Cassie dropped her eyes, remembering the last visit from Uncle Arvid. Even if he hadn't said it, she could tell he'd been out of sorts about something. In the morning, he'd been gone, as was his usual mode. "And, we don't even know where he is," she finished.

"Life is funny, you know," Grace said. "Sometimes it brings us the strangest things. You see, my papa is the minister here in Rosenthal. He's old now, but when he was young, my mama died, too."

She glanced at Cassie before going back to her work, "I was just seven years old at the time. We struggled along by ourselves for a few years, but it was hard. I tried to take care of him and the household and also go to school. A girl needs a mother around to teach her about the world. And about life. How to be a lady and what men expect from them. Men don't think the same way we do at all." She laughed. "God made us quite different, and I'm not speaking about the obvious difference."

Cassie felt her face warming. She liked Grace and felt a kinship growing.

"So, he married again, giving me a mother." She glanced at Cassie. "She passed on three years ago from influenza."

"Siss…"

At the barely audible call from the other room, Cassie dropped the fork she held and bolted from her chair, running to Josephine's side.

"Josephine!" she pleaded, picking up her sister's hand. "Did you say something? Josephine, are you awake?"

Grace and Annabelle hurried after Cassie and went to Josephine's other side.

"She called for me. Did you hear it?"

Grace and Annabelle shook their heads. Josephine's face was warm but she no longer had beads of perspiration on her forehead.

"I didn't hear anything," Grace offered, with an apologetic look. "But that doesn't mean *you* didn't. I'm going to get the tea and poultice. They both should be ready by now."

Sam came through the door at that moment, his hat dangling from his fingertips. The brass hinges squeaked as he closed the door gently behind him. He looked into Cassie's face.

Chapter Twenty-Four

"Sam," Cassie breathed, her eyes searching his face, and the hint of a hopeful smile playing at the corners of her mouth. "Josephine is waking up."

"That's the best thing I've heard for three days." The sight of even a glimmer of happiness in her eyes did funny things to his insides. "I've been worried about her, and that's no lie. But the truth is, more trouble is headed this way soon enough. None of you women are to leave this building. This afternoon, when we have the funeral, will be the only time. Cassie, I'll have one of the boys stay here with you and Josephine."

"What's this I hear about the funeral?" Grace asked. She came into the room carrying a white porcelain bowl with a spoon protruding over the top. "What time?"

"Three o'clock," Sam answered. "Someone's bringing a coffin over now and others are at the cemetery digging—well, uh, taking care of things."

Cassie hovered around Josephine, seemingly unaware of the others in the room. She stroked her sister's cheek as she whispered into her ear, "Come on, Josephine, open your eyes. I know you can do it, sweetie. I heard you speak just moments ago. Come on, honey—do it for me."

Grace set the bowl on a cabinet behind Cassie. "As soon as Cassie and I have this poultice on Josephine's arm, I'll prepare his body. I haven't had a chance as of yet."

Sam put his face close to the bowl and sniffed, pulling away quickly. "I thought I smelled something rank." His eyebrows arched and his mouth pulled down in a grimace. "What is that, anyway?" He quickly stepped away. "Never mind. I'll take care of the doctor; you three take care of Josephine."

When Grace opened her mouth to object, he put up his hand. "No arguments. I'm the new sheriff, and I'm calling the shots."

"Sheriff?" Cassie asked, surprised.

He was still standing by the bedroom door. "Oh, I guess you haven't heard. The men have appointed me sheriff while we're dealing with the outlaws."

"Sheriff," she murmured, turning back to Josephine. "That sounds plenty dangerous." Cassie took a small amount of the warm poultice and gently patted it in place on one of the welts. She repeated the process several times, then wiped her hands.

Grace was back with a china teacup and clean dish towel. Cassie began slipping an arm under Josephine's shoulders.

"Here, let me." Sam came forward and lifted Josephine's head and shoulders up slightly, freeing Cassie to do the rest. With a teaspoon, Cassie dribbled a tiny amount of the tea between Josephine's lips. "Come on, take a little. Try to swallow it, Josephine. It's good."

The liquid just leaked out the side of her mouth, and Cassie's face clouded unhappily. The need to do something overwhelmed him.

"Josephine, this is Sam. Sam Ridgeway," he said briskly as he stroked her hair.

Cassie looked up at Sam's persuasive tone.

"I want you to start minding your big sister!" He cleared his throat and then began again, using his sternest voice. "Drink this tea. She's only asking you to take a couple sips, and you're being headstrong and ornery. Mulish, even."

"Ummm."

Josephine's eyes were still closed but this time there was no denying she'd made a sound.

"Sam!"

"I heard it. See if she'll take some tea."

Grace hovered close behind, and Annabelle, who was the quietest woman Sam had ever encountered, waited with a cloth ready to dab the child's mouth.

"Cass..." The partial word was wobbly. "Cass...," Josephine began again, and then slowly opened her eyes. When Josephine saw her big sister, she began to cry.

Sam leaned in close. "Shhhh, honey, shhhh. You're going to be fine, now," he whispered into her ear as Cassie hugged her.

A fragile hush descended as they watched Josephine take another sip from the spoon Cassie held to her lips, spilling more down her chin than she got in her mouth. "You're going to get better," Cassie said, smiling into Josephine's face. "Here, take a little more."

A banging at the back of the house made all three women jump. Something heavy dropped onto the porch.

"That'll be the coffin," Sam said, looking at Grace. She rushed away and returned, followed by Jonathan. The young man hurried to Annabelle's side.

Sam signaled Grace. "Can you take over here?" he asked, looking down at Josephine's body cradled in his arms. She took the child from him as Cassie continued spooning in the warm liquid.

Sam opened the door to Annabelle's bedroom, "Jon?"

Jonathan stepped away from Annabelle and followed Sam. Sam closed the door.

Both men stared for a few moments at the sheet-covered body lying motionless on the bed. When Sam pulled the covering down the doctor's face was a mass of dark black and blue bruises. It was a shame Annabelle would remember her father like this.

"Those sorry excuses for human beings," Jonathan said between clenched teeth. "He wouldn't stand a chance against a flea, let alone a gang of outlaws. It's disgusting, is what it is."

Sam pulled the sheet back up. "You go up and grab some clean clothes. And be quick. No telling when those outlaws are going to make their move."

"You think your plan will work?" Jonathan asked, still looking at the body of the doctor motionless under the sheet. His face had lost a little of its color.

"Has to." Sam jammed his hand through his hair in frustration, hoping that what he said was true. He himself wasn't a killer and didn't want to become one, if he could help it. But their options seemed limited. "Those men are cold-blooded murderers." He tipped his head toward the body. "Proof's right here. They'd just as soon shoot you as say hello."

Sam went to the window on the opposite side of the bed and pushed the curtain to the side. All was quiet. He caught a glimpse of Jasper and Pug coming down the boardwalk. They opened the door and went into the Blue Bell Café.

He turned back to the bed just as Jonathan was about to leave the room. "I'm relieved we got all the things down at the jail put into place. I'll feel a whole lot better when the farmer returns with the logs. How far out is his place?"

"About half an hour," Jonathan mumbled. "Depending on how long it took him to find something suitable, he should be getting back anytime now. I'll keep my ears open. He'll pass by here on his way down the street and I'm sure he'll make a racket."

"Good. Now, off with you. I'll have the doctor's body ready when you get back with his clothes."

Jonathan left and for a moment Sam listened to the quiet conversation coming from the examination room. He thought he could distinguish Cassie's voice amid Grace's southern drawl and Annabelle's soft, high tones. Josephine had come around. The thought brought a rush of happiness. When had those two girls become more important than his dreams?

Sam went to the water pitcher and splashed some water into the bowl and dipped in a cloth. Wringing it, he noticed Cassie, or someone else, had put her old hat and a few of her things atop the polished mahogany dresser along the wall. Next to the piece of furniture, on the floor in a heap as if thrown down in a hurry, were both his and Cassie's saddlebags.

For just an instant he felt the old pull of the gold claim. His gaze stayed on the leather bags as he listened to Jonathan in the upstairs bedroom. But the pull was faint, and he barely noticed it. Other things were more important now. Like Cassie. As he'd held her in his arms last night all time seemed to stop. He longed for that again. Her goodness. Her smile.

And, of course, there was Josephine. That tough little angel who'd sneaked her way under his skin. It would be some time until she was well enough to actually sit her pony, but the thought of her smiling up into his eyes was enough to make him dance. And, he didn't even know how to dance—had never learned.

Sam shook himself out of his thoughts to get back to things at hand. He stripped the torn shirt from the doctor's body and washed his face and arms. Looking around, he spotted a comb. He contemplated the hair a moment, then swept it over to the right and curled some long stands around the doctor's ear. That was as good as it was going to get. Moreover, though he could hardly believe it himself, he was also concerned for all the people he'd met in this town. They were depending on him to figure out how to bring the outlaw in the jailhouse to justice without anyone else having to be buried alongside the good doctor and the sheriff.

Jonathan burst into the bedroom. "Brox is back with the logs. And they're big ones. Come on, he's just coming around the corner."

Outside, the farmer came around the bend of the street where a little one-room business called The Knitting Basket stood. Long reins trailed behind him as he slapped the horses' sides. "Get up, Samson. Haw, Delilah."

Danny walked behind, intently watching the straps that held the harness to the logs. The horses strained forward, their black coats glistening with sweat. Brox pulled them to a halt.

Sam went out to meet them. "These are huge," he said with satisfaction, patting the mare on the neck. Great streams of air bellowed from her flared nostrils. "Just what I envisioned. Place one here at the crook of the street where it can't be seen from the bend."

The farmer nodded and relaxed his shoulders. Danny walked up to his side.

"Put the other on the opposite side of town where the road leads to the sheriff's office. Around the corner of First and B Street, so it's not visible until you make the turn."

Broxton and Jonathan smiled, having caught on to what Sam was planning.

"Frankie and Bill?"

"They're in place," Jonathan answered.

"Good. All we can do now is wait. I'll be here at the doctor's if you need me, Brox. Can you take care of placing the logs?"

"Sure 'nuff."

Sam and Jonathan finished dressing Dr. Hershey while Grace set a table with cold meat and bread for their noon meal, although few felt like eating. The time crawled by. At three o'clock Sam felt hesitant about leaving Cassie while the rest of the town went out to the graveyard next to the church.

"We'll be fine," Cassie assured him as she held Josephine's hand. Josephine was awake now, but weak. "Bill assures me he's a good hand with a gun. Besides, how long will you be—fifteen minutes or so?"

"I'd just feel a lot better if we had this whole business over with. As much as I hate leaving you here, I don't want to abandon those town folks out there like birds at a turkey shoot. I *have* to go."

"Of course you do." She shoved him toward the door. "Go on, now. If you don't hurry they'll be done with the funeral before you get over there."

***

Arvid Angel exited Miss Hawthorn's deserted boarding house and slammed the door so hard the walls rattled and the welcome sign hanging above the door clattered to the porch. Broken Branch was a ghost town. "Where the devil did everyone go?" he spat angrily. He descended the steps and walked out into the vacant street. "It hasn't been more than three weeks since I was here." *And hid the deed in Cassie's drawer for safekeeping,* he thought. Now the town was all but empty and his two nieces were nowhere to be found. If that older gal had gone and lost it, there'd be hell to pay.

Anger and frustration scalded him. He slammed his fist into his palm. "Same ol' stinkin', rotten story of my life!" If it hadn't been for Sam Ridgeway trailing him so closely, he'd have ridden straight through to Coloma, and filed the papers on the claim before Sam could get there. Now he had to keep clear of him *and* find the girls.

The ring of metal on metal split the air. He looked down the street at the shops and buildings, but didn't see anyone. Again the sound disrupted the silence and Arvid started off toward the livery. At least the Sherman brothers were still in town.

He stepped into the smithy and took stock. Bristol held a horseshoe in a clamp as he heated it in the forge. Klem was slumped in a chair, his feet propped on a stool, watching.

"Boys," Arvid said as hospitably as he could muster.

Both looked up surprised, unaware of his approach. Bristol's eyes narrowed as he straightened to stand. He wiped his hands on the towel draped over his belt.

"I'm looking for Cassie and Josephine," Arvid continued.

Klem stood quickly but not before Arvid noticed the decrepit condition of his boot soles. He'd be hard pressed to scratch a match without burning his feet.

"You stole my watch," Klem accused, his face turning red.

Arvid began to sweat. He thought Klem was too dumb to notice. "What're you talking about? I did no such thing."

"You're a *liar*."

Klem stepped forward, but Bristol caught his arm. "It was broke, Klem, and not worth a plugged nickel. You can fight if you want, but I ain't tendin' you later."

Arvid wiped his sweaty palms on his pants. "I'm just concerned for my nieces' safety," he said, nimbly changing the subject. He needed to find out if Sam Ridgeway had come this way.

"That girl is the last person who needs lookin' after. She ain't defenseless. She shoots better'n Klem here."

"That's horse manure and you know it!" Klem retorted heatedly.

"I wish I did know it," Bristol said, "then maybe you'd be of some use to someone."

Arvid felt pretty sure he wasn't going to get any further, but he had to try. "Did a man named Sam Ridgeway come this way?"

"You're jist full of questions, ain't ya?" Klem sneered, settling himself back into his chair.

"Shut *up*, Klem!" Bristol barked. "If information is all you want, Arvid, this store is closed." He went over to the forge and picked up the hammer and began banging away.

Arvid walked back down to the boarding house, stewing. He knew little more than when he rode in. He searched the girls' room from top to bottom, making sure Cassie hadn't hidden the claim before leaving, with the intention of coming back for it later. He was going to find Cassie and the claim if it was the last thing he did. He'd risked his life stealing it from Ridgeway's saddlebag, and then spent every other dime he owned staying three steps ahead of him. In a sense, he'd earned the claim—it belonged to him! And all the gold in it, dammit!

Chapter Twenty-Five

The sun was low on the horizon when Jonathan barged through the hallway and into the examination room. "They're coming!"

The women jumped to their feet and Josephine struggled up to her elbow, her eyes big with fear.

"How many?" Sam asked.

"Just saw two. From the upstairs window. They're sneaking down the hill behind the livery, on foot."

Sam pushed everyone from the room and herded them into the kitchen. "Cassie and Annabelle, you know what I want you to do. Jon, you go over to the saloon and tell whoever's there to take their places. Go on, all of you. And be quick."

"Come with me, Grace," Sam said as he went back into the examination room. He picked Josephine up easily and bounded up the stairs. He placed her on the doctor's bed. "You be good and mind the adults," he said to her. "No shenanigans."

Back downstairs everyone hustled about. Sam jammed his hat onto his head and moved to the door. Cassie met him there.

"Be careful," she said, standing close, her hair falling softly around her face as she regarded him intently.

There it was. The light. The warmth deep in her eyes he'd seen before. And something else? Was she starting to feel this attraction that had begun to hound his thoughts? He looked away to keep himself from pulling her into his arms.

"You be careful, too. If you're faced with a choice, go on and shoot."

"You know I will, Sam. I can take care of Josephine and myself. It's you I'm worried about."

As he opened the door to leave a shot rang out, the bullet sinking deep in the floorboard between them. Sam dove behind the water trough as Cassie slammed the door. Sam drew his gun.

"If you set our man free no one will die!" called a voice.

Sam looked up and down the sidewalk. All was clear. He tried to make out where the voice was coming from.

"You hear me?"

The report of a gun blast was followed by the splintering of the wooden plank directly above his head. Sam rolled to the side to avoid the stream of water.

The voice had come from an alley two buildings over and across the street. Sam knew Walter was over on the boardinghouse rooftop by the jail and Mr. Fennimore, with his one leg, directly across the street. He'd instructed them not to shoot until, and if, he gave the signal. He needed to get farther up the street for a better view of the alley.

Sam dived, rolling across a narrow side street. He dashed into the building that housed the Padua Press, a monthly newspaper, and a leather shop. Inside, he took the stairs two at a time, then crept up to the window. With his back against the wall, he peered out to the street below. Seeing nothing, he unlocked the latch and swung the window wide, stepped through the tall opening and crept to the edge of the roof. When he jumped to the next building, a gun discharged several times and bullets scattered around him. With his pistol, he broke out the pane of a window in the new building and reached inside to unlock it. He was back down the stairs in a moment and onto the boardwalk, shielding himself with the wide banister from the barbershop. He gave a birdcall and heard one in return down by the jail.

All of a sudden Spencer's voice shouted from his cell, "Hurry up, you dung beetles. I've been rottin' away here for too long. Get me out!"

Two men emerged from the alley directly across from Sam and looked around. "This here town is full of women, is all," one said to the other. "There ain't a man between 'em. Look, they's all scairt 'n run away."

"Zat so?" Chester's unsteady voice called out from his assigned hiding spot. "We'll just see about that."

He fired two shots and the outlaws darted back to where they came from.

Sam shook his head angrily. Until now, he'd been the only target. "Darn you, Chester," he hissed.

A horse nickered. Then a barrage of bullets hammered the face of the small bank where Chester was hiding. When the shooting stopped, a long whistle pealed through the air followed by two short ones. That was the signal letting Sam know more riders were headed to town from the north end.

Now that Sam knew which direction the outlaws were coming from he felt a bit more confident. The road would bring the gang right past the two outlaws holed up in the alley, and end up in front of the jailhouse. It was a good two blocks from where he was and if he didn't hurry all could be over in just a few moments.

He holstered his gun. Grabbing the reins of a horse at the hitching rail, he took hold of the saddle horn with both hands and swung onto the animal's back. A barrage of firing erupted as Sam galloped toward the jail, some shots narrowly missing him, while others went wild.

Sam rode straight into the livery stable opposite the jail. Without slowing, he leaped from the saddle directly onto a ladder, scrambling up to the loft. From the barn window he saw the leader on the piebald galloping pell-mell toward the town. Two mounted outlaws followed close behind.

Just as he'd hoped, the three riders hit First Street at a dead run. When they rounded the corner at B Street the bulky logs lay solidly in their path. The piebald was quick, sailing over easily, but the other two horses sat down on their hocks, sliding to an abrupt stop and flinging their riders over their heads. The men landed with a thud. Across from them, Sam covered Walter and Broxton as they ran out and clobbered the outlaws on the head with their pistols and dragged them back into the building where they'd been hiding.

"Get this over with! What's takin' you so blasted long?" Spencer screamed from his cell.

From the corner of his eye, Sam saw a man in the alley crawl behind a watering trough and lie flat. The leader, still mounted, was in front of the jail. He pulled his rope from his saddle, expecting cover from his friends who were no longer there. He tossed the rope to the window and Spencer grabbed hold. Sam aimed and fired, hitting him in the shoulder. The outlaw jerked and slumped forward, spurring his horse into the safety of the livery, directly below where Sam was hiding.

All was quiet again except for the hysterical commotion by Spencer. A string of curses filled the air as he demanded yet again for his men to set him free.

Sam heard a moan from somewhere underneath him. Then came the sound of the wounded outlaw falling from his horse. He had to proceed carefully, for any movement would cause hay and dust to fall, giving him away. There was a scrambling sound and then voices.

"Seamus, you hurt?" The voice was high-pitched and wobbly. It didn't sound like a hardened killer.

"Yea, Billy, I'm hit. Drag me over there where I can get a look out this door."

"But, you need doctorin'!"

Coarse laughter turned into a sputtering cough. "Ain't no doctor goin' to patch me up, you dummy. Besides, did you forget already we beat the doctor to within an inch of his life? They buried someone out in the cemetery today. My guess is it was him. But, forget about that. We need to bust Spencer out of that jail before I lose the little blood I got left. Come on, pull me over there!"

Sam lowered himself quietly to the loft floor and tried to see between the boards, but they were too tightly set. He slowly pushed aside straw until he found a knothole. A small noise beside him made him turn his head. Ashes moved to his side and she rubbed adoringly against his head. Sam gritted his teeth. *Not now, you dang cat!* He tried to push her away with his shoulder, but she started to purr. It was then he noticed dust floating from the knothole and over the two outlaws.

"Ah, ah, ah, *choo*." The younger man sneezed, and then wiped his arm across his face.

Sam held his breath. A couple well-placed bullets through the old loft boards would easily kill him.

The young outlaw dragged the bigger one over behind some hay where he'd have a view of the jailhouse. As he propped the wounded man's back against a wall, the leader grabbed his underling by the shirtfront and viciously pulled his face to within an inch of his own. "That brother of Spencer's don't have the guts to break his own kin out. Besides, I don't know where he went. Maybe he's dead. It's going to be up to you to get out there and get it done. I'm telling you now to shoot anyone that comes within your sights. I don't care if it be man, woman or child. Just kill something, and the rest will run and hide."

Seamus shoved Billy away and spat out a glob of blood, wiping his mouth with the back of his hand.

Sam heard shouts from out on the street and then a shot. He wished he could go back to the window, but moving now would be suicide.

When a couple more shots sounded, the wounded man hissed, "See who that is!"

While Billy scooted to the door, Sam took the opportunity to move carefully over to the loft ladder himself.

"Well?"

"I cain't, I cain't," he stuttered. "I cain't see anything."

Sam inched toward the ladder.

Billy turned and looked up.

Chapter Twenty-Six

"Shoot, you idiot," Seamus bellowed. "Shoot!

Billy froze, his gun pointed at Sam's chest.

Their eyes locked and Sam dared not take a breath. Thoughts of Cassie filled his heart. He might never see her again. Or hold her in his arms. Never get the chance to feel his lips on hers. Never say I love you! Billy's hand wavered and Sam could see the sheen of perspiration on the young man's forehead.

"If you don't shoot, you lily-livered toad, *I'm going to kill you!*

Billy's face hardened.

Exactly at that moment, Ashes jumped from between some sacks of grain stacked on a platform and raced between Billy's boots, startling him. The blast from Billy's gun split the air and a lantern hanging above Sam's head exploded, raining glass down around him.

Seizing the moment, Sam hopped down the ladder, and then leaped from six feet up. He knocked Billy down and the two men rolled around the dirt floor. They slammed up against a support post, and Sam was knocked against it hard, hitting his head. Shaking it off, and with a thrust propelled by adrenaline, he pitched Billy off him and jumped to his feet. With a handful of Billy's shirtfront, Sam hoisted him up and smashed his fist into his face, holding nothing back. There were sounds of commotion outside, too.

The young outlaw was no match for Sam. The punch sent him reeling across the hay-littered floor and he crashed to the ground.

Seamus grabbed wildly at his bandolier but the bullets he extracted slipped in his bloody fingers as he tried to jam them into the chamber of his six shooter. Sam pulled his Colt 45 and blasted the gun from Seamus's hand. The outlaw cried out in pain.

"I'm saving you for the hangman's noose," Sam said. He closed the distance between them and picked up the outlaw's gun. "You and Spencer can swing side by side." He stepped close and, with his gun, knocked the man out cold.

Enraged screaming came from inside the jail. Sam ran over and pushed inside. Jonathan, Walter, and Chester were there, the latter holding his bloody arm to his body. The last outlaw rolled on the floor, his face in his hand. His cries of pain were pathetic. Beside him was the board with the broken bottles attached and scattered glass all around.

"I saw the whole thing happen," Jonathan said, his face gritty with dirt and sweat. "It was just like you figured, Sam. When he came through the door all the broken glass on the floor threw him off and he never saw the trip wire or the board until it hit him in the face." He slapped Sam on the back and let loose a nervous laugh. "Congratulations! You captured them all. You're one clever cowboy. Downright brilliant."

Sam looked around at the relieved faces. His gaze stopped on Chester, the only one who was hurt. "Sorry about that arm, Chester. But if it's the only casualty of the day, I'll be a happy man."

All the men nodded.

***

Cassie couldn't sit still another second. She could see the commotion at the jail was winding down and the men were milling around, talking and laughing. She bounded up the stairs and went into the bedroom where Grace and Annabelle watched over Josephine.

"How is she?"

"Sleeping now," Grace replied softly. "But I'm sure she's on the road to recovery. She's much cooler. And look here."

Grace gently picked up Josephine's arm. The scratches were still red but their intensity had lessened, and the marks weren't quite as puffy. "I believe she's out of the woods."

Annabelle was looking stronger, too. Her eyes were still bloodshot and anguished, but she was up and about, doing for Josephine. "Did you see anything, Cassie?" she asked quietly.

"Yes. Looks like we whooped 'em good. I'm not sure yet, but I think everyone is okay. And, in case you're wondering…" She paused and draped her arm around the younger girl's shoulder and pulled her close, "I just saw Jonathan talking with Sam on the boardwalk at the end of the street."

That brought a smile to Annabelle's face and Grace nodded with pleasure.

"I'd like to go down to the jailhouse and see what's going on," Cassie said.

"Of course," Grace responded. "Then you can bring us back the news."

Cassie bounded down the stairs and out onto the boardwalk, which was still wet from the bullet-pierced water trough. Hopping over the mud, she hurried toward the jail, anxious to see Sam. She couldn't wait to touch him and prove to herself that he really and truly was safe. When all the shooting had started she wanted to be out there with him, protect him. She'd had to push every bad thought from her mind, telling herself that he was still alive, still a part of her life.

Just what *did* Sam mean to her anyway? She was depending on him more and more these days. When he'd held her in the moonlight last night she'd wanted to run her hands over his chest and loop her arms around his neck. Lean into him, feel his body against hers. She'd wanted him to kiss her in the worst of ways.

Well? Who *was* Sam in the scheme of her life? Did he fit in with her dream of becoming a baker with her and Josephine's own bakery? That's all she'd wanted for as long as she could remember. Her mother used to tell her all sorts of wonderful stories of when she was a little girl helping *her* mama bake. Cassie's grandma, Cookie Foster, had been a successful businesswoman. She'd wanted that dream her whole life. And the gold claim Uncle Arvid had given them would provide the means to make that dream come true. It was all she needed in this life—or so she'd thought.

"Cassie! Over here!"

Sam was at the livery, waving to get her attention.

At the sight of his disheveled appearance her heart somersaulted. She wanted to run and jump into his arms. Feel his lips against hers. His heart-stopping eyes made her breath catch. His shirt was torn and there was straw in his hair, but his smile—wide and warm and inviting—made her insides do funny things. She smiled back quickly and waved, hurrying across the street to meet him.

The moment she was close, Sam pulled her into his arms and cocooned her to his chest. "Everything all right down at the doctor's?"

She nodded, still marveling over her revelation that Sam had made his way into her heart. He wasn't like the men her mother had warned her against. He was honest, and good. She wrapped her arms around his middle, hugging him back. She inhaled deeply loving his scent, scruffy or not.

"Josephine will be up and around soon," she answered, looking up into his face. "The scratches are looking a lot better even in such a short time. The goldenseal tea and poultice did the trick. Oh, Sam, I'm so happy!"

"I can see that in your face. I'm happy, too. For Josephine and for how we collared all those murdering outlaws. It feels real good not to have that threat hanging over our heads anymore." He loosened his hold and she stepped away, instantly missing the warmth of his body.

He chuckled and shook his head slowly. "I really don't believe it."

"What?"

Sam pointed to a dilapidated wagon next to the livery wall. "Come on, I'll show you."

When they got close Cassie could see Ashes circled up on the wooden seat. Sam reached for the cat and held her in his arms. He even rubbed under her chin and the cat lazily opened her eyes.

Cassie couldn't believe her cat and Sam had finally made their peace. "Sam?"

149

"This mangy animal saved my skin. That outlaw would've shot me dead if not for her. He was just pulling the trigger when she raced between his legs and blooey! The shot went wild."

"Really?" She laughed and reached for her cat, holding her lovingly in her arms. "Good girl," she crooned. "Josephine will be excited to hear how you saved Sam's life."

Ashes mewed softly.

"Sam," Jonathan called, walking toward them. "What're your thoughts concerning the outlaws? We're still waiting on the circuit judge and a new sheriff. I've asked all the other men and everyone is agreed about wanting you to stay until they arrive, and act as sheriff. And, you know…if you're willing and all, be our sheriff for as long as you like."

Chapter Twenty-Seven

A rush of pleasure coursed through Sam. He liked these men! Felt a closeness with them, a bond of brotherhood. But sheriff? No. He had a claim to dig. Gold to discover. A ranch to build and horses to breed.

"Sam, what do you think?" Cassie studied him, her expression blank. He wished he knew what was going through that head of hers. "Do you want to stay on? It is a beautiful little place. I could see you settling here."

She stood tall in her boy's clothes, her hair tucked behind her ears, the cat cuddled in her arms. Her cheek, soft and fair, begged to be touched. Her eyes sparkled. She was so darn pretty Sam was sure he'd never forget the way she looked right now.

Then a realization smacked him hard in the core of his being. When that outlaw had had him in his sights, one heartbeat away from death, all he'd wanted in the world was one more moment with Cassie. To be with her. Laugh with her. Feel her hand in his. He hadn't given the claim a passing thought. Now he was stunned to realize he never wanted to be anywhere Cassie wasn't. The claim was important, yes—but not as important as Cassie, or winning her heart!

As tempting as these feelings of attraction were, as beautiful as she was standing there gazing up at him, he had to remember she wasn't going to be happy when she learned the reason he'd begun this journey to Coloma with her and Josephine. In all honesty, she would probably hate him for the deceit. And could he blame her? He'd do well to keep his sights on getting them all to the claim alive, and *then* work out the truth about everything. He wasn't sure what he would do or how, but he'd navigate that stream when he got there.

He glanced at Jonathan and then at the jailhouse where Brox, Walter, and the rest of the men were watching to see what his answer would be.

"No, I'm going with you, Cassie, until you reach your destination. I'm not changing horses in the middle of this stream."

"You sure? You don't owe us anything. Or our Uncle Arvid." She seemed to let go a breath she must have been holding, for her shoulders relaxed and she smiled making her eyes come alive. "I'd think twice if I—"

"Hush! I'm not letting you go on without me. Look at what happened to Josephine." He hadn't meant to sound so stern, but why the heck was she trying to get rid of him? "I can always come back if I change my mind."

Jonathan shrugged. "I was afraid you'd say that. You sure? Rosenthal is usually peaceful. A nice place to sink your roots and start a family. You'd come to like it here pretty quick."

The men were sincere and Sam felt a jab of regret at having to turn down their offer. He'd only been eight when his mother had passed away, and since then he'd never really felt as if he belonged anywhere. He and his brother, Seth, had helped her the best they could eking out a living by washing other people's clothes. Then when she passed on, Clemen Miller, who'd always been around with sacks of potatoes and flour for their dinner, chopping wood for their fire, took the boys in and taught them how to ride. How to spot good horseflesh and how to patiently bring along a two-year-old so as not to sour or spook him. In essence, he taught them how to be men.

Clemen, Sam was sure, had had a soft spot for his mother. Would have married her too, if she hadn't already had a husband. Brewster Ridgeway always stood in the way. After years of abandonment his mother finally received a letter telling them Brewster Ridgeway, as part of an outlaw gang, had been tried and found guilty of armed robbery. Incarcerated for life. Sam remembered how, even at that young age, he'd been glad to hear the shocking news. If he'd been able, he would've gone and laughed in his face.

Jonathan laid his hand on Sam's shoulder. "No, Jon. I'm not staying."

Jonathan turned to the waiting men and shook his head. They dispersed slowly, talking amongst themselves.

"What now?" Cassie asked, as Ashes jumped out of her embrace and trotted a few feet away.

"I figure it'll be a little while before Josephine is fit to ride again. I think we should just rest up until then."

They strolled down the boardwalk back toward the doctor's office. Sam tipped his hat to a woman who was standing in her doorway, watching them approach. "Ma'am."

"Thank you, mister, for helping our town. If it hadn't been for you, who knows what would've happened. We're grateful."

Sam felt his face heat up. He wasn't used to so much attention. Didn't much like it.

"No thanks needed, ma'am." He took Cassie's elbow and continued down the walkway.

"Sam, you *sure* about not staying? You could start your new ranch here, couldn't you?" Cassie asked.

"Well, Cass, I suppose I could now, at that," he quipped sarcastically. His jaw clenched so hard it hurt. An unexplainable irritation twisted his gut at her insistence. "But what about you and Josephine? Are you going to ride out and set up claim on the river without help?"

He glanced back at Ashes bringing up the rear. "What'll happen when more men like the ones we just locked up find out it's just you and your little sister and this here little cat? What's to stop them from killing you and taking over? Or even worse?" He smacked a post with his open palm and frowned.

Cassie stopped and turned to face him. "Why are you being so cross?" Her hand came up and fingered the lump of whatever it was she always kept hidden under her shirt.

He folded his arms and glared at her, agitation percolating within. Was she actually trying to get rid of him? "What is that, anyway?" he asked crossly. His curiosity had gotten the best of him but he was glad the question was finally out. "Well?"

"A cameo—if you must know."

"Where'd you get it?"

Her expression hardened and she took a step back. "It was a gift from...Charles Smith. My intended."

Sam's stomach clenched.

"*Your intended*! You're engaged to be *married*?"

She looked off down the street for a few seconds in silence. Her nostrils flared before she turned back, leveling him with a purposeful gaze that scorched him to the bottom of his boots.

"Why so surprised, Sam? Is that so impossible? I wear pants and shoot like a man. Is that what you're thinking?" She reached up and fluffed her hair from behind her ears and shook it out. It swished around her face. "I'm not woman enough to find a husband?"

"Of course not!"

Ashes leaped to the railing and looked at them.

"Even if you can't envision such a ridiculous notion, Sam, I was engaged for a short time. Charles was a wonderful man. Handsome, too...and, uh, rich. Why, his family owned half the town. He was tall and had muscles,"—she made a gripping motion with her hands— "and was stronger than anyone I've ever seen. And, he was smart. He'd completed all his grades and was working on becoming a United States senator."

Cassie turned and started walking toward the doctor's office. "Charles gave me this brooch as a reminder of our commitment to each other. He died before we could marry."

Sam felt foolish—and boorish. Poor Cassie! She'd lost so much. She'd suffered more at the hands of fate than anyone ever should. "Forgive me for prying."

"It's all right." Her chin tipped up and she didn't look too sad at her loss. "I wear it always for courage. And to feel *his* nearness. I'll *always* wear it."

Sam nodded. They were almost back. He didn't want to end the conversation on this sour note, but there wasn't anything he could think of to lighten the moment.

Cassie let Sam open the door for her, all the while chastising herself. The lie she'd just told was outrageous. He'd sounded so accusing it had just slipped out. And once she'd got going it had snowballed into a whopper. Looking up, she gasped.

"Cassie," Josephine cried out, and held out her arms. "You're back." Josephine was sitting in the rocking chair. A soft quilt covered her lap and shoulders. A big grin creased her face when she saw her sister.

Cassie laughed and rushed over. Her relief was overwhelming and tears sprang to her eyes. "Yes, you little muskrat, I'm here." They rocked together in a tight embrace, neither one willing to let go first.

"I hope you don't mind we brought Josephine down," Grace said. "Her fever is practically gone and it's only a matter of time before she's completely better. She really wanted to run down to the jailhouse but I told her she'd have to wait for you here."

"No, I don't mind," was all Cassie could get past the lump in her throat. She wiped away tears with the back of her hand, and then pulled back so she could look into Josephine's face. "You gave us a scare, you know. I don't know what to do with you."

Josephine just giggled. A silly grin appeared as she looked up at Sam. "Hi, Sam."

"Hi, yourself. I'm glad you're feeling better. How's that arm?"
Josephine pulled up her sleeve to show everyone. "Better. See?"

To Cassie the scratches still looked nasty, but her smile never wavered. "They sure are, aren't they Sam? So much better than before."

"Why, I can hardly see 'em," Sam replied, going along with her. He nodded to Grace and Annabelle. "You did a...fine job," he said almost inaudibly. He seemed in deep reflection looking at Josephine, as if struggling with an inner thought. "Thank you," he added after a moment.

"Meeeooooow." Everyone heard the pitiful crying at the front door, followed by a light scratching.

Josephine's eyes widened. "Is that Ashes?"

Sam was the closest to the door so he reached over and opened it. Ashes took stock of everyone in the room, then carefully stepped in as if she had all the time in the world. She stopped just past the threshold.

Josephine scrambled from the rocker before anyone could stop her and ran the few feet to where her cat waited. She scooped her up.

Grace and Annabelle couldn't hold back their laughter any longer. Happy voices filled the room. There was a knock on the door and Jonathan stepped in. He went straight to Annabelle's side.

"Sounds like good news," he said, reaching for Annabelle. They embraced momentarily and then faced the group. "I see things are turning out here as well as they did down at the jailhouse."

"They are," Grace replied, giving him a quick squeeze too. "Josephine is feeling stronger and her temperature is all but gone."

"Well, I'll be!" Jonathan looked down at the cat in Josephine's arms. "Who do you have there?"

Sam heaved a sigh. "The mangy creature that started this whole business in the first place."

Cassie reached down and stroked the cat's dark gray fur. "Remember what you told me, Sam, not a half hour ago.

157

This mangy critter saved your mangy hide when that outlaw was fixing to shoot you."

"Really?" Josephine asked, her eyes widening. The cat looked unperturbed. "Is that right, Sam? Did Ashes help you?"

"As much as it pains me to admit it, yes, she did. She jumped out of the shadows just as the outlaw aimed his gun at me and darted between his boots. His shot went wild and missed me by a country mile."

"She's a hero! She's a hero!" Josephine shook with happiness. "Cassie, can I get her a cup of milk for helping Sam with the outlaws? I think she deserves one, poor kitty."

Annabelle started for the kitchen. "I agree with Josephine. I think it's the least we can do for such a brave cat. I'll get a nice big saucer of milk. Josephine, you stay there."

Jonathan followed Annabelle and the two disappeared into the other room. Cassie and Grace exchanged a knowing look. Sam smiled.

"It's a shame David isn't here to give away his daughter's hand away in marriage," Grace said. "I doubt those two will wait much longer."

Sam shifted his weight from one foot to the other. "I suspect you're right. I also think it would be a good thing to get Annabelle's mind off the grief of losing her father."

"Why, Sam!" Grace said as she went about putting away the things they'd used in nursing Josephine. "I didn't know you were such a romantic. That's astute of you." She smiled and cleared her throat softly. "I'm surprised that some lucky woman hasn't snapped you up for a husband before now. What are *you* waiting for?" She handed him the extra lantern they'd gotten down the night before, not waiting for his answer and asked, "Can you place this up there, Sam? It's a little too high for me to reach."

Cassie had to look away, as she was sure Grace was batting her eyelashes at Sam. Swallowing uneasily, she directed her gaze to the top of Josephine's fuzzy head and kept it there. What was Grace up to? Was she prompting Sam and her, or did she have designs on him herself?

Chapter Twenty-Eight

The room was closing in on Sam. Now that the showdown with the outlaws was over, he'd just as soon get back on the trail. Unfortunately, because of Josephine, it might be a few days before that would be possible. He moved to the door. "I'm going over to the livery to check on Blu and the other horses. Don't know how well Split Ear is fitting in over there being he's such a cantankerous sort."

"Is Pepper there, too?" Josephine asked.

"Yeah, all the horses are there. I just want to make sure they're getting enough to eat." He really just needed out of this room filled with females.

"Here we are," Annabelle said, as she and Jonathan came back into the room and placed a saucer of milk on the floor.

"I'm off, too," Grace said, reaching for her shawl, which hung on a hook by the door. "I'm going home to fix supper for you all. I have everything I need so please don't be fussing over anything. I think it'll do everyone good to get out of this office and sit at a nice dinner table set with china. It's important to remember some of the finer things in life."

Sam opened the door and held it for Grace.

"Supper will be on the table at seven-thirty. It'll be hot so don't be late." She passed through the door under his arm.

Sam looked at Cassie as he pushed his hat down on his brow. "I'll be at the livery if anything comes up." He tugged the brim. "If time runs short and I'm not back here, I'll just meet you over at Grace's. By the way, where is your house, Grace?"

"One block over, second house from the corner," she said, waiting on the boardwalk for him. "You can't miss my flower boxes and little white fence. I'll point it out to you from the livery. Cassie, it's easy to find. It's bright yellow, next to the church."

"I need to go too and check on things at the jail," Jonathan said. "Those men are still a dangerous bunch, even locked up." He put his hat on and moved toward the door. "I won't rest easy until there's a sheriff in town and those men are either in prison or hanged. Either way is fine with me."

"Bye, Sam," Josephine shouted as the door closed behind the three people. "Pet Pepper for me. Or, give him an apple!"

"Shhh," Cassie admonished. "I'm sure Pepper heard you all the way from here." She turned to Annabelle. "Do you think Grace would like me to take something over for dinner? It's kind of her to do all that work. I hate to think about her cooking for so many people all by herself, especially since..."

Cassie stopped herself before she mentioned Annabelle's father.

"She's fine. If she'd wanted you to bring something she would have asked. She's a really fine cook and does this every Sunday evening for my father and Jonathan and me. Until Daddy..." Annabelle's face clouded. She gathered herself and continued, "Her own father is elderly and eats like a bird. I suspect Josephine doesn't eat all that much either so it's really only two more to prepare for than she's used to."

Cassie thought about everything Grace and Annabelle had already done for her and Josephine. They were such good friends. Instantly she felt badly about what she'd been thinking about Grace and Sam just a short time ago. Sam wasn't her beau even in the remotest sense and she'd best remember that. Traveling together had a way of bringing people together, though, whether they intended it or not. For some reason Sam seemed to feel responsible for getting her and Josephine to the claim in California. He and Uncle Arvid must be close friends.

"Cassie, do you mind if I lie down for a while? I suddenly feel tired," Annabelle said, her eyes searching.

"Of course not! Please, take as long as you like. Josephine and I will go upstairs to the room I rested in, if that's okay with you."

"Consider it your room until you go."

"But, it's your father's room. Where will you stay as your father was in yours?"

Annabelle reached down and stroked the cat that was now finished with her milk and washing her face with her paw. "While you were down checking out the happenings at the jailhouse Grace and I changed the sheets in both rooms, and freshened everything up. Gave us something to do besides twiddling our thumbs. We figured you'd be staying for a couple of days at the least."

Again Cassie felt overwhelmed with gratitude. "I wished you'd waited for me to help. You all have already done so much for us. We're indebted to you."

"Don't be silly. You'd have done the same for us, I'm sure."

Annabelle moved to the door of her room. "If you need anything just make yourself at home." Yawning, she rested her head on the door jam. "Now, I'm going to get a nap before dinner tonight. I think you could use one too, if Josephine feels generous enough to let you sleep." She went in and closed the door.

"Come on, you." She bent down and picked Josephine up. "We're going upstairs."

Cassie took the steps carefully, one at a time, until she was on the upstairs landing. Ashes trotted up behind.

It was evident Grace and Annabelle had made the room homey. Her and Josephine's coats hung on a peg and their saddlebags sat neatly next to the dresser. The pillows on the bed were fluffed and the corner of the quilt turned down invitingly, exposing immaculate white sheets. A jar of water with drinking glasses, and a vase of flowers, finished off the room. Suddenly Cassie felt exhausted.

"Are you tired at all, Josephine? I don't think you can be after all the sleeping you've been doing. I'd like to take a little rest myself. What will you do if I sleep for a while?"

"I can sit in the chair and play with Ashes." She climbed up into the big chair. "Here kitty, kitty, kitty," she said, patting her lap. "I'll stay *right here* until you wake up." The cat jumped up onto Josephine's lap and started rubbing back and forth. "I won't move an inch."

Cassie arched an eyebrow. On her way to the bed, she stopped in front of the mirror, gazing at her reflection. Lacking. That was the word that best described her. She ran her fingers through her shoulder length hair, trying to fluff it. If only it was still long and she had her blue dress with the white eyelet. Well, she didn't. All the wishing in the world wasn't going to change that. Sighing, she winked at her sister

163

as Josephine watched her in the reflection. "We are what we are," she said and nodded. "Be a good girl. I won't sleep long."

Chapter Twenty-Nine

Cassie awoke with a start. She glanced about. Not finding Josephine, she jumped from the bed and ran down the stairs in a panic. She found her sister in the kitchen sitting on top of the table. Flour covered her from head to toe as she moved a big spoon around a porcelain bowl.

"What are you doing?"

Josephine jumped at the sound of Cassie's voice. Her face turned red. "I got hungry, Cassie. Don't be ma…"

Relief that her sister was actually back to her normal, mischievous self, chased away Cassie's irritation. "Well, Grace is going to have a beautiful dinner for you tonight." She smiled. "Now run upstairs and change into your clean shirt while I straighten up this mess. Don't forget to wash your face."

A half hour later, Cassie held Josephine's hand as she knocked on the door. Grace had been right. It was impossible to miss her home. Besides the bright yellow color, it was as immaculate as a storybook house, as was the darling little church that stood to its left, set back a hundred feet or so from the street.

Annabelle had slept into the evening, and insisted that the girls go on ahead so they wouldn't keep Grace waiting. She'd said Jonathan would stop by to pick her up shortly.

Cassie knocked again, hearing noises coming from within. Nervously, she glanced around, looking for Sam. He hadn't returned to Dr. Hershey's before it was time to leave and she wondered what had kept him away.

"Come in. Welcome," Grace said, sweeping her arm wide so the two could enter. "I'm so happy you made it."

The entry was attractive, with yellow striped wall covering and a beautiful hand-woven rug. Two wall lanterns burned on either side of a large gold-rimmed mirror, and tantalizing aromas of meat simmering and coffee brewing made Cassie's mouth water.

"Thank you, Grace." Cassie released Josephine's hand and helped her little sister out of her coat. Then removing her own, she hung them up on the hooks on the wall.

"And how is Josephine tonight?" Grace said, pulling the little girl into a hug. "It seems like days since I've seen you although in reality it's only been a couple hours."

Cassie smiled. "She's much better. No fever and she's hungry as a horse." She'd have some scars to remind them all of how close she'd come to dying, but that seemed her only ill effect from the episode. She was once again rested and full of vim and vigor. She'd be running around tomorrow, Cassie had no doubt.

Josephine's bottom lip jetted out. "Cassie wouldn't let me bring Ashes. She said it's not polite to bring a pet over to someone's house. I had to leave her locked on the back porch. Could she have come to dinner, too?"

Graced laughed and released her hold on Josephine, walking toward the sitting room. "Follow me. There's someone I'd like you two to meet. I think it just might answer your question."

In the next room was an old man resting in a big plaid chair with a white dog, no bigger than a minute, sitting in his lap. The dog's ears were pricked, his little obsidian eyes watched intently as they walked into the room.

"I'm not sure if my father's dog would've appreciated you bringing Ashes, Josephine. I *do* know it'll be a much quieter evening without the two of them, um, getting to know each other."

Josephine shrugged. "Guess you're right."

Grace beckoned them closer. "This is my father, William Hearthgrove. Papa, this is Cassie and Josephine Angel, the girls I've been telling you so much about. Without them and their friend Sam Ridgeway, our town would've suffered so much more at the hands of those evil outlaws. We're indebted."

William Hearthgrove smiled, his face becoming a maze of wrinkles, running this way and that. The gray hair on his head was thinned to the point of being a distant idea of what it might once have been, and he had few teeth. But his eyes shone brightly and it was impossible to look away. Cassie wondered if she'd ever met anyone so old who had such exuberance of youth.

"I'm pleased to meet you." He stood and held out his hand to the girls while holding his dog in the other.

Surprising Cassie, Josephine went right up to shake his hand, and then petted the little dog, totally unafraid. "I like your dog."

"His name is Buddy," the man replied with a smile.

Buddy wagged his tail vigorously and licked Josephine's hand when she extended it. "He's really friendly," the man continued. "Would you like to hold him?"

"Is it okay?"

As Grace's father passed the little dog over to Josephine there was a knock on the door. Grace hurried off to open it. Cassie heard Grace's greeting and Sam's deep voice saying something back. Excitement zinged this way and that as she realized she was excited to see him. She missed him during their hours apart.

Sam stepped into the sitting room almost bashfully, his hat dangling in his fingertips. It was obvious he'd gone somewhere and bathed and shaved and it even looked as if he'd gotten his hair trimmed, too. His starched blue shirt looked new and his expressive dark eyes were unreadable as his brows arched up in the same amused way as when he'd first seen Josephine boxing the cat. His rugged male aura filled the room and Cassie had to look away for fear he'd know what she was thinking.

Question was, what *was* she thinking?

"Evenin'," he said, his deep voice enveloping Cassie like a soft, warm blanket. Cassie forced a "hello" from her throat.

"Sam, this is my father, William Hearthgrove. Papa, this is Sam Ridgeway."

"Hi, Sam," Josephine interrupted. "This is Buddy." She approached Sam with the dog in her arms. She looked tiny next to him.

"Cute little fella," Sam said, stopping with his hand halfway toward the dog, a faux worried look on his face. "You sure he won't bite me?"

He winked at Cassie and she felt a thrill course through her body and warm her face. How she wished she owned a pretty dress! Something to show Sam she was more than a tomboy. At the moment her boy's clothes felt all the shabbier.

"Buddy would never hurt a flea, would he, Mr. Hearthgrove?" Josephine squeezed the dog so tight his black button eyes widened. "His heart is beating faster than a squirrel after an acorn."

Everyone in the room laughed at Josephine's amusing expression. She looked around quizzically.

Sam scratched the dog's head, then made his way over to shake Grace's father's hand.

"Dinner's almost ready," Grace said. "I wonder where Jonathan and Annabelle are?"

At that moment the door opened and Jonathan's voice called out, "We're here."

Grace smiled. "Ask and you shall receive." She passed the young couple on their way into the sitting room and gave each of the newcomers a hug. "I'll put the food on the table. I hope you're all hungry."

"Can I help you?" Cassie called out softly after Grace.

"You stay and visit," Annabelle said, catching Cassie's arm as she was about to go in search of the kitchen to help. "I'll go. I have something I want to tell Grace anyway." She smiled into Cassie's eyes. "Relax."

That was easier said than done. Why was the sight of Sam so flustering tonight? She'd ridden next to him for hours on the trail, eaten with him, laid on a blanket looking at clouds, even slept next to him and a campfire. Why did it feel so different tonight?

When Sam laughed at something Josephine had said a light giddiness fluttered in her stomach. Just being in the same room with him put her world to right. But she needed to stop thinking like this about Sam. He was a friend. Her uncle's friend. Nothing more.

She glanced again and caught Sam looking at her. He nodded slightly, and she could feel the warmth in his eyes from where he stood. And there was something else in his eyes, too, but she couldn't quite pin it down. What was going on with him? He was different but she couldn't tell exactly how. Whatever it was, her heart liked it very much.

Chapter Thirty

A pulse of pleasure rippled through Cassie as Sam stepped closer and whispered next to her ear. "I think Ashes has some serious competition." He chuckled and briefly touched the small of her back, letting his fingers linger a moment longer than necessary. He smelled of warm spice and freshness and on his breath was a hint of peppermint candy.

Sam raised an eyebrow. "I think that ol' cat will have a jolt of panic when Josephine comes home covered in unidentifiable dog scent." He nodded toward Josephine, who sat quietly on the sofa, speaking with William. Cassie had to tear her gaze from Sam's face to look over at her sister. The dog was planted on her lap, sleeping or seeming to, as her hands stroked his back.And in that moment Cassie knew what the difference was tonight.

Sam himself.

His expression. His nearness. The intimacy of his gaze. He was thinking things he hadn't when he'd left them this afternoon. She felt it to the depth of her core, leaving nothing to wonder about. She looked back at him in amazement.

Sam shifted his weight from one foot to the other as Jonathan walked to his side. "Cassie?" She was gawking at him as if he'd just sprouted pink fairy wings. What had he said that was so startling to her? She looked beautiful tonight, even in her boy's clothes and boots, and he was certain he'd be a happy man no matter if she never went back to wearing dresses. Her hair had been brushed to a high sheen and glistened as it swung freely around her face. He liked her, no; he loved her, just the way she was.

"Cassie, what's wrong?" Jonathan asked. Now they had his attention, too.

"Nuh…nothing. I was just wondering where Sam had gone off to today. You were gone a long time, Sam. I was worried."

Her last three words pleased Sam. These were new feelings for him, knowing that someone actually cared for his well-being.

She leveled him with a no-nonsense stare, but he could tell it was all bravado. A blush had appeared and her teeth slowly pulled on her lower lip. He smiled at her, bringing another look of confusion. "After checking on the horses, and making sure everything was under control at the livery, I went over to the jail to see how things were going."

"That he did, Cassie," Jonathan added with excitement and came closer, shrinking their circle of conversation. "I was there too and we have some news to report."

Sam leaned closer still, wanting to tell Cassie himself before Jonathan blurted it out. "A telegram arrived late this afternoon. The circuit judge is on his way and could be arriving as soon as tomorrow. It won't be long before Rosenthal will be finished with this whole ugly episode, and life can get back to normal. The judge is bringing with him a paddy wagon to take the men he finds guilty to the prison. That is, if they don't hang them here." He shrugged.

"I'll rest easier when it's over," Sam continued. "I don't like thinking about all those men locked up over in that jail just dreaming up ways to break out and take revenge."

Sam was excited, yet nervous, too. Ever since his soul searching earlier this evening, while he was bathing, he was a man transformed. A man on a mission. A man who wasn't going to accept the word "no." He and Cassie were a good team, and yet so much more. He didn't think he could live a day without her in his life. His heart gave a slight shudder just thinking about how it could be between them.

"So true," Jonathan agreed. "Walter and Brox are on guard duty until we get back over there. Sam and I are going to stay the night."

Sam nodded, still unable to take his eyes off Cassie. She meant more to him than any gold claim ever could! Barely able to concentrate on anything since he'd acknowledged that fact to himself, along with all the earth-shattering changes it would mean, he'd set about thinking of a way to get her to see things his way.

"You are?" She still looked confused.

"Yes, because if they're going to try anything, it'll be tonight. But don't worry your pretty little head; we have them locked up tight. Lock, stock and barrel." As he talked, his mind raced. He couldn't believe everything had gotten so clear so suddenly. He was sure now that he loved her, wanted to share his life with her, no matter what. If he was correctly judging her reaction to him, she felt the same for him. How would he explain the claim to her, though? That was going to be hard. Could he really let it go to win her love? It meant so much to him and Seth. Besides, he was the rightful owner. Doubt tried to wiggle its way into his heart. There had to be a way.

Cassie laughed and looked away nervously. "My pretty little head? Sam, what's gotten into you tonight?"

Jonathan joined in, slapping Sam on the back. "Relief has a way of firing a man's blood, isn't that right, Sam? We're all just so thankful there wasn't more killing and bloodshed. This town has seen its share in the last week."

"Yes, that's so," Sam replied. "Violence like that makes a man yearn for the good things in life. Makes him dream of peace and happiness." The thought of wedding Cassie and becoming a true family was everything to him now. What a perfect ending to his problem with the claim, too. Even though that was a minor issue to him now, he was glad there was a good solution to this dilemma he found himself in, one without having to crush her dream or his.

"And love!" Jonathan added.

Cassie laughed nervously.

Sam smiled at Jonathan, nodding. After they were married he'd protect and love her, and Josephine, all the days of their lives. It shouldn't be all that hard, he thought, as he looked directly at the cameo pinned under her shirt. He was up to the challenge.

"Come to the table," Grace called from the other room. "Supper's ready!"

Annabelle came into the room and laced her arm through Jonathan's. "Can I steal him away from the two of you?" she asked softly. They approached Grace's father and, taking the old man by the hand, helped him to his feet. "Ready for supper, sir?"

"I sure am, more than ready. Come along with us, Buddy."

The dog, now awake, stood on Josephine's lap. He barked once, leaped off, and trotted after William, his little toenails clattering on the hardwood floor.

"Over here, Josephine," Cassie said, pulling out a chair. "Grace wants you to sit by her."

Sam pulled out the chair next to his own, on the other side of Grace, and waited until Cassie was finished seating her little sister. "Cassie?"

She looked up at him suspiciously. Could she know what he was thinking? She moved slowly and then sat as he pushed in her chair.

"Thank you, Sam" she said quietly.

"You're welcome. I do have a little couth and manners."

Everyone was now seated and putting their napkins in their laps. All except Josephine, who was looking at the pretty china and serving dishes on the table with curiosity. "What's couth, Sam?"

"It's knowing how to be a gentleman, or a lady."

"Like this," Annabelle said softly from Josephine's other side. She took Josephine's napkin from her plate and placed it in her lap.

Josephine looked delighted but Sam could feel Cassie's tenseness. The exchange had embarrassed her. He wished he could think of something to make her feel better without being too obvious.

"Please start passing before everything gets cold," Grace said. "I didn't work all afternoon for you not to be able to enjoy it properly."

With anticipation they passed around the dark, golden brown pot roast with its blackened edges and chopped garlic cloves peeking from every crevice, seasoned new potatoes, and butter-coated green beans. Sliced carrots in a sea of honey followed, plus a gravy boat filled to the brim. Grace excused herself to the kitchen for a few moments to slice the bread, warm from the oven. When she returned and was again seated, she said, "Papa, will you please say grace for us?"

William bowed his head, and everyone else followed. "Heavenly Father, we thank you for this wonderful meal, good friends, and the roof over our heads. We keep in mind and prayer our beloved brother David, who has recently passed into everlasting glory. Amen."

"Amen," the group echoed. Grace's eyes remained closed a moment longer, her head bowed.

Jonathan took his knife and gently tapped on his water glass. "May I have everyone's attention, please? I know you want to get to your supper but Annabelle and I have an announcement."

A smile crept onto Grace's face and Annabelle looked as if she might faint.

"As some of you know and others of you don't," he laughed, "Annabelle and I have been planning to be married in a few months. But, with the events of late, we don't want to wait any longer. So we've decided to do it tonight! As William is a minister, albeit retired, we're having our wedding right here after supper. You're all invited!"

A din of happy voices filled the room. Jonathan couldn't stop grinning and Annabelle giggled like a schoolgirl.

"Cassie, they're getting married! Tonight!" Josephine called out loudly. "I've never been to a wedding before."

"Well, this is exciting news if I do say so myself," Grace's father exclaimed. "I haven't performed a wedding since Reverend Greenmire took over Charity Church. I'm honored and delighted. Matter of fact, I still have some wedding licenses sitting in my drawer."

As Sam glanced from one face to another, an inspiration started to grow. He looked at Cassie, a beautiful smile beaming on her face. Did he dare? For a moment he shoved the idea from his mind, thinking it outlandish, but instantly felt the overwhelming loneliness that had been his world for the last few years. He strengthened his resolve. Would Cassie consider making it a double wedding tonight? He couldn't think of one reason to wait. Would she laugh in his face? After her reaction to him in the parlor, he didn't think that would be the case. She was warming to him, no doubt. "Congratulations, you two," he said, a bit distracted.

"Yes, Annabelle and Jonathan, congratulations," Cassie said. "I'm surprised—but not too much. It's wonderful you've made it possible for us to share your special event."

"Cassie, that's actually one of the deciding factors for us choosing tonight," Annabelle said. "We knew you, Josephine, and Sam would be leaving us soon and we feel as if you're family already. We hoped you'd stand up with us as witnesses."

Sam felt encouraged. These were perfect circumstances to get Cassie thinking along the right lines of becoming Mrs. Sam Ridgeway.

"We'd be honored to do that," he replied. "Wouldn't we, Cassie? And, to think this has all happened so fast. When opportunity strikes, one should seize the day, I guess." Maybe he was laying it on a might too thick, but he felt time was of the essence. With the announcement at hand he better act fast. No sense at all in stalling.

"Can I talk to you privately?" he whispered in her ear.

Her look was one of disbelief. "*Now?*"

He nodded.

"What could possibly be so important that you'd need to talk to me now?"

All conversation had stopped and everyone looked at them.

"Trust me, it is." Sam stood and helped her to scoot her chair back. "Will you all excuse us for just one moment?"

"Well, I guess," Grace replied, curiosity shining in her eyes. "But only for a moment, as you say. I'll never forgive you if you two go off and let this dinner I slaved over get cold."

Chapter Thirty-One

"Have you lost your mind, Sam?" Cassie asked as he herded her into the sitting room, far away from the others. "What on earth are you up to?" He had a look about him, something she'd never seen before, a vulnerability that made her want to take him into her arms instead of admonish him. Still, excitement shot through her body as she wondered what it was that was so important he would interrupt the dinner party directly after Jonathan and Annabelle's important announcement. Remembering how he'd earlier caressed her back, her heart trembled.

"I want you to hear me out with an open mind." Facing her, he took both her hands into his and held them. "Then, when I'm done, you can give me your answer. Just promise me you won't cut me off before I'm finished saying what I have to say."

"Sam," she said, glancing at her hands in his.

"Promise me."

Looking up, she searched his eyes for any hint to what was going on. "Sam?"

"Promise or we forget it. Your food's getting colder by the second." A few moments ticked by. "Well?"

He was so disarmingly handsome tonight.

Especially his eyes.

And his expression.

How could she not promise him?

"Okay. I promise not to interrupt you."

His obvious intake of breath made her duck her head momentarily to hide her smile. Whatever it was he wanted to tell her must be really important. Unease filtered through her. Maybe he wanted to ride on without her and Josephine? Or, more likely, he'd decided to stay here in Rosenthal after all and be the new sheriff. She certainly couldn't blame him for that. This was a wonderfully welcoming town, one anyone would like to call home. At the thought, her heart plunged to her feet. It would be a sad day without Sam by her side. Or, just maybe...

He stared at her as if he'd totally forgotten what it was he wanted to say.

"Sam, our dinners? Remember? Let's not be rude. What is it you want to tell me?"

"I—" he stopped.

"Yes?"

He gazed into her eyes with an intensity that almost frightened her. "I want you to marry me."

"*What!*"

He didn't flinch at her outburst and his gaze never left her face. "I want you to be my wife."

"Sam, *what* are you talking about? You *have* lost your mind!"

"I want you to marry me *tonight*. Don't you feel it, Cassie? This thing between us? I do, and it's been on my mind and I can't think of anything else. It's driving me crazy. Besides, you know—we make a good team."

180

Cassie felt as if the wind had been knocked from her lungs. Sam's expression was so earnest she was sure he wasn't playing some sort of joke. But it was impossible to get any thoughts in her head to come into focus.

"Marry you?"

"Yes."

"Now?" she squeaked.

"Tonight. In a double ceremony. I'm sure Jonathan and Annabelle won't mind."

Panic took over. A hundred reasons ran through her head why Sam's idea was crazy, as her mother's warning about men vied for attention. Still, when she looked in his eyes she saw happiness, love, and more. This was Sam. Her hero. Josephine's hero. A good man who'd been caring and truthful. "I—I don't know. We've only met a few days ago."

"I'm asking you to become my wife. I don't want to lose you. I realized today when I was looking down the barrel of the outlaw's gun that I can't live without you. Life is short, darlin'. I don't want to have any regrets."

Suddenly Josephine appeared by their side. "What are you two doing?"

"Nothing," they said in unison.

"Grace says you're to come back to the table this instant. Your supper is cold."

"Tell her we'll be right there," Sam said, touching Josephine's cheek. "Away with you now."

As Josephine walked away, Sam straightened. "Well, this didn't go quite as I hoped it would. You're saying *no*, then?"

As unbelievable as it was to herself, Cassie wanted to say yes! She couldn't deny her feelings and attraction to him any longer. He was right—life was short and sometimes one just had to jump in with both feet. Had to forgo warnings and doubts. Had to grasp for the brass ring.

Sam ran his hand over his face. "We have to go before Grace herself comes looking for us with a wooden spoon. Your answer *is* no, then."

"No. My answer is *not* no. I just needed a moment to let what you said sink in. Yes, Sam Ridgeway. I'll marry you. I'll be your wife." She laughed. "Three minutes is a fast courtship."

Sam pulled Cassie into his arms. When his lips covered hers the whole world faded away. He was warm, and tasted good. Her body tingled as every nerve ending fired with delicious excitement. He loved her! Wanted to marry her! Unable to stop herself, she leaned in boldly, acutely aware of the hardness of his muscles and feel of his body. His head tipped and he pulled her even closer.

Cassie's heart thudded so hard she feared the others in the dining room would hear it. Throwing caution to the wind, she ran her hands up Sam's back and over his strong shoulders, reveling at the feel of his muscles beneath her fingertips.

Sam buried his face in her neck and took a deep breath. "There, it's sealed," he breathed into her ear. "Let me take care of the rest."

They returned to the table hand in hand. Their expressions must have given them away because Jonathan slowly stood. "Well?"

Sam cleared his throat and the anticipation in the room hummed.

"Sam, spit it out," Grace said excitedly. "You're killing us." Laugher erupted at her uncharacteristic lapse in manners.

"Cassie and I are getting married, too. Tonight, if Jonathan and Annabelle don't mind."

Jonathan stepped forward and grasped Sam's hand, pumping it up and down in excitement. "Mind? We'd be honored! It would make the day even more special. Isn't that right, Annabelle?"

Annabelle and Grace hurried over and hugged Cassie as Josephine squeezed in amongst everyone.

"Let's do it right now!" Annabelle cried. "Our dinner can wait—but I can't! I won't be able to eat even the tiniest bite just thinking about it."

William nodded. "We can do that."

"Actually, I think it's a fine idea. David would be pleased," Grace echoed. "What's dinner compared to a double wedding? But, the brides will need a few minutes to get ready." She took Annabelle and Cassie by the arm. "You boys can put the meat and potatoes in the oven to keep warm. We'll be back shortly."

Upstairs in Grace's bedroom, Annabelle and Grace whipped Cassie's boy clothes off so fast Cassie didn't have a moment to protest. Grace then slipped a beautiful, creamy yellow gown, made from an incredibly soft fabric, over Cassie's head, letting it cascade all the way to the floor. It hugged Cassie's body almost indecently, making her feel like the most beautiful, most desirable woman in the world. The neckline scooped down to the swell of her breasts, and long, fitted sleeves went past her wrists. Glancing at herself in the mirror, Cassie shivered, not recognizing the girl who looked back.

"What about my boots?" she whispered, watching Grace in amazement. The woman was a human whirlwind.

Grace plopped Cassie onto the bed and quickly unlaced the first. "You can go without."

Cassie wiggled her toes. "Barefoot?" she said under her breath.

"We must hurry!" Grace took a brush from her dressing table. "Flip your head over, Cassie. Thank the heavens you wore your Sunday best today, Annabelle. You already look lovely."

Without taking her attention away from the job at hand, Grace gave Josephine, who was behind her, a gentle nudge. *The woman must have eyes in the back of her head*, Cassie thought. "Stop gawking at your sister, sweetness, and help Annabelle lace that ribbon in her hair. Your little hands need a job." She turned Cassie around and pinched her cheeks several times, bringing the color up.

"Ouch!" Cassie rubbed the offended spots.

Grace laughed softly, her apologetic expression asking forgiveness. "It won't be but a moment more and the men will be calling for us to come down. They just don't understand the importance of a woman's appearance." She stepped back and admired the two young women. "There! You're both as pretty as a picture."

"I ain't never seen you so purdy, sissy." Josephine ran her little hand down the soft fabric over Cassie's backside.

"I agree," Annabelle said, giggling mischievously. "Just wait until Sam gets a glimpse of his bride."

Lord Almighty! Sam almost gasped aloud when he first saw Cassie standing at the top of the stairs. He'd known she was beautiful, but—but…

"Sam, get a grip!" Jonathan whispered into his ear. They stood by the fireplace with William as the two girls came down the stairs together, side by side. Grace played softly on her piano and Josephine danced happily around the room, looking like a pixie. "If you don't get your eyes back in your head Cassie's going to think she's marrying a frog."

Sam gulped. "Thanks. You're right."

"Here you go. Stand here and here," William said, placing the brides in their proper places.

Sam glanced down when Cassie took hold of his arm, her soft touch branding him hers forever. His heart expanded almost painfully. *This* was Cassie. The *real* Cassie. To have and to hold—*tonight!* Happiness, desire and protectiveness ricocheted around his mind, then through the rest of him, as he marveled at how lucky he was to be marrying her.

If Sam wasn't at her side, helping her stay steady on her feet, Cassie thought she just might crumple to the floor. When a small quiver moved slowly through her body, Sam looked down into her face and winked. Placing his palm over the hand that was tucked tenderly in the bend of his arm, he gave a gentle squeeze. Jonathan and Annabelle were almost finished with their vows. Cassie felt beautiful, and cherished. William looked at her and nodded, smiling.

"Do you, Cassie Angel, take Sam Ridgeway to be your husband? To have and to hold, from this day forward, till death do you part?"

Sam's look was sincere and she warmed.

"I—I do."

"Do you, Sam Ridgeway, take Cassie Angel to be your wife? To have and to hold, from this day forward, till death do you part?"

"I do." His voice was confident, strong.

"Then I pronounce you all husbands and wives. You may kiss the brides," William said with a chuckle. Buddy barked excitedly, Grace wiped at the tears welling in her eyes and Josephine shook with eagerness as Sam took her sister into his arms.

This kiss was warm and exciting, but paled in comparison to the one that had spurred her imagination into flight just fifteen minutes before, when they'd been alone in the hallway. The memory, still vivid, made her fingers curl around his arms. Anticipation of the coming night had her breathless.

Cassie leaned over and hugged Josephine who was now tugging on her sleeve, not wanting her to feel left out. This was a big day for her, too. Her world had changed, as well. Who would have ever thought she'd find someone like Sam. Her mother would be so happy for her. Sam was nothing like the men she'd been so fearful of. No, Sam was a knight in shining armor.

Grace clapped her hands over her head to get everyone's attention. "Now, before the meal is completely ruined, can we *please* sit down and eat?"

The meal was almost finished when a loud knock on the door interrupted the happy conversation. "Oh, my stars," Grace said, dabbing at her mouth with her napkin and pushing out her chair. "When it rains it pours. Who on earth could that be now?"

Sam and Jonathan both stood at the same time with the intention of seeing who it was. Grace stopped them with a wave of her hand. "You two just keep eating. We'll never get through this dinner if you don't. I'll see who it is." She swished out of the room and was gone. The sound of her opening the door and then an exchange of words floated in from the entry to the dinner table. Moments later she entered the room, followed by a man.

Buddy, who'd been napping beside his master's chair, jumped up and crossed the room in a flash, letting go a rat-tat-tat of barking. He launched himself at the newcomer and grabbed the man's pant leg, growling viciously and refusing to let go.

Chapter Thirty-Two

"*Uncle Arvid*!" Cassie and Josephine cried at the same time.

"Get this mangy rat off my leg!" he bellowed, hopping about. He shook his leg vigorously several times and kicked out, but Buddy hung on with the tenacity of a wolverine, his teeth holding tight to the fabric.

Sam jumped up so quickly that his chair toppled over and rolled on its side with a clatter. Cassie didn't know what to address first, the dog hanging off her uncle's pant leg or the utterly surprising rage she saw glittering in Sam's eyes.

"Buddy! Here!" William called, his voice barely audible over the animal's attack. "Come here, boy!" He clapped his hands together loudly several times, adding to the cacophony.

Grace followed Arvid around and round, trying to grab her father's dog. "Stop," she implored the man. "Stop and I'll get the dog."

Arvid's face was contorted. Ignoring Grace, he grabbed a heavy iron trivet from the buffet and raised it over Buddy's head.

"No!" Cassie was close enough to jump forward and grab his arm in full swing. The force propelled her around a few feet before Sam snatched her up and placed her behind him, shielding her with his body.

Grace quickly pulled Buddy from Arvid, ripping his pant leg in the process, and ran out of the room, the little terrier still growling and carrying on.

The room fell silent except for everyone's heavy breathing.

Arvid Angel ran his hands down one leg and then the other as if to see if his body parts were still intact, then took stock of the guests in the room.

"Well, isn't this just a sight for sore eyes," he drawled. "Here I was worried sick about my dead brother's girls disappearing without leaving me a note, or any message whatsoever, or even a by-your-leave. I sure didn't expect *this*."

Sam came around and placed his face just inches from Arvid's. "Arvid, we finally meet again!"

By his tone Sam was anything but happy to see Uncle Arvid. If she ventured a guess, Cassie would think they were bitter enemies. She poked her head around Sam's body. "Hello, Uncle, how did you find us?"

"Wasn't too hard. Not that many young'uns running around the countryside. Just did my due diligence. I see you went and cut off your hair. Both of you. What's that all about?"

Cassie reached up and tucked her hair behind her ear, but not before she saw Josephine duck her head in shame.

Grace was back, a flustered look on her face, wisps of hair falling over her brow, and a rip in her right sleeve long enough to expose her arm from elbow to wrist.

"I'm so sorry, Mr. Angel," she said, her fingers pulling the fabric of her sleeve together. "Let me assure you that this is the first time Buddy has ever attacked anyone. I have no idea what has gotten into him. How is your leg? Did he break the skin?"

"Don't think so."

Grace held the back of her wrist to her forehead. "Thank God. I hope you can forgive us."

"I'll try," Arvid drawled, still looking at Sam.

Grace ran her hand down the front of her dress. "This gentleman said he's your uncle." She addressed Cassie and Josephine. "I can see by your faces he was telling the truth."

"Of course I'm telling the truth," Arvid snapped. "Girls?" He held out his arms in invitation. When they didn't move, he added, "Come give your Uncle Arvid a hug. I've missed you both."

Cassie hesitated a heartbeat, glancing at Josephine, and then went to him. She couldn't help but glance up to see Sam glaring. Josephine moved slowly forward.

"Come on, slow poke," Arvid said, "I ain't got fleas."

Josephine inched over and he gave her a brief, uninterested squeeze. "Now, I demand to know what my sweet little nieces are doing having supper with this thieving gambler?" He stood on tiptoe and looked Sam straight in the eyes.

"*I'm* not the thief. You are," Sam said in a controlled voice.

Cassie was confused. "Sam, what's going on? You said you and my uncle were close friends. And that you were traveling with us out of kindness for him and…"

"Is *that* what he told you?" Arvid's laugh was smug. "Oh, he's a smart one, all right."

"Now, you wait just a minute," interjected Jonathan. He helped an agitated William to his feet, and the sound of Buddy's insistent barking was heard from the second floor.

They came around the table and stood next to Sam. "I don't like you throwing accusations around about my good friend Sam," continued Jonathan, his square chin jutting out aggressively.

William cleared his throat and laid his hand on Jonathan's forearm. "There isn't anything you can't work out with words."

Cassie looked between the men, bemused. "Tell me what's going on, Sam? Why are you so mad at Uncle Arvid?"

Sam hesitated, looking from Cassie to Arvid and back again.

"I can see he don't want to say nothing, and I know why," Arvid sneered. "He's trying to steal that claim I gave you girls for safekeeping right out from under your noses. He's tried thrice before. He's getting into your good graces and then he'll steal it, just like he tried from me."

"The claim?" Cassie turned slowly and stared at Sam, unbelieving.

Sam's jaw clenched several times as he looked down at her. "Don't you believe him, Cassie," he said. "I met Arvid in a game of poker with several other fellows. The claim was in the pot. I won. Later that night he stole it from my saddlebag."

Cassie looked from one to the other, a sickening feeling tightening her chest. The claim. The claim Uncle Arvid had given to her and Josephine. At least, she'd assumed he'd given it to them. But, now, it all made sense. Sam showing up in Broken Branch out of the blue. Sam offering to ride with them to Coloma. Him snooping in their bedroom. Him trying to open her saddlebag...him wanting to *marry her*! All so perfectly planned out. She felt like vomiting. She glanced down at her beautiful yellow wedding dress with embarrassment and shame. Her face flamed painfully. In a swift motion, she slapped Sam across the face with all her might. "*That's* for lying!"

The room went silent. Sam's granite hard gaze never wavered. "Don't believe him, Cassie," he gritted out. He shook his head slowly as a red welt began to rise on his cheek. "He's not telling the truth."

"Pack up your things, girls. We're getting out of this town tonight," Arvid interrupted. "Even though I'm dead tired from riding night and day to find you, I don't like the feel of it here."

"You're not going anywhere with my claim," Sam retorted. "I'm being civil now out of respect for the women present, Arvid. But be warned. I'm not letting you waltz away with what is legally mine."

He stepped toward Arvid but Jonathan grabbed his elbow.

"It's my word against yours," Arvid growled. "And, the claim is in our possession. You don't have a pot to piss in." Arvid snickered, pleased with his cleverness. "In case you don't know it, possession is nine-tenths of the law."

"You don't have the claim either. Cassie does."

"Same thing. I put it in her dresser drawer. She knows the claim belongs to me. What's mine is hers and vice versa. It's the Angel family claim now, and belongs to all three of us," he said angrily, his voice rising.

Arvid was smarter than Sam gave him credit for. Saying the claim belonged partly to the girls made it more difficult for Sam to take it back. Well, that might be true, but he'd never let Arvid have one tiny flake of gold from it, even if it was fool's gold. He'd walk away from the claim for Cassie and

Josephine's sake, but never for Arvid's. His sneaking, lying ways reminded him too much of his own father's dealings. No, he'd not give in to him. One glance at Cassie told him volumes. Her stricken expression conveyed better than words just how much he had to lose.

"As you know," he continued. "I won it from the Swede fair and square, with a full house. You tried to bluff with two pair." He looked at Cassie, but his words were falling on deaf ears. Her eyes smoldered with hurt and disbelief.

"Show me your bill of sale," scoffed Arvid.

"You know very well I don't have one."

"Gentleman," Grace said, her arms holding tightly to Josephine's shoulders. "Please. There must be a way to settle this civilly. Some of us are getting upset."

Sam glanced down at Josephine and a knife sliced through his heart. Her face, a contorted mixture of fear and sorrow, was one he wouldn't soon forget. Cassie walked over and picked Josephine up and the little girl laid her head on her sister's shoulder without taking her eyes off her uncle.

"Grace is right," Jonathan said. "We'll wire the previous owner—the Swede, as you call him—and have him send a bill of sale. That will settle this once and for all."

"That's impossible," Sam replied. "We were all on the move. There's no way of finding him."

Weary from standing so long, William sank back down in a chair. He cleared his throat to get everyone's attention. "Well, you'll just have to settle this the mature way."

Everyone turned and looked at him.

Chapter Thirty-Three

"Enlighten us, William," Sam said through a clenched jaw. "We're listening."

"With a competition," he replied, looking around from face to face. "Whoever pulls the most gold out of the claim in one month will be the rightful owner. The other party can keep what he worked for, but forfeits all rightful ownership."

"But the claim already belongs to Sam," Jonathan said heatedly. "That's like stealing it from him all over again."

Arvid went to the table and picked a piece of meat off the center platter, stuffing it into his mouth. "You don't know what you're talking about," he said around the mouthful. He chewed for several moments, and then took a glass of water and guzzled down several swallows. "But," he added, wiping his mouth with the back of his sleeve, "no matter what you think, he can't prove it and I say he don't own the claim."

Sam tried to take Cassie's hand but she jerked it away. "Can I talk to you?" he asked.

Her eyes narrowed. "I don't think so, Sam. You've done enough talking already for one day. For one life! Don't you think?" Her eyes had opened wide, and now anger had muscled out the hurt. "I like Reverend Hearthgrove's idea. I'll agree to it if you will. Me and my family against *you*."

"I'm the voice of the Angel family claim, Cassie, and the Angel family in general," Arvid countered. "The claim is ours already! We don't need no competition to prove anything."

Sam hesitated. Did he dare to voice the obvious? He turned to Cassie. "You're my wife, now. The claim belongs to *us*."

Arvid choked on whatever was in his mouth. "The hell you say! What's this about you and Cassie being married?"

"It's true. We got married tonight. What's hers is mine and mine is hers."

"Sam!" Cassie spoke up. "That's absurd. The wedding was a sham and you know it—nothing more."

William held up a hand for silence. "If we put it to a vote right now, who we believed about the ownership of the claim," he said softly, "Sam would win our four votes to your three. And truthfully, I'm not sure you'd even have three. Should we go ahead with a vote and settle the dispute here and now?"

Arvid slammed his hand down on the table, making everything rattle and jump. Josephine whimpered in fear.

Sam grasped him by the shoulder. "Knock it off, Angel! My patience is about gone. Either we hold a vote this minute, or you agree to the competition. I'm not handing my claim over to you just because you say it's yours. That's just not going to happen!"

The blood flowed to Arvid's face with such force Sam thought the older man's eyes were going to pop out of their sockets. He shook his shoulder free. "I guess I got no choice," he hissed at last. "I agree." He turned to go.

"Where're you going?" Cassie asked.

"Never you mind. We'll meet up tomorrow so we can plan our departure." Without another word he walked out the door.

Well, thought Sam, the big problem hanging over his head about Cassie and the claim was now out in the open. At least he didn't have to worry anymore what she'd do when he told her the claim was really his. His heart twisted at the pain in her eyes at his perceived betrayal. He could see only too well what she thought of him now

"Sam, I'll write up a contract tonight, with all the particulars, so after you leave here nobody will be able to go back on their word," Jonathan volunteered.

"Thanks, Jon, I'd appreciate that."

Cassie busied herself with the clean-up, anything to keep her thoughts off two-faced Sam, and what she'd so carelessly done. Well, they'd undo that wedding as quickly as they'd made it. Surely, all they needed to do was rip up the paper they'd signed. Grace went upstairs to retrieve Buddy, settling Josephine and the dog in the sitting room in an effort to take the child's mind off all the upheaval.

Grace came back, her brows drawn together in worry. "What are you going to do with Josephine when you go to the claim?" she asked Cassie in a hushed voice.

"What do you mean?" Cassie had been clearing the table, but stopped at Grace's question, two plates and the gravy boat in her hands. She glanced at Sam in a deep conversation with Jonathan and shame overcame her all over again. How could she have considered, even for a second, the idea of marrying someone she'd known for such a short period of time? Had she forgotten her mother's warning so fast? Was it the kiss? All the considerate things he'd done? Shockingly, the feel of his lips on hers was still so vivid she was sure the memory would never fade.

Grace took the dishes from Cassie's hands and placed them on the drain board. "A river is a dangerous place for an adult, even under normal circumstances. It could be deadly for Josephine. During the competition all three of you will be working night and day, trying to beat the other and win title to the claim. Who will watch over her? If you're mining, Cassie, you won't be able to keep her under foot or even close. Have you given that any thought?"

"Yes." Grace was right. What kind of a guardian had she been so far? Just look how sick Josephine had become because of Ashes. She also could have fallen off the cliff to her death, or been killed by the mountain lion. And now a river? "But what choice do we have? We'll get by somehow, because we have to. Uncle Arvid will be there now to help, too."

"Yes, your uncle Arvid. So true." Grace's tone was gently laced with sarcasm. Then she looked at Cassie meaningfully.

"Would you consider leaving Josephine here with me and my father for the month when you and Sam will be so busy with the gold panning? She could go to class with me every day and get caught up with her schooling. She'd have a bedroom of her own, with a nice, clean bed to sleep in, and a hot, nutritious supper every night. I'd love her and spoil her as much as I could. The claim is no place for a little girl." She closed her eyes momentarily as if looking for the right words. "I don't mean to be unseemly, but mining towns are full of men. Unlawful men. I'm worried about you, but I'm terrified for Josephine."

Cassie nodded, a lump in her throat. She agreed completely with Grace's description of where she was headed.

Although she knew everything Grace was saying made excellent sense, her heart screamed a resounding *no*. What if Josephine never wanted to come back to her? She'd promised her mother to take good care of her sister. But...where would Josephine be safer, happier? The answer frightened Cassie.

"I'm sorry," Grace said. "I can see what I've suggested has shocked you. Don't answer now. Just think about it?"

Cassie nodded.

Grace stood before Cassie, love and worry shining from her eyes. "One more thing and then I'll drop the subject. I promise." She stepped closer so only Cassie could hear. "Sam seems like a good man at the core. I think it would behoove you to give him a chance. A *real* chance."

"Grace, you don't know what you're saying. From the very beginning he's done nothing but try to trick me. The first day we met, he told me a big fat lie about being friends with my uncle. He was sneaky and..." She couldn't finish her thought. Although she'd never trust Sam again, she couldn't make herself say such things about him either. She just couldn't.

Cassie turned and looked out the window, staring into the black night beyond. Grace was right. The place she was taking Josephine was no place for a girl, of any age! When she was running from Broken Branch this all had seemed like such a good idea. The answer to her prayers. Now she wasn't certain.

And what if Sam *was* telling the truth about being the real owner of the claim? Because of her uncle, his whole life had been altered, and he'd been dragged across the country by her and her sister. It wouldn't be the first time that Uncle Arvid had lied for his own benefit. On the other hand, she and Josephine were all that their uncle had left in the world. He'd lost his only brother when her father had passed on and if he wanted to have any family at all, it had to be her and Josephine. Unquestionably, he could have won that claim fair and square too. Couldn't he?

A deep voice startled her from her reverie.

"Cassie?"

There was no mistaking who was behind her. Turning, Cassie found Sam in the doorway to the kitchen. He looked uncomfortable, and the smile that had brought her such happiness only an hour before was nowhere to be seen.

"I think I'll go and check on Josephine," Grace said. "She must be worn out from all the happenings." She withdrew quietly from the room.

"We need to talk," Sam said, coming into the kitchen a few feet and stopping. "Whether you like it or not, we have things we need to work out. And I have some things I'd like to explain."

Cassie nodded, avoiding eye contact as an overwhelming sadness descended upon her. This is where Josephine needed to be. Here, safe and warm. Here with Grace.

Sam stepped forward quickly and pulled out a chair. "Cassie?" He took her arm and gently sat her down.

It was as if the whole world were tumbling down around her. She couldn't breathe, or even think. And she definitely couldn't look Sam in the eyes.

Chapter Thirty-Four

The sight of tears welling in Cassie's eyes was too much for Sam. Leaning forward, he captured her fisted hands, which were now pushing on the tabletop. "I'm sorry about all this," he said softly. "I lo—."

She ripped her hands from his. "I'm not crying because of—*us*! There never was an *us* and there never will be an *us*. If you must know, you're the last person I'd waste a tear on. Remember one thing, Sam Ridgeway. I'll never, *ever* believe a word you say."

He rocked back, giving her space as he digested her statement. It was founded, considering what had just happened. He'd give her time. "Okay. If it's not us, then what? If it's that insufferable uncle of yours—I'm going to nail his worthless hide to the wall and shoot it full of buckshot until there's nothing left." She looked at him, the anguish in her face enough to make him want to strangle Arvid to within an inch of his life.

"It's not Uncle Arvid. And it's not you and me." *But isn't it? I thought we had something wonderful. Something really special. A love to last a lifetime.*

"Then what?"

Tears began to trickle down Cassie's cheeks. She drew in a slow breath and her shoulders wobbled.

Sam hunkered down by her chair and pulled her into his arms. She turned her face into his neck. He noted distractedly that her hair smelled of lilac. A violent shivering wracked her body and he began to feel genuinely worried.

"Cassie?" He massaged her back and kneaded the taut muscles of her neck. Softly he asked again, "Why are you crying, sweetheart?"

"First of all," she said between breaths, "don't call me sweetheart. I'm *not* your sweetheart." She sat back and brushed angrily at her tears. "It's Josephine," she finally finished. "Because of all the danger I've already put her in and what I was thinking about the claim."

"What do you mean?"

"From day one, the idea of taking her to Coloma was a stupid and risky thing for me to try to do. She's just a little girl."

Sam gave her a nudge so she'd sit back and he could look into her face. Her nose was red; her eyes, puffy and wet. She was beautiful.

"Yes, she is. And you're just a young woman. So? I still don't understand."

Cassie ground her eyes with the heels of her hands before she continued. He could hear Josephine and Grace in the sitting room laughing about something, plus a murmur from Jonathan.

"I should've been more careful with her. She almost died! But what hurts me most is the thought of leaving her here. *She'll never want to come back to me!*"

A new rainstorm burst from her eyes and coursed down her cheeks. Sam pulled out a chair and sat next to her.

"You're leaving her here?" he asked, handing her his handkerchief.

She blew her nose. "Grace wants to take care of her while I'm at the claim. She thinks—and so do I—that Rosenthal would be safer for Josephine. She'll take her to school and church. Cook good suppers, give her constancy. Plus," she waved her arm around, "look at this beautiful home. Who wouldn't want to live here? Grace can be a much better mother to Josephine than I could ever think of being."

Sam's eyebrows tented over his eyes in surprise. This was a great idea. He'd been concerned by the thought of the child hanging out around the river. It *was* too dangerous a place for her.

"Cassie, I'd have guessed you'd think this was the answer to a prayer." He reached forward and tucked a wayward tress of hair behind her ear. "What better solution could there be? It's only a month and then you can decide what you want to do. This gives you freedom to work things out without worrying about her. Agreed?"

"It's still hard, Sam."

"Life is hard. Growing up is hard."

"You're right about that."

She took a deep breath and seemed to be holding it. Now that that crisis was past, at least until the time came for leaving her little sister behind, he knew she'd get to the subject he'd been dreading.

"How could you do it, Sam? How could you lie to me like that?"

How he wished he could turn back the clock and confront her with the facts way back at the beginning, the moment she slapped the cold rag over her battered face, the very point at which he realized they were kin to Arvid and most likely had his claim. But, he hadn't, and changing the course of the last few days was out of his power.

"It just happened. Then, one thing led to another. I wanted to tell you several times. I didn't think you'd believe me. Do you now?"

"How can I?"

That comment slashed him to the quick. Good question. Almost everything he'd told her, about the important stuff, had been untrue.

"I needed to find Arvid, or whoever else it was that had my claim. Is that so hard to understand?"

Cassie looked at him but he couldn't read her expression. Disappointment? Anger? Disgust?

"You believe your uncle over me?" He involuntarily clenched his fist resting on his thigh and shook his head in disbelief.

"He's my uncle."

"You're my wife."

"No. I'm not."

She glanced to the wall for a moment then back at him, her expression now resembling Josephine's when in a petulant mood.

As if on cue, Josephine came into the room. She wedged into the tiny space between them and stroked her sister's hair. "It will be okay, Cassie. Everything will work out." She looked closer at her older sister's tearstained face. "Have you been crying?"

Cassie sniffed and sat up straighter. "I have."

"Why? Do you have a tummy ache?"

Cassie pushed her chair out and pulled Josephine onto her lap. She hugged her tightly until Josephine leaned back.

"No, my stomach feels fine. It's my heart that's hurting me."

Sam stood and ran a hand through his hair, knowing the big talk between the two girls was coming. Josephine held her arms out to him and waited expectedly, not understanding the enormity of the situation between him and her sister. He shook his head. Cassie wouldn't be able to bear it; she needed her sister's closeness to get through this conversation. "Your sister has something to tell you."

"What?"

Silence was the only answer.

"What? Am I in trouble?" She took Cassie's face between her two palms just inches away from her own.

Cassie leaned forward and kissed her forehead. "No. Never. I've just been thinking about the gold claim and how difficult it'll be. And cold. All the hard work we're going to have to do every single day for hours on end. I'm sure food will be scarce so we'll be hungry a lot of the time, too. I'm just debating…"

Josephine popped happily out of her lap. "If you still want to go? We don't have to if you've changed your mind. I don't mind if we stay in this town. I like it here."

"Do you?" They were eye to eye.

"I do. Grace and Annabelle are nice. I like Buddy a lot, too. I'm going to take him on a walk sometime."

Cassie started crying all over again. Sam pulled her up and into his embrace, knowing she wouldn't resist. He turned her around to face Josephine. "Go on."

Josephine's uncanny ability to sniff out danger was working overtime. She grabbed Cassie's hand and pulled hard. "What is it?"

"You're going to stay here with Grace and live in this big, beautiful house while Sam and I and Uncle Arvid go to work the claim. Isn't that great news?"

It took a moment to sink in. Josephine's little face contorted as if she'd been stung by a wasp. "You're going to leave me here? Alone?"

Cassie forced a chuckle, trying to lighten the mood. "No, silly. You'll be here with Grace and Annabelle. Don't forget Jonathan and Mr. Hearthgrove. And Ashes! A whole bunch of friends are going to be with you. And it's only for a little while. One month. Then we'll decide where we want to go from there."

Josephine threw her arms around Cassie's middle, smashing her face into her pretty yellow dress. "No! I don't want to stay without you," she said in an angry voice, laden, Cassie knew, with all sorts of pain from her past. "I don't really like this town at all. Besides, we're sisters. You promised Ma before she died you'd never leave me. I heard you. Remember, sissy? Remember your promise? The night she died you told me many times that we'd always be together. You did. You did!"

Cassie thought her heart would break. How could she stand this? How could she leave Josephine behind?

"Shhhhh," she whispered as she rubbed Josephine's back. "I know I promised that, Josephine. I did. And we *will* be together. It's not as if I'm leaving you forever. Things have changed, and it's only for a short time. It'll be so much better knowing that you're safe and living in a nice place, with nice people. And going to school and to church. So much better than where I'm going to be."

Still clutching Cassie's middle in a bear's grip, Josephine looked up at her, her little face bathed in tears, her eyes beseeching. "Please don't leave me, sissy. Please don't."

"It's getting late," Sam said gently. He picked Josephine up and she buried her face into his neck. "Why don't I walk you two over to Dr. Hershey's and get you tucked in? It's been a long day for everyone. Tomorrow everything will look brighter."

Chapter Thirty-Five

Cassie knelt on the cheerful green-and-blue rag rug, her head bent over folded hands, feeling anything but happy. "Lord, please watch over Josephine. As you know, she tends to get into mischief. Don't let anything else happen to her," she whispered, not wanting to wake her sister, who was already asleep just inches from her face. For the past two days she and Josephine had been staying with Annabelle and Jonathan, while Sam stayed with Brox. Arvid was at the boarding house.

Tomorrow, they'd leave at daybreak. They'd collected provisions, mining tools, and other amenities, all paid for by Sam. Cassie had a few funds but Sam wouldn't think of letting her use them, no matter how hard she argued. Arvid had pulled his pockets inside out, letting them know they'd not get any help from him. Josephine stopped bringing up Cassie's promise to their mother, but the weight of her culpability was heavy in her little sister's eyes.

Ashes, who'd been curled up next to Josephine, came down off the bed in one long, easy stretch. She rubbed up against Cassie's thigh, mewing. In a single motion, Cassie scooped her up and rolled around so her back was against the bed and her knees were pulled to her chest. She cuddled the cat.

"You've come a long way with the two of us, haven't you?" Ashes began to purr. "You're a good friend. Please watch over Josephine just like you did with Sam."

The cat's whiskers tickled Cassie's face. Her purring seemed louder than usual, vibrating her whole body as she massaged forward and back with her paws, her claws slipping in and out of Cassie's nightshirt, snagging the fabric and catching her skin.

"Ouch."

"What're you doin'?"

Turning, she saw Josephine looking down over the side of the bed. "Did I wake you?"

Josephine nodded. "But I don't mind. Are you talking to Ashes?"

Cassie smiled and nodded. "Yes, I guess I am." She handed her up to Josephine. Rising off the floor, Cassie sat on the bed next to her sister, who was making an indentation in the quilt for the cat to lie in.

"You're going in the morning."

The statement was an arrow to Cassie's heart. "Yes, we are. I want to talk to you about that."

Josephine's little hand glided gently over Ashes' head and all the way down her back, to the tip of her tail. The cat's contented eyes were just slits in her face. Josephine never took her attention off her beloved pet as Cassie felt her heart tear in two.

"When I promised Ma I'd watch out for you, take care of you, I meant what I said. Never in my wildest dreams did I ever imagine circumstances would arise that would warrant that I leave you behind."

Cassie lay down and pulled Josephine into her embrace. Her gaze rested on the slatted beams criss-crossing the pinewood ceiling. They stayed like that quietly, just cuddling. After several minutes, Cassie felt her sister's chest rise and fall with a deep breath.

"Cassie?"

"Yes?"

"I miss Ma. I don't tell you because I know it will just make you feel sad, but every night I cry for her in my mind, before I fall asleep. I miss Pa, too."

Sorrow stabbed inside her chest. She reached for Josephine's hand. "I know what you mean, honey. I miss them, too. I had them a lot longer in my life than you did."

"I'm afraid I'll forget about them." Josephine had rolled to her elbow and was looking down into Cassie's face, the weight of the world reflected in her eyes. "What if I do?"

"Well, *that's* not going to happen, silly. I won't let you forget because I'm going to keep telling you about all the good times we had together. How much Ma and Pa loved you, and cared for you. How much they loved each other. And God won't let you forget them either. He's put their love in your heart to remind you. Always."

Josephine snuggled back down onto her arms. "I hope you're right."

"Aren't I always?"

She felt Josephine nod her head sleepily.

"About my promise…"

Josephine's arm was slung across Cassie's body and her fingers gently played with her big sister's hair. "I know you think all this leaving is for the best." Josephine yawned, her other hand feeling around for the sleeping cat. "It's okay. I let you out of the promise."

Cassie bit the inside of her cheek, gazing up at the knotholes dimly visible in the amber light. Only for now. She was only breaking the promise for one month.

"How come you're so much older than me?" Josephine's voice was low now and she knew her little sister would be falling asleep any moment.

Fragments of the past shuddered through Cassie's mind, bringing sharp stings of grief. Her mama struggling to survive. Her mama kneeling at a tiny graveside. Then another. And another. Her mother's face looking as if it were chiseled from marble, her body thin as a reed. And finally, her mama too weak to fight off influenza, dying.

"Because our mama lost three babies in between you and me. Do you remember us talking about that?"

Josephine nodded.

Cassie smiled and hugged her closer. "Three boys. Ezra, Winston…"

"And Chester. Where are they now? I mean, their bodies?"

"Back in Colorado. That's one of the reasons Ma was excited when Pa told her he wanted to come to Nevada. That he'd found a place that needed strong laborers. She wanted to start fresh, without the sad memories. She told me once that she didn't want her girls—that's *you*, you know," Cassie said, nudging Josephine to make sure she was listening, "to have a sad mama, but a happy one. One that liked to make dresses, have tea parties and bake cakes. One that laughed, and smiled, and gave kisses all day long." Cassie hesitated. She wanted Josephine to remember the good parts, not the hard times. "She told me to laugh every day, no matter how I feel inside. She believed that life was too short to be sad or unhappy. Do you remember us doing any of those things?" She felt no guilt painting a pretty picture for Josephine, planting the seed that Ma and Pa had a storybook relationship. Cassie knew Pa was a big disappointment to Ma, but her innocent little sister didn't have to know. Sam popped into her thoughts.

Her heart lurched. *How could he have done that to me? Marry me for the claim.*

"Some," Josephine answered softly. "I think. She and Pa are with our brothers now, right?"

"Absolutely."

Ten minutes passed. Cassie was sure Josephine had long since fallen asleep. She wished she could too.

"I'll bet they're all really, really happy." Josephine's voice was little more than a whisper and Cassie was surprised that she was even still awake thinking about it.

Cassie kissed the top of her sister's soft blonde head. "I'm sure they are. Now, go to sleep, sleepyhead, before morning is here and you have to get up." Cassie traced a little cross on her forehead with her finger.

Josephine would be all right, wouldn't she? What would happen if they didn't win the claim contest and she came away empty-handed? What then?

Chapter Thirty-Six

Sourdough Creek, Coloma, California

"**W**ell, Cassie, what do you make of her?" Arvid asked. "Isn't she just the prettiest sight you ever did see?"

The two of them sat their horses at the edge of a bluff. Cassie looked down to the river below. She was sore and tired, and more than ready to be finished with this trip. It had taken a few days longer than expected as the weather, turning blustery, had let loose a deluge. After the first onslaught, the rain had eased into a soft, shimmering veil, causing the following days to be a sloppy, soggy mess. It had cleared and hopefully would stay that way for a while.

"Aaahhh…choooo!" Cassie blew her nose on the handkerchief she kept in the gullet of her saddle, and then stuffed it back next to her horse's withers. Her slicker had kept most of the rain off, but when she looked down, reaching for the canteen looped over her saddle horn, a rivulet of water poured off her hat, down the slicker, and directly into her right boot. She stifled a groan.

What she wouldn't give right now for a hot bath and steaming cup of tea! But the work was just beginning. There would be time later for comfy chairs, goose-down quilts, crackling fires, and hot stew. Right now she had a contest to win.

Sam, who'd been trailing them a good ways back, reined up alongside her, the creaking of his saddle and a morning dove's call off in the distance, the only sounds. She wasn't talking to him much anymore. He'd become quiet over the past days too, speaking only if Uncle Arvid asked him a question. *Probably embarrassed for what he'd tried to pull.* He'd ridden last in line, bringing up the rear and leading Split Ear with a long rope.

With each mile she relived every moment they'd shared since meeting back in Broken Branch. It played over and over in her head and she berated herself for her foolishness. He'd hoodwinked her, plain and simple. Her imagination over the kiss had run away with her, and she vowed not to make the same mistake again.

"Hungry?" Sam asked from a few feet away.

She shrugged. She'd not tell him her stomach was turning in on itself. "Not bad, actually." A quick glance found him watching her. "I've been eating jerky." She held up a soggy strip of meat for him to see.

"Well, I'm damn starved," Arvid barked out grouchily. He stood up in his stirrups, stretching his legs. "Never have cared for camp cookin'. And you, girl, have a lot to learn."

Cassie tried to ignore the hurt as she took in the panoramic view of the California wilderness. The river came down through the valley in twists and turns. It was rimmed by hills on both sides that grew larger the farther out they went. To the east was a majestic mountain range.

A little quiver niggled up Cassie's spine, reminding her of the time the mountain lion had awakened her in the dark of the night. The feeling of knowing something was wrong before it became clear. She shook it off and continued to admire the loveliness in every direction. Statuesque oaks, silvery-green water crashing over rocks, treacherous but lush-looking poison oak, with its lacy, ginger-colored leaves moving in the breeze. Plus, in the valley, a carroty carpet of poppies as far as the eye could see. Still, as beautiful as it was, it was also more desolate than she'd ever imagined.

In Hangtown, they'd filed the needed papers, including the officially signed and sealed agreement concerning their state of affairs with the claim. They'd stayed over one final, glorious night in the Berry House, to enjoy a hot bath, a sumptuous supper, and the comforts of a warm bed one last time before coming out to the Sourdough. Without a doubt, this was going to be an exceptionally long month.

On their way out of town, they'd seen miners of every age, squatting at the river's edge, their suspicious eyes watching them pass. Chinese immigrants were everywhere. Families, with children filthy from head to toe, looked as if they'd not bathed in a month of Sundays. As the road narrowed to a single lane, and then a pebble-strewn trail dotted with deer droppings, they saw fewer and fewer people. Soon there wasn't a soul to be found.

"Cassie, you listening to me?" Arvid asked impatiently. He'd swung around in the saddle and glared at her. "Always off somewhere daydreaming about something. Well, it better not be that claim-stealing cowboy sitting by your side. That marriage was bogus, and I'd never have allowed it. You best remember that. Now, I asked if you liked the river!"

"Yes, it's pretty," she managed to get out in a semi-civil tone. A flash of irritation at Arvid's condescending attitude flickered through her, but she was too tired to stand up to him now. Let him know he couldn't get away with treating her that way, uncle or not. What was even more maddening, and galled her to all get out, was that Sam continually occupied her thoughts. Was she the weakest woman in the world? Would it take a sharp blow to her noggin to knock some sense into her? From the corner of her eye she could see Sam, his forearms crossed over his saddle horn as he inspected the river below.

Her mother had been right. From now on she'd not depend on any man – or any men – uncle or love. Her strong back would deliver her and Josephine's bakery. When a cold blast almost blew her hat off, Cassie reached up quickly to keep it from flying away. Was she kidding herself? Could she actually make their dream come true? Or was it just that—a dream?

"Good. Because I don't like repeating myself. Today we set up our camps. Tomorrow the mining begins. We'll pitch our tent over there on the sandy part of the west bank by the manzanita. It looks like easy access for firewood and has bushes for our private needs." He laughed when Cassie turned away. "Don't go getting all delicate on me now," he added unpleasantly.

He reined his horse to start down the fifty-foot hill.

"That's too close to the river," Sam said forcefully.

Arvid pulled up. "Pitch your tent anywhere you like, Ridgeway. You didn't hear me inviting you, did you? There's a lot of land between our markers from there," he pointed west, "to there," he pointed east.

"I know the boundaries. I'm just saying where you want to make your camp is unsafe. I don't like it."

"Well, you don't have to like it. If we get washed away the claim will be all yours. Haaw," he shouted, booting his horse in the ribs and proceeding down the steep embankment.

Cassie was too tired and too wet to make a fuss about anything with anyone. She just wanted to get unpacked and the horses staked out so she could get a fire going. Warmth to her bitterly cold bones was all she could think about.

Turning, she followed Arvid down the side of the bluff. She leaned back in the saddle and gave Meadowlark her head as she slid down. The mare sat back on her haunches. It was slick and Meadowlark slipped, almost catching her nose on the ground before recovering her footing.

"Come on, slowpoke," Arvid yelled. "Over this way."

Arvid had dismounted and was walking around a level area, inspecting it. "This is the spot." He went over and uncinched his horse's saddle after pulling off his bedroll. He removed the bridle, then haltered the gelding and tied him to a tree. "When you get your horse unsaddled, take mine out with yours." He pointed to several big rocks. "Those will make good stones for the fire; be sure to gather them up."

Still at the top of the bluff, Sam watched. As usual, Arvid barked out orders faster than Cassie could comply. She took her tent and bedroll and hauled them over close to the hill, out of his line of sight. Next, she took the two horses twenty feet into a small meadow east of their camp and hobbled them, leaving them to graze.

Being with Cassie these last few days had been hell. They'd lost so much. And yet, her feelings were written all over face every time he came close. She didn't trust him anymore. He'd hurt her badly, and he doubted it was something that could be repaired in the days ahead, if ever.

Discouraged, Sam clucked softly to Blu and gave her plenty of rein. They started down the embankment, with Split Ear following a few feet behind. They slipped and slid until they were safely at the bottom. The only access to where he wanted to make camp across the river was through the area where the two were setting up theirs.

"This ain't Main Street," Arvid complained as Sam rode through their camp and into the meadow where the two horses grazed. He ignored the man and continued through a dry bed of rocks to the riverbank where it widened out and looked shallow. Blu and Split Ear picked their way across the cold water to the opposite side. Sam went through the meadow of flowers a good hundred feet, across an outcrop of shale and up onto a plateau with some open space. There was also a dense growth of manzanita before a big stand of trees.

"Whoa." Sam looked around and dismounted. He unloaded the supplies and put the horses out to graze. He gathered as much dry wood as he could find and picked out some round stones for his campfire. Pitching his tent under some trees, he rolled out his bedroll, which had stayed surprisingly dry, and arranged the few personal things he'd brought with him inside his tent.

Later, he'd take the mining supplies over to the Angels' camp after he'd unpacked his coffee pot and utensils, made a fire, and put on some water to boil. He'd toss in a few strips of jerky and a potato or two, in case Cassie didn't have anything handy. She looked plum worn out, and he wished she'd accept a little help from him.

When he finished, and the so-called miners' stew was bubbling softly in a pot over the flames, he hefted the pack containing two gold pans, a few glass vials for the gold, a hammer and nails, and a pair of lady-sized gloves he'd picked up in town in case Cassie found she couldn't take the ice-cold temperature of the spring runoff. He'd also bought a Derringer and intended to give the last two items to her tonight—and was not going to take no for an answer.

He slung the heavy pack across his back, and with his other hand grabbed the two picks they'd brought along. He set out toward the other camp.

At the crossing, there were several large rocks and with carefully placed steps, he was able to get across without getting wet. He arrived in their camp only to find it deserted. "Hello?" He set the pack down and looked around. "Cassie? Arvid?"

It had taken him a good hour to get his place set up, and now he wondered where the two of them had gone. Their tents were pitched close to the overhang, separated by fifteen feet. A tiny campfire crackled nearby.

He looked up river and spotted Arvid along the bank, gazing down into the water. Where had Cassie gone off to? Feeling uneasy, he walked toward her tent.

Chapter Thirty-Seven

"Cassie?" Sam said again softly, realizing she must have fallen asleep. It was no wonder. Arvid worked her hard. He stepped closer to the tent's opening. "You in there?"

He waited a few moments, wanting to give her ample time to respond if indeed she was. He pulled the flap back. As he'd thought, Cassie lay rolled in a blanket on top of her bedroll. Her hands were pillowed under her face and her knees were drawn up. Her clothes hung off a jury-rigged peg of sorts—her attempt at drying them.

As he slowly backed away he picked up her breeches and shirt. Gathering some sturdy branches, he took the hammer and nails and made a makeshift rack for drying her clothes. He searched out some dry wood, enough to last a few days, and got a big blaze going. Within the hour he had things looking the way he'd wanted.

Arvid came into camp and stopped short when he saw Sam. "What're you doing here?"

"Come on, Arvid. We may not like each other, but I think we have no other choice but to band together when we aren't panning. Cassie is worn out. She needs help. If she doesn't get some rest she's going to get sicker than she already is."

"I helped her pitch the tents," he retorted angrily. "Who're you to be telling me about how to care for my own niece?"

Sam controlled his temper and kept his voice low. "In case you've forgotten, Arvid, this claim is mine. We both know it. I'm being amenable *only* because of Cassie. I didn't want to kill her only living male relative in case *just maybe* you might be some kind of help to her."

"Oh, you're some big talker. I'm shaking in my boots."

Sam took a step toward him. "You better be." He pointed a finger in Arvid's face. "I'll be watching you. I'll know if you pick a hair from your nose." Frustrated, he pitched the hammer aside. "And, let's not forget Cassie is my wife!"

Arvid laughed. "That confusion is done. The old preacher said it was the first thing he'd do."

Sam glared, knowing Arvid spoke the truth. He wished it were otherwise. William had said the licenses were numbered, and that he couldn't just rip it up. At Cassie's insistence he had promised to file the proper cancellation papers the following week.

"What's going on out here?"

Cassie stepped from her tent dressed in the new set of clothes they'd purchased in Hangtown. The warm breeze ruffled her hair and the untucked tails of her shirt. Except for the redness under her nose, her skin was flawless in the early evening light. When she noticed the clothes drying on the rack, the blazing fire, and the stack of wood her cheeks blossomed pink, making him pleased he'd taken the time to help her.

"Just discussing things," Sam replied, trying not to stare. He'd been a darn fool not to acknowledge his feelings for her sooner, before things had become so complicated. Before her uncle showed up, poisoning her against him.

"Things? What things?"

She glanced from him to Arvid.

"Uncle?"

"Nothin'."

She shrugged yet again, a reaction he'd never get used to seeing. He clamped down the prickly irritation that rolled in his belly. With Arvid, she was always on the losing end. Her uncle was breaking her spirit, one snide comment at a time. "Okay then, I'm going to the river to get some water to make supper with."

Sam cleared his throat. "I brought you some over there."

She gave him a long look. "I wish you wouldn't do that, Sam." She placed her hands on her hips trying to look stern, but it only accentuated her small waist. "But, I thank you all the same."

He raised both his brows. "Welcome."

"I'm perfectly capable of getting water, or anything else we may need." She took her shirttail in hand and gave it a good shake, so he'd look at the oversized man's shirt she was wearing. "Just think of me as *Cassidy*. Remember those days?"

She went to the bucket Sam had left by the fire and a nice feeling of accomplishment snaked through him as she set about gathering supplies. *I surprised her.* "Tomorrow I plan to go hunting. Early morning," he said. "There's deer scat everywhere."

Cassie rummaged through the food and pulled out a sack of flour and a small canister of sugar. "That's a good idea. Tonight I'll make some sweet biscuits."

"I have a pot of watery stew simmering over on my side of the river. It's not fancy, by any means." He couldn't help but smile at how that sounded as he went over and tested the dryness of Cassie's clothes. "It should be done by now. I'll go get it." He hitched his head, "These are done, too."

She went over and took them off the rack, and moved the contraption away from the flames. "Thank you," she said again a bit brusquely.

"Welcome."

Arvid rolled his eyes and went into his tent.

Sam stepped closer. "I have something I want to give you."

She looked up from the mixing bowl she'd picked up, a spoon in one hand and a puff of white flour on her cheek.

He pulled the Derringer from the pack of other mining tools and held it out to her. The gun was no bigger than a small bird. She just looked at it.

"I have my Colt, Sam. I don't need that."

"Yes, you do. To keep on you at all times."

"You're being overly cautious."

"Not so. Your Colt is too cumbersome to carry while you're mining. This will easily fit in the pocket of your trousers. " He nodded toward the cameo pinned under her shirt. "Just like you always wear that. I must admit, a gun is not nearly as endearing as a promise cameo, but...I think it's even more meaningful. Just humor me, please."

"Sam..."

He was looking at her angel cameo now, a funny look on his face. She needed to tell him the truth. Even if the words would be bitter to taste, especially after her reaction over his deceit. He'd think her a silly girl, but perpetuating the lie just to let it continue on with a life of its own didn't feel right. Besides, what did it matter? Their relationship was already over, having gone through the worst possible betrayal.

"Sam," she began again. "There's something…"

"I'm not taking no for an answer! This is untamed territory. There are still Indians making trouble for settlers. And, actually, I don't really blame them. I'd be darn mad if someone was running me off my homeland, as well as all the other wretched acts that are being perpetrated against them. And it's not only them I worry about. There're cougars, like the one that almost attacked you and Josephine, and bears, too. And let's not forget about other miners. We might not see them now, but I'm sure they're out there."

She took the small gun from the palm of his hand and turned it over, feeling its weight, hefting it gently up and down.

"I think you're being ridiculous." She looked at it, and then pointed it out toward the river. "It's so tiny. Would it even do anything?"

"It wouldn't kill a large animal, but the blast and sting would make it think twice about attacking. A person at close range wouldn't stand a chance, though." He handed her a pouch of bullets.

"Oh, for goodness' sakes!" She didn't want anything from him. He'd already done enough. He'd not worm his way back into her good graces.

Were his narrowed eyes and hard-set mouth his attempt to scare her? She almost laughed.

"Cassie, stop being a stubborn mule."

She glared right back.

"I won't sleep a wink this whole month with you over here and me on the other side of the river. I know Arvid won't budge about this camping spot, but that doesn't mean I'm going to like it." A sweep of his arm took in the expanse of the camp. "For one thing, you're out in the open, easily seen from the bluff. And, like I said before, much too close to the water. There ain't a fool like an old-brainless fool."

She stomped her foot, which Sam didn't even seem to notice, but pain radiated up her sore muscles. "Sam!"

"It's true. And he's a liar and a thief—and doesn't give a hoot about—"

"Sam Ridgeway," she interrupted before he could say the hurtful truth. "I won't stand for you defaming my uncle every chance you get." She wished she could tell Sam he was wrong about her uncle, but she wasn't completely sure anymore. "You did your own lying, too. You were going to steal the claim from me. Why, you were willing to marry me just to get your hands on it!"

"Bloody hell," he said under his breath. "It was already mine. *Is mine*," he corrected. "And what about you, Miss On-the-Up-and-Up. Weren't you trying to trick me with your boy get-ups? That's different, right?"

He turned to go. "Had something else to give you too, but I've changed my mind. I'll be back shortly with the stew."

He's mad. Well, good! She placed her hands on her hips and watched his wide back as he strode toward the river. "Fine, then," she called loudly. "By the time you get back these sweet biscuits should be done!" Going over to the fire, she scooped a large dollop of lard from the can and flung it into the hot skillet appeasing her anger some. She waited a moment till it settled, then ladled in batter making four mounds.

A high-pitched whinny, more like a whistle than a neigh, sounded from across the river, barely audible over the rushing water.

Cassie looked up to see Sam turn back and wave her over.

It only took a moment for her to run to his side. "Look," he shouted, pointing down the valley of poppies.

Both of Sam's horses stood with their heads held high and ears pricked. Wind lifted their manes and tails as they intently watched something.

"What? I don't see—" She leaned closer to Sam, trying to see what he did.

Chapter Thirty-Eight

Sam chuckled as his mare snorted and pranced around, hobbles and all. When Split Ear nudged up close, she squealed and kicked at him with her left hind leg.

"A stallion," Sam said, pointing. "Don't you see him?"

He extended his hand and helped her scramble onto a boulder, giving her some height. "*Now* I do. He's beautiful!" In the excitement she pointed, too. "Look. He's rearing."

"Blood bay," Sam stated under his breath, in awe.

Cassie laughed at the stallion's bold behavior as he tried to gain the mare's attention. After a short sprint, he slid to a halt and stood tall, motionless. His confidence, as tangible as the rock Cassie stood on, rippled towards them. His gaze shifted from the mare to where Cassie and Sam watched.

"He's the most beautiful creature I've ever seen, Sam. One mass of muscle and energy. I hope he comes closer. Look at that chest! It's massive. His hindquarters are too."

The animal's nostrils flared with excitement as he tossed his head.

"Actually, I heard about him in the saloon in Hangtown," Sam said, staring. "He was purchased years ago as a colt by a rich Spanish landowner and brought out here all the way from Texas. He's a descendent of Steel Dust, a stud well-known for siring all kinds of great horses. Some wild mustang snatched his mother from the remuda, with him still at her side, along with several other good mares. They said men have been trying to re-capture him for years. To this day no one knows where he keeps his band."

"He doesn't want to come too close."

"Give him time. He'll try for Blu and your mare, too. He'll wait for the right moment. The cover of darkness."

She looked at him in earnest, worried. The old Cassie. The one he'd held in the moonlight after she'd fallen asleep on Meadowlark. Her eyes searched his. Her kissable mouth tempted him.

"What can we do? We'd be stranded without our horses." Sam was sorry when she looked away, back at the marauder. "Besides, I'd never want to lose Meadowlark."

"As long as we're diligent about keeping the horses hobbled, and close, we should be okay. We'll tie one to a tree in camp every night; the others won't go far."

The stallion spun a full circle and pawed the ground with a powerful foreleg, digging through the damp earth and sent a clump of sod flying.

Sam laughed heartily. "Looks like he means business."

The stallion trotted a few feet closer, prompting another round of squeals from Blu, and forcing Split Ear to hold his ground by pinning his ears and snorting.

"Poor Split Ear," Sam chuckled. "His only girl has abandoned him."

Sam took out his pistol and fired one shot into the air, which brought Arvid running from his tent, gun in hand. The stallion raced away before Arvid could see it.

"What's going on?" He was breathing hard by the time he reached the riverbank. "Injun?"

"No. Stallion. He's interested in our mares."

"I'll take care of him," Arvid said, waving his gun around.

"You wouldn't!" Cassie jumped down from the rock and faced her uncle, her brow furrowed.

"Why wouldn't I? I defend what's mine."

"Because it's not right! He was here first and this is his home."

"Women. They're always so over-romantic." Arvid stomped back toward his tent. "Call me when supper is ready. I'm starved."

"Okay, now I'm really off," Sam said, disliking the man even more, if that were possible. "Don't worry too much about Arvid and the stallion. That animal is a mature horse, cagey enough to have avoided the lariat for this long. I doubt your uncle could kill him even if he tried."

"That doesn't make me feel much better. How can anyone think like that?"

Sam tried to keep the knowing look off his face. Especially as Cassie's expression said she wanted to bite her own tongue for proving his point.

Cassie waited by the bank as Sam walked away, feeling very small in the bigness of the land. The breeze chilled her. Upstream, the river careened around a bend and crashed down a short waterfall into a big, black pool. It continued on to the shallower spot where Sam was getting ready to cross. Farther down, it widened for a few yards, and then narrowed into wicked looking rapids.

When Sam had hopped his way across the rocks and climbed the far bank, she turned and headed back to the fire. With a pot holder in each hand, Cassie dumped out the scorched biscuits she'd been frying before the stallion arrived. With a degree of difficulty, she wiped out the hot, weighty skillet with a dishtowel. Setting the utensil back over the fire, she scooped another clump of lard and this time carefully plopped it in. At home, she could have managed the skillet one-handed, but here, on the trail, it took two—and it was three times as tricky.

She sat back on her heels and watched as the fat melted into a clear liquid. She'd yet to get the hang of cooking over a campfire. When they'd first started their journey together they had eaten the supplies they brought with them: jerky, baked bread, and fruit. Now that most of that was eaten, food preparations fell to her shoulders.

But tonight, their first supper on the Sourdough, Sam was graciously bringing over something he'd put together. How nice of him, she conceded. Thoughtful, indeed. Whatever it was, she didn't care. The fact that there was going to be something to fill her gnawing belly was a blessing. And one she greatly appreciated. Staunchly, trying to hold onto the hurt she still felt every waking moment, she shoved away any nice feeling about him.

If only she had a table to work on. Even a log would be an improvement. She looked around. A fallen tree not that far away had been stripped of its branches by someone else. If she could get it over here it would serve as a work-top of sorts. Walking the short distance, she bent her knees and gripped onto the trunk, giving a serious tug. It moved slightly. She'd need help to get it over to the fire.

"Uncle Arvid, can you give me a hand out here?"

She waited for him to respond. "Uncle?"

Arvid poked his head out of his tent. "What? Is supper ready? What's taking so long?"

Taken aback by his angry tone, Cassie glanced away for a moment before putting a smile on her face. "Could you help me drag this log closer to the fire? It'll make cooking a lot easier."

Arvid disappeared back inside. He emerged moments later pulling his suspenders up over his shoulders. "Seems like a lot of work to me. Always something with you, girl."

She felt awkward. "I can get it later with my horse if you're rather not do it now. I didn't realize you were resting."

He sat on the ground and pulled on his boots. "Just taking a nap before supper. Got to rest when I can."

Cassie had to clamp her mouth shut to keep from saying something. What would happen if they weren't able to move the log? If it was too heavy? She'd seen his temper several times during their trip, explosive enough to make her insides quake. Then, his laziness began to grate on her nerves. Who was Uncle Arvid? Really? Other than being her father's older brother, she realized she didn't truly know him at all.

Arvid came up and took a hold. "Go on and get that end," he directed her. "On the count of three. One, two, three—"

Cassie shoved for all she was worth and the log moved forward several feet. Arvid lurched back, but caught his heel. He fell hard on his backside. The log was ripped from Cassie's hands.

Arvid screamed out like a tortured animal, writhing in pain. Cassie ran to his side and dropped to her knees, not knowing what to do.

Chapter Thirty-Nine

"Don't touch me, girl!" Arvid screeched. "Don't touch me! You've done enough harm already. I think my back's broke." His arms were drawn up to his chest, his fingers resembling the crooked talons of a bird. Pain contorted his face as he glared at her.

"Uncle Arvid, let me help you," she gasped. "I'll get you back to your tent."

"No. Not 'til the pain stops." His eyes rolled back in his head as he groaned.

"I'll get Sam. He'll be able to help better—" Cassie gulped down a sob as she stood. The spectacle of her uncle on the ground held her spellbound. "I'll be back as fast as I can. He'll know what to do."

Cassie took off toward the river, running as fast as she could. She paused at the river's edge looking for the path Sam had taken, then dashed across. The last rock was covered in slime, and she slipped, plunging her foot into the icy water before she had a chance to catch her balance.

Scrambling up the opposite side, she ran all the way to his campsite where she fell to her knees, struggling to catch her breath.

Sam heard someone running across the ground, heard harsh breaths interspersed with the footsteps. Was it Cassie? He bounded from his tent. "What happened? Is the stallion back?"

She shook her head, unable to speak, her breath still a tangle within her chest. Sam took her by her arms and pulled her upright so he could see her face.

"Go on, take a deep breath."

"It's Uncle Arvid. He's hurt bad. Please come."

Sam grasped Cassie's hand and pulled her along behind him as they ran down into the meadow, spooking the horses. When they arrived at the river's edge he gave her no time to protest, but scooped her into his arms and carried her across. They made it back to her camp in minutes.

"There." Cassie pointed.

Sam went over and dropped to one knee. "Arvid. Arvid. Can you hear me?"

The old man's eyes popped open, blazing hot with anger. Sam jerked back in surprise. "I can hear you, you piece of dung! I just can't move!"

Sam stood up slowly and turned to Cassie, whose face was ashen. "What happened?'

Her teeth chattered violently, making it hard for her to answer. "We were trying to pull this log over by the fire, so I could use it for a table. He tripped and fell. I had asked for his help. It's my fault he's been hurt."

Sam gently tipped her face up with his finger. "Accidents happen, Cassie. But still, we need to get him into his tent where he'll be more comfortable. You go in and straighten it out so I can lay him down."

She nodded.

"Arvid, this is going to hurt," Sam said, kneeling down again by his side. "But we have to get you somewhere where we can take care of you. So," Sam found a stick and placed it between Arvid's teeth, "bite on this if it hurts too bad. I'm going to pick you up and put you on your bedroll."

Arvid's eyes grew large with fear. He rolled his head back and forth.

Cassie was back. "It's ready."

"Bite now," Sam said, slipping one arm under his shoulders and one under his knees.

"Aaaarrrggggg!"

"Bite the stick!"

"Acccckkkkgggg!"

"Keep biting!"

In six smooth strides, Sam had Arvid on his bedroll. As he laid him down, the older man moaned, his arms and legs stiff, as if frozen in pain. Carefully, Sam straightened out his limbs and removed his boots. He covered him with a blanket. Cassie waited at the opening of the small tent, crestfallen.

Arvid's head rolled to one side and he spat out the stick. "Whiskey."

"Where is it?"

Arvid moved his eyes toward his saddlebag. Sam unbuckled the leather pouch and fumbled around until he felt a bottle and pulled it out. With a twist, Sam jerked out the cork and lifted Arvid's head, holding the bottle to his lips.

"Take a long drink."

Arvid gulped down several swallows and closed his eyes as some of the amber liquid dribbled down his chin. "More."

They repeated that process several times until Sam felt certain Arvid had a good bellyful. Sam wiped off the older man's chin and laid him back on his bedroll, satisfied when his eyes remained closed and his breathing evened out.

He slowly backed out of the tent.

Cassie waited for him, her eyes stricken.

"What are we going to do, Sam?"

"I don't know yet."

"He's in so much pain; it's horrible. I can hardly stand to look at him."

"When he wakes up we'll talk to him and see what he wants to do. If he'd like to go back to town to see if there's a doctor, I can make a travois and we'll take him. It'll be painful, but it can be done. He may want to wait it out, knowing how best to deal with this himself, if he's had back pain before. We'll just have to be patient to see what he feels up to doing."

Sam looked around, trying to decide what to do. It'd be hours before Arvid slept off his drunken stupor, and he was glad for it. It would be best if he could get Cassie's mind off Arvid until they actually had to figure out what they were going to do.

"Go catch up your horse," he said.

Cassie looked surprised.

"I'll saddle her and move the log so you can use it to work on. Right now, while you get her, I'll retrieve the stew. I don't know about you, but I'm hungry."

"Sam, I couldn't eat..."

"You may not be able to eat, but I can. I haven't had a bite since this morning. Go on, do as I ask and I'll be back before you're done."

Along with the stew, Sam gathered up his bedroll and a few other things he'd need for the night. Cassie was scared, and he didn't blame her. Arvid was in a bad way. Sam had never had any back problems, but he'd seen fellows that had been crippled for life by falling from a horse and landing the wrong way. They suffered horribly from the pain, without much to help except strong liquor and prayer. As much as he disliked Arvid, he wouldn't wish that on anyone.

Sam started back with his arms full of his gear and the pot dangling from a finger. At the river's edge he made two trips across to be sure he didn't slip and lose what little dinner they had.

"Hey, I'm back."

Cassie glanced over her shoulder at him as she worked at the campfire. She'd caught and saddled Meadowlark, and the horse was tied to a nearby tree. Arvid's chestnut gelding, the animal that her uncle just called Horse, had followed them over, and was nosing around on the outskirts of camp.

"Said I was going to saddle her," Sam offered, trying to understand the way her mind worked. "It would only take me a second, and you have enough on your mind."

"I know. I needed something to do."

Shaking his head he asked, "Has he woken up?"

"No." She stood. "I haven't heard a peep from him. Sam, I've been thinking. This could be awfully bad. He may be paralyzed." She paced back and forth, looking at the ground. "What was I thinking? I should have waited for you."

"Cassie, stop. We're going to wait and see how he is. It's unfortunate this has happened, but things could be worse..."

He tried to think of something worse than being unable to move, even an inch, without devastating pain gripping your body, but was stuck. "I agree it's pretty bad—but, thinking on the bright side, he could be dead."

She gaped at him. "Don't say that."

"Okay, I won't. But you have to agree to stop thinking the worst until we know more. Let's concentrate on moving this tree, and getting this camp set up so it's livable so no more accidents will happen."

Cassie stopped her pacing. "Fine." She took the stew from his fingertips, looking questioningly at the other things Sam had bundled in his arms. When she looked into his face he tried not to smile.

Chapter Forty

Sam shrugged. "I thought it best if I moved over here in case you need help with Arvid when he wakes up. It could be in the middle of the night." He set the things he was holding on the ground. Even in the dusky light of evening Sam could see Cassie's face taking on a pinkish hue.

"Thank you, Sam," she said softly this time. "I appreciate your help more than you could know."

"Don't mention it." He smiled, hoping she would see that all he wanted was to help her, love her. Spend the rest of his life with her.

"There's something else," Cassie said.

He was surprised at the pain moving across her face. "Yes?" he prompted.

"I'm sorry about slapping you the night we got..." She paused, unable to go on as if the thought of them getting married was just too painful. "I'm not sorry for what I said, because I meant every word of it. But, I am sorry that I hit you so hard."

She was softening to him. He was sure. He brought his hand up and covered the offended spot as if it still hurt. Her brows crunched into a remorseful frown. "That's okay, Cassie. I understood why you did it."

He glanced down into the frying pan. There were two yellow biscuits bubbling in the hot oil, their outer rims turning black and crispy.

"Those look, uh—good."

"The biscuits!" Cassie wrapped a dishtowel around the hot handle, pulling the pan away from the flames. "I can't believe this. I burned these, too. I can't seem to get anything right, lately."

"They aren't burned, just a little crunchy. Serve 'em up. We'll get to the tree after we eat."

Cassie poured Sam's concoction, which resembled brown water with bits of potato into two tin bowls, and placed them on tin plates. With her spatula she slid a biscuit alongside. "Should I keep a little back for Uncle Arvid?" She handed him his plate.

Sam headed for the log that had started all the trouble. He sat down. Cassie followed.

"I doubt he'll have an appetite when he finally comes to. I'd wager he's going to want more whiskey."

She looked at her plate for several long seconds. "I'm not really hungry."

"Well, eat it anyway," Sam said. "You'll be hungry later if you don't." He took a bite of his biscuit and followed it with a spoonful stew.

Cassie stalled. "I wonder how Josephine is doing."

Sam chewed a few seconds. "I'm sure she's fine. You know how young'uns are. They adapt quickly. She's probably going to school and enjoying herself." He stuffed the second half of the biscuit into his mouth. "No need to worry with Grace and Annabelle taking care of her."

He was right. There was no need to worry. But that didn't stop her from missing her. It had been hard falling asleep without her by her side. They'd slept in the same bed ever since their ma's death, when Miss Hawthorn had taken pity on them and let them move into the boarding house. Cassie was used to Josephine's cold, little feet.

"Cassie? What are you thinking?"

"I know you're right. I just have to keep reminding myself of it."

They finished in silence and as Cassie put the cooking supplies away and cleaned up, Sam moved the tree with the help of Cassie's horse and his lariat. He chopped a number of saplings and nailed them across the top. It was crude, uneven and wobbly, but if one was careful, it held plates and other wide-based objects. She was thankful.

In the dark, Sam moved his two horses over the river to Cassie and Arvid's side, to keep them safe from the marauding stallion and any other large animals looking for prey. He snubbed Blu to a tree and said his goodnights.

Dawn was just breaking when a loud string of cuss words jarred Sam out of his sleep. He met a sleepy-eyed Cassie in front of Arvid's tent. She reached for the tent opening.

"No. Let me," Sam said, pulling back the flap to find Arvid looking at him from his bedroll with cherry-red eyes and rumpled clothes. The look on his face would wither a cactus flower.

"How's your back?" Sam asked.

"How do you think?"

"I bet it hurts like hell," Sam replied evenly.

"Where's Cassie?"

"Right here, Uncle Arvid," she called past Sam. "Can I get you something to eat? Some water? Can you move?"

"I don't know what hurts worse, my back or my head. No doubt you got great satisfaction drowning me with my own whiskey."

Sam silently counted to five, restraining his anger. "You asked for it. Do you want to try to come out? Sit for a while?"

"Yes. Hurt or not, I'm going to have to do my business sometime."

Sam almost groaned out loud. What in the world were they going to do with Arvid all the way out here?

Cassie touched his arm to get Sam's attention. "I'll start a fire if you'll bring him out," she whispered quietly. "Do you think you'll need my help?"

"No, the tent's too small for all three of us."

"What do you think I should do? What will he want to eat?" She was wearing a long nightshirt and wrapped in a blanket, with her boots poking out beneath. She looked beautiful.

"Make anything that's quick and easy."

"Okay, and…"

"Come on and quit your yabbering," Arvid called out angrily. "You think I'm deaf? I can hear you talking about me. If I don't get to the bushes soon it won't be pretty."

Cassie's face scrunched up in horror and embarrassment. "Sam, I'm sorry."

Sam gritted his teeth and looked out over her head at the bluff. "Don't mention it."

While Sam helped Uncle Arvid, Cassie ran and got dressed, and then started a fire. She laid a few slices of bacon into the frying pan, and made biscuits. The coffee was just finished perking, the rich aroma making her mouth water. She assembled the plates, cups, and eating utensils on the makeshift table Sam had made the day before.

"Here, Uncle, sit here," Cassie said, patting the log near the fire as he and Sam inched slowly into camp. Sam had a firm hold on his right arm as Arvid shuffled along. Sam's face was a blank mask, but Uncle Arvid actually managed a smile.

"Thank you, girl."

"Bacon and biscuits are almost done."

Sam poured two cups of coffee, holding one out to Arvid.

Arvid reached for it, but stopped, his face grimacing as he pulled his limb back down into his lap, leaving Sam standing there. "When I first woke, I hurt like the dickens. But, being up and moving seems to have loosened me up some. Still hurts, mind you, but if the absence of tingling in my legs and neck is any indication, I think I'm on the mend."

"I'm happy to hear that," Cassie replied. She sat next to him with a plate of food and took the cup from Sam. She carefully put the coffee to his lips to give him a sip. "Just take a little, it's pretty hot."

He sipped and swallowed, his face screwing up tight. "Ooooweee, that's *strong*! If that don't grow hair on my backside, nothing will. Woman's work is just not your thing, niece."

Cassie felt stung. In light of everything else, his comment cut her to her core. The coffee was the same as she'd been making for days. "I guess my thoughts were distracted this morning and I added too much coffee. Do you want me to make another pot?"

"Do I have to ask twice?"

Sam's face was hard. "Tastes fine to me, Cassie. I don't know what he's talking about."

Arvid sighed. "Oh, he's probably right." He cast cheerless eyes to the dirt at his feet.

Frustrated, Cassie tossed the coffee from her uncle's tin cup into the bushes. She turned for the pot.

Arvid cleared his throat. "Waste not, want not," he said, giving her a knowing look of chastisement. "That coffee is costly, mind you."

"Oh, for the love of Pete! If you weren't already hurt I'd throw you in that river!" Sam said angrily. "I'd like nothing better than to see you bobbing away never to be seen again."

Confused, Cassie looked at the pot in her hands. "But you asked…" Backing away, she hurried off to the river. When she returned she found Sam hand-feeding her uncle. She quickly made another pot and put it in the hot coals. "Let me do that." She took Arvid's plate from Sam, who relinquished it readily and stepped away. She sat down in his place.

Cassie put a piece of bacon up to Uncle Arvid's mouth and his lips stretched out greedily.

"Mmmm, that's good bacon."

"I think I should take Arvid back to town where someone can care for him properly," Sam said. "In a house with a bed. It's the prudent thing to do."

Arvid stopped chewing. "I'm not leaving my claim," he said around the clump of pork in his mouth. "You can just forget about that! I'm here to prove my rightful ownership of the place."

"How're you going to do any work?" Sam replied heatedly. "Tell me. You can barely even walk."

"Until I'm up to it, I have Cassie. She was going to help me anyway. What's the difference?"

"You can't expect her to do the work of a man, and care for you night and day. That's not possible."

Cassie's face grew hot. Did he think she was a shrinking violet? "What are you talking about? Of course I'm going to work the claim. My gosh, Sam, before you and Uncle Arvid showed up I was planning on working it myself, with Josephine."

Sam swung his arm wide, taking in the expanse of the wilderness. "Can you see now how impractical that stupid notion was? Just one night here and someone, a grown man at that, is hurt seriously. Josephine wouldn't have lasted a day." He frowned at her. "Do you even know what a flake of gold looks like? This whole idea was foolish! And I'm the biggest fool for going along with it in the first place. I can't believe I agreed. It'll be a miracle if you find any gold at all without killing yourself first."

Cassie tossed her uncle's empty plate into the wash bucket. "I'll be back in a while, Uncle Arvid, to help you back to your tent." She stomped over to the pack that held the mining gear and pulled out the gold pans. Taking one, along with a small glass vial, she hefted a pick and headed down to the river. "We'll just see about that."

"Cassie, get back here!"

"Not on your life, Sam Ridgeway, not on your life!"

Sam looked at Arvid, who smiled and shrugged his shoulders. "Takes after her uncle."

"Hardly," Sam shot back. *She's the complete opposite of you—you selfish, deceitful disgusting son of a warthog*! Sam picked up his own mining things, following Cassie. He needed to calm her down so they could map out a plan. Several things, like swapping out the horses and going hunting for some fresh meat, had to get done before he could even think about panning for gold. If she'd let him, he wanted to give her some pointers to keep her safe while she did what she felt in her heart she had to do.

Cassie was on the riverbank looking at the water, her pick dangling from her hand.

"Cassie, we need to talk."

"No, we don't," she answered without turning around.

"There are things I need to do to support us here, like do some hunting, before I can join you. Please, will you turn around and talk to me?"

When she turned to face him Sam couldn't miss the tears sparking in her eyes.

Chapter Forty-One

"Are you crying?" Sam asked, his mouth going dry at the sight of her tears.

"Only because I'm so mad. I can't believe everything that's happened. Uncle Arvid showing up at Grace's house and ruining Jonathan and Annabelle's wedding." *And ours, too.* "His accusing you and you accusing him, all the while I thought the claim was mine. Now, because of me, he's gotten hurt so badly you have to take care of him even though you two hate each other. This whole debacle is so frustrating I could scream."

Sam heaved a sigh of relief. He could argue with a mad Cassie, but he couldn't deal with a crying one. He knew a lot of what she was leaving out of her little speech was her hurt over what had happened between them. She thought all he'd wanted to do was to dupe her. Play with her heart and then throw her away after he had the claim. Would he ever be able to regain her trust?

"I hear what you're saying," he said gently, nodding. "It's pretty unbelievable what's happened, I agree. But, I'm concerned about *now*. Right now. I need to go hunting. That may take hours, or the whole day." He let his gaze drop to the ground where her boots made an indentation in the soft grass.

"And?"

"Thing is, I'm uneasy about leaving you working in the river alone. Can you wait to start panning until I get back?"

Cassie let out a harsh laugh that Sam was sure was a result of dealing with the situation at hand. "Wait? I'm trying to beat you, remember? We're not working together."

"What if you slip and fall in? No one will be here to pull you out." He pointed to the rapids.

"Who says you're responsible for our food situation and that you have to go hunting? I have enough flour to keep making biscuits for weeks. And we have bacon and coffee."

"Just thought some fresh meat might be nice."

"Cassie!" Arvid yelled from camp. "My back is plum wore out from sitting. I need to get back to my bed. Come up here and help me." Cassie clamped her eyes closed. "Girl," he shouted louder, "can you hear me down there?"

Sam had a hard time hiding his smile. He looked out to the meadow where the horses were grazing peacefully.

"Go ahead, laugh all you want," Cassie said as she walked away from him up the trail toward camp.

"Cassie? Can you hear me, girlie?" Arvid called again.

"I didn't say a word," Sam called to her back. "You need my help with him?" The chirping birds and rushing water were his only reply.

After settling her uncle in his bedroll, Cassie took the better part of an hour to clean up the camp dishes and straighten up her own tent and belongings. Standing on the log that started the whole dilemma, she could see Sam down on the river's edge, mining away. *So much for going hunting.* Oh, well.

She'd be down there soon enough and was actually excited over the prospect of perhaps finding some gold. She plopped her hat on her head and started toward the river.

"And she returns." Sam pushed the rim of his hat up with his thumb; the only finger that wasn't a muddy mess, and smiled. "How'd it go up there?"

"Fine."

He'd rolled up his pants; his boots were soaked. He took a kerchief from his pocket and wiped his brow, leaving a few little wet blobs of dirt clinging to his temple. "This is harder than it looks."

"Mmhmmm."

He turned and sat with a plop on the edge of the bank, and set his pan down. "Come on, don't be angry. We're going to be working side by side for a month. No reason we can't be friends."

Cassie struggled to hold onto her irritation. When he smiled like that all she could think about was the kiss. That first one in the hall. The one that had her body tingling from her crown to her toes, even now. How many women had he kissed like that? she wondered. His eyes gleamed, as if he had the greatest secret to tell her, and his brows arched knowingly over his thickly lashed eyes. Without a doubt, Sam Ridgeway was the most disarmingly handsome man she'd ever seen.

"Truce?"

She bent and rolled up the cuffs of her dungarees. "Why should I?"

"Because it will make life so much nicer."

"I think life is as nice as it can get." She carefully inched down the bank until she was standing on a rock in the shallow water. He seemed inclined to just sit where he was and watch her.

"Hah! That's a joke. Did you see I switched out the horses while you were helping Arvid?"

"I saw," she answered. She felt around the side of the bank, trying to decide where to start. "Thought you were going hunting?"

"Guess I got involved. I'm planning to go in a while. Here." Without getting up, Sam hoisted the pick and made a hole right where she was looking.

"Sam! I want to do this on my own. Now if I find a big nugget I'll feel responsible to give you half."

"Sorry."

Squatting, Cassie reached into the broken earth and took a handful of the cold dirt, setting it in her pan. She grimaced when a long, fat worm wriggled into view. Moving quickly, she plucked it out and dropped it into the river, averting her eyes. Then she dipped the edge of her pan down and took in a small amount of water. It turned the clump of earth instantly to mud. She gave the murky water a tentative swish, but in the process lost her balance momentarily. While righting herself, the mud spilled over the side of her pan into the rushing water.

"Darn, there goes my gold nugget…"

Sam picked up his pan and stood. Bending, he took a fist full of the gravelly dirt off the bottom of the river where the water ran shallow and put it into his own gold pan.

"Like this." He dipped his edge and swished the water so a small amount escaped over the lip. "It takes a while to get the hang of it. The trick is not to try to drain the pan too fast. Slowly, she goes…"

Cassie watched him carefully as he moved the gold pan around and around. It really was quite beautiful how he did it, rhythmic and slow. He made it look easy. The water took a little more dirt out of the pan with it each swish. Soon there was only a tiny bit of gravelly soil left as the lighter dirt had been washed out. "As you know, the density of gold makes it very heavy. It stays in while the other gets washed away."

She came closer and looked into his pan. "Have you had any luck so far?"

"Not yet." He brought the pan up close to his face and poked around at the leftovers with his finger for several long minutes. "Nothin'."

He tossed the dregs out and dipped his pan into the river, washing it out.

"Just like that?" Cassie said, under her breath. "Doesn't seem too hard. How many times have you done it already?"

Sam pointed to a big hollow in the side of the bank where his pick lay on the green grass. The aroma of rich, dark soil pervaded the air. "More than you'd care to know."

He laughed and she couldn't help but smile. "Are we crazy?"

"Could be." He nudged her with his elbow. "You give it a try."

Sam stood by her side as she worked pan after pan, giving her suggestions and encouraging her whenever she got disheartened. A good hour elapsed without the hint of a sparkle, as Cassie's teeth began to chatter like the dice in a gambler's cup before he threw down. For what seemed like the millionth time, she peered at the bottom of her pan. Then she gasped.

"Sam! What's that?"

Chapter Forty-Two

Sam crowded close to Cassie and looked into her gold pan. Concentrating on her task was difficult with Sam's hard body smashed up close to hers. His warm breath caressed her cold face. He scooted in a bit closer still. "Let me see, Cassie. Where?" A moment passed. "I don't see anything."

Their heads bumped together as they examined the inky black soil. "*There*!" she exclaimed. "There! Do you see it? Is that gold?"

"Eureka!" Sam shouted, smiling into her face. "You found the first flake. Congratulations." He patted her back several times, as she laughed. "Get your vial out and open it up."

Once the vial was open, he took her shaking hand in his own and pressed her little finger onto the tiny flake, pushing down hard. They brought it up together. It was so small she was hard pressed to see it on the tip of her pinky.

"Scrape it off in here," he said, holding up her vial. "Careful. Careful. Go slowly now. You don't want to lose it."

"Are you teasing me?"

"Heck no! This is exactly how fortunes are made. One itty-bitty flake at a time."

Cassie scraped it off her finger and into the container half-filled with river water and screwed the lid on tight. She shook it and held it up to the sun, turning it back and forth. The flake floated around ever so slowly in the bottom of the vial.

"Isn't it pretty, Sam? So shiny. So—*gold.*"

She was so excited she could hardly stand it. Her dream was actually coming true! She and Josephine would open a modest bakery in some little town. With the profits, Josephine would have all the finer things in life—an education, a cozy home, plenty of food on the table each and every evening…all the things her little sister deserved. This little flake of gold was the beginning of all that.

"You might not want to keep it in your pocket, do you think? Might fall out."

"You're right."

Cassie proudly carried her reward up to the top of the bank clutched in her hand, and looked around.

"Just set it over there, where we can see it easily, and where it won't get lost. Tomorrow I'll bring something down with us that will keep our vials safe."

Cassie bounded back down the riverbank so fast that her foot caught on a rock and she slipped onto her backside. When Sam reached down to help her up she was shaking from the cold. Her blue lips encased chattering teeth and her hand felt like a chunk of ice.

"You're frozen. I think we've done enough for our first day out. Arvid's got to be hungry by now, and we're both going to be sore in the morning from all this bending and digging. If you go fix him something to eat, I'll take Blu and see if there's any game close by."

"But it's still early, Sam, and you haven't found any gold yet. I think we should just try a few more pans before we call it quits." She reached down and grabbed a handful of mud.

He knew if he pushed the point she'd get all huffy and stay on her own, fingers miniature icicles or not, just to be stubborn. Her jaw clenched over and over as she tried to stop the chattering, but it wasn't working.

"Okay, one more," he said.

"Two?"

"I'm just thinkin' of your uncle. Poor fellah can't even move."

Her eyes turned dark and she glanced toward the camp. "All right, just one more try. But tomorrow I think I should make up some lunch and put it in with Uncle so he can eat when he's hungry, and not have to depend totally on me." She swished her pan with confidence and familiarity now, smiling up into his face. One thing was certain: Cassie Angel had been bitten by the gold bug, and he wasn't going to be able to squash her enthusiasm very easily.

On his knees, Arvid peeked from between his tent flaps to see if the coast was clear. The top of the shabby structure sagged down, touching his head like a hat, and his belongings were lying all around in a messy heap. The air inside was hot and pungent from his being inside for so long.

He needed to relieve himself in the worst way, but didn't want his niece, or Sam Ridgeway, to see that he was capable of taking care of himself. Actually, this arrangement could work out quite well, if he played his cards right. Cassie was as stubborn as they came when she set her mind to something. She'd win this contest for him without him having to lift a finger. He'd done some mining when he was a younger man, when he had more brawn than brain, and knew what backbreaking, freezing work it was. He hadn't been looking forward to standing in that frigid spring runoff for hours on end, picking through the mud and gunk.

No, he'd rather relax on his bed doing nothin'. Young'uns were supposed to earn their keep. He laughed, marveling at his cleverness. It was too bad he'd never had a chance to run for a public office of some sort. He'd have made a wonderful politician.

Since the camp was deserted, he slipped from his tent and slowly made his way into the bushes. He relieved himself and was just starting back when he heard Cassie's humming as she came up the trail to the camp. She laughed once and said something he couldn't hear under her breath and resumed humming. He'd miscalculated! She would be in camp in seconds. He froze, trying to decide what he should do.

"Uncle Arvid, are you awake?" Cassie said quietly next to his tent opening, not fifteen feet from where he lay, stomach down on the ground, between the manzanita and shrub brush.

"Uncle?"

"Aaarrrggg. Help me, Cassie! Please! It hurts somethin' awful!"

The cry pierced Cassie like a hot poker, sending her heart straight up her throat. She'd been ready to pull back the tent flap to make sure her uncle was sleeping. Turning in the direction of his voice, she ran a short ways and found him. Uncle Arvid writhed back and forth, gasping and whimpering. His hands clawed at the sky and his back arched up in a bow so far that he was supported only by his heels and his head. His eyes were squeezed closed.

It was a full minute before he finally grew quiet. Cassie dropped to her knees but was apprehensive about touching him, fearful she would cause more pain.

"Uncle, what happened?"

One eye slowly opened. Then the other. Spittle had collected on his beard, and he was drawing deep, shaky breaths.

"I couldn't wait another minute. You've been gone so damn long a turtle could crawl to town and back." He reached for Cassie's arm, but his arm fell back onto the earth with a thud. "I just couldn't wait no more, honey. I hope you will forgive me for being a foolish ol' man. I thought I could make it on my own. On my way back my wobbly legs gave way and I fell. Now, every dang limb I have has gone numb again."

Cassie looked around.

"Can you get Sam to come help me back to my bed?"

"I can't. He's gone hunting. We'll have to make it on our own."

His bottom lip wobbled as his face beseeched her.

"We can do it, Uncle."

"I don't think so. It'll hurt too much."

"I can't just leave you here," Cassie said softly. He stared at her for a moment. "Give me a stick to bite on like Sam did yesterday. Then when you lift me I won't scream in your ear and break your eardrum."

"Okay."

Cassie found a strong stick and placed it between his teeth.

"Well, let's get going," he said with difficulty, gripping the branch in his mouth. "If it hurts I'm sure it won't kill me."

"Please, don't talk like that."

He spat the wood from his mouth, and glared, fairly shaking with anger. "Geez, girl! Just get moving and get me to my bed." His tone wasn't soft and sorry anymore, but irritated and impatient.

"Yes, of course." Her defiance wanted to rear its head, tell him to be quiet, but she beat it back with a mental shove. He was hurt! He had a right to be short with her. How heartless could she be?

Cassie bent down, and with surprisingly little effort on her part, helped her uncle stand and regain his balance.

"Here we go." She tried to smile.

Arvid hobbled next to her as she held his arm. Every once in a while his foot would drag, causing him to teeter dangerously to one side.

"Almost there, thank goodness. I bet you'll be glad to be back on your bed."

Before he could answer, he cried out sharply and spun out of her arms. He landed in a heap, screaming in pain. "See what you done to me, girl! See what you done! I'm never gonna be the same. I'm gonna be a cripple. A cripple!"

The tears that had been pooling behind Cassie's eyes since finding her uncle on the ground now came out in force. She sobbed once, then pushed the tears away with the back of her hand as she went to help him up.

"No! Get away. I'll crawl in on my own."

Cassie stood in silence as Uncle Arvid creped inside slowly on hands and knees until the flap closed behind him. There was a rustling sound and then nothing more. She stood for ten minutes just staring at the flap and listening to the sounds of the wilderness. The rushing river. The call of a hawk. A dark cloud of gnats passing over her head and were gone. She wished Sam was here. She felt completely alone.

Chapter Forty-Three

"Easy, girl," Sam soothed. The small deer carcass draped across the back of his saddle made his mare more skittish than a youngster at bath time. Dangling on both sides of her flanks, the young buck's legs jiggled with each step Blu took. Eyes wide with apprehension, Blu flicked her ears back and forth, and she snorted repeatedly. Sam smiled to himself at the thought of her trusting him so implicitly and reached down to scratch her withers. The mare slowly made her way through the trees and came out of a copse, just over the rise from the camp.

The stallion, once again, crept into Sam's mind. From what he'd seen, the animal's conformation was flawless. He'd make any ranch an outstanding foundation sire. Plus, his intelligence was evident, outwitting the number of men trying to capture him so far. Wouldn't he love to have a horse like him?

Cassie would be pleased with the deer. The thought of fresh venison, thick and hot straight from the fire, made his mouth water and his stomach clutch with hunger pangs. After it was smoked, would keep them well fed for days to come.

Sam had had more luck than just bringing down a buck, too. He'd also run into a miner who was pulling up stakes. Tired of living like an animal, the man was heading back to civilization. Besides providing some helpful information, he'd sold Sam the remainder of his provisions.

The two large bags hanging from either side of his saddle horn contained beans, salt pork, bacon, oatmeal, some moldy white cheese, flour, and the like. He'd even procured a small bag of sourballs, a pouch of tobacco, and small jug of apple brandy.

Tonight, they'd celebrate. Their first flake of gold from the mine, lots of fresh deer meat to last them for days, and a sip of apple brandy to delight the taste buds before retiring. He was looking forward to it.

He pulled up to a quiet camp. Dismounting, he looped his reins around a scrub oak, and looked around. It was still light enough that he could see Cassie down by the river's edge, sitting on a rock.

Gosh, he'd hoped there would be at least a *little* something cooking. He hadn't eaten since morning and his stomach was achingly hollow. But the fire was out and there was no sign of Arvid.

Sam untied the leather straps holding the deer to Blu and slipped it off over her rump. She gave one last hump of her back and, with plate-sized eyes, sashayed to the side, snorting her protest at having to carry such frightening cargo. After laying his kill out nearby, removing the bags of food and loosening Blu's cinch, Sam started toward Cassie to see what he could find out.

"Cassie?"

She looked around. In the dusky light he couldn't see her expression. Scrambling off the big rock, she fairly flew into his embrace.

"What is it?"

She wrapped her arms around his middle and buried her face against his chest. "I'm so glad you're back, Sam."

This was a huge change for Cassie. He wondered what was behind it. "What happened?"

"Uncle Arvid tried to come out on his own. He fell. When I was trying to help him back, he tripped again. He's really hurt. I've ruined his life, Sam, forever. He's going to be a cripple now, and he hates me for it. I can't blame him in the least."

Sam took her face in both of his hands and looked into her eyes. "He doesn't hate you, Cassie. That's silly. You're his niece. Hasn't anyone ever told you that accidents happen? And besides, if I remember correctly, he was much better this morning and I'm sure if he had a set-back it'll just take a day or two longer before he's better. It'll teach him not to go venturing out on his own anymore."

She pulled from his arms and turned back to the river. "No. It's really bad." Her voice was small. Hurt.

"I believe you. But I think you'll feel better when you get out of those dirty clothes from this morning, and get something hot into your belly. Come with me right now."

Sam took hold of her hand, almost smiling when she didn't resist, and started up the path to the camp. They came to where Blu was tied and the new provisions sat nearby on the ground, still the focus of the horse's attention.

"Look at what jumped out and bit my bullet?"

"Why, he's only a yearling." She knelt by the deer and ran her hand down its long neck. "You did well. Thank you."

Her words sounded hollow. Whatever dad-blasted Arvid had said to her had cut her to the quick.

"I have another surprise, too," he said. "Close your eyes and open your hand."

"Sam…"

"Just do it."

She did. She stood in the near dark with her eyes closed and palm upturned. He was tempted to take the opportunity to kiss her, but knew she'd be fuming mad if he did. And he was too tired to fight.

"Keep 'em closed," Sam warned. "This might take me a second. No peeking." He went to the bags and dug through the first one as fast as he could. Unsuccessful there, he opened the second. He heard Cassie shift her weight from one foot to the other.

"Don't be impatient. You're gonna like this." He fished two candies from the small bag, tied it again and put it back.

"Sam?"

"Here." At the same time he placed one sourball in her hand he slipped another between her lips. Her eyes popped open.

"What?" Surprised, she opened her mouth wider; then, getting a taste, she closed it, and started savoring the treat. "Mmmm. Oh, that's good. What is it?" A little laugh slipped out. "It makes me feel like puckering up."

He laughed too, happy that this was making her feel a little better. "It's a sourball."

"Where on earth did you find sourballs out here in the wilderness?"

"I came across a disgruntled miner who was packing up and going home. He sold me his provisions for next to nothin'. A bag of candy was among my spoils."

Blu snorted loudly and pawed the ground, making Cassie and Sam laugh again. "Poor horse has been traumatized by having to carry the dead deer on her back. Horses don't like the scent of death. I need to get her out to graze and the deer strung up and bled out. Will you be all right on your own for a while longer?"

"Of course. Now that you're here I—"

He gaped at her, surprised at what she'd almost said. "Yes?"

"...feel so much better. I do. I'd be a liar to deny it. I'm going to get you a lantern to work by. After that I'll take care of your horse. If you don't mind bacon and biscuits again I can have that ready pretty quickly."

"That sounds good, Cass. Don't worry, everything is going to be fine, and that includes Uncle Arvid." Sam couldn't believe he'd just called that stinkin', slimy snake uncle, but he'd do it for Cassie.

She smiled. "I'll be right back with a lamp."

"I'm going to make a fast trip over to my camp before I start the butchering, and haul the rest of my things over to this side of the river. That might take a few minutes."

He might be seeing things in the evening light, but he thought he saw her eyes light with pleasure.

"Can I help you?"

"You sure can. By fixing me somethin' hot to plug this hole smoldering in my gut."

Sam circled the hind hoof of the deer with his lariat and looped the rope over a sturdy branch. Hand over hand, he pulled until the carcass, hung nose down, just inches from the ground. He tied the rope off on the tree trunk. To ward off nocturnal hunters that might smell the kill, he roughened up the earth beneath the buck to make it accepting of the blood and fluids that would come from the incision he was about to make.

By now it was dark, but the lamp Cassie brought over to him cast just enough light to enable him to see what he was doing. She was busy over by the campfire, mixing her biscuits and frying the bacon. The smell was tauntingly aromatic, distracting him all the way over where he was working.

Sam wondered about Arvid. What the heck was the man doing in that tent? No one could sleep hour after hour, even if they were hurt. Sam wiped his hands on a cloth Cassie had supplied, done with the deer until morning, when he'd skin and butcher it. It was time to get washed up for dinner and check on that uncle of Cassie's—whether he wanted to or not.

Chapter Forty-Four

Cassie was just taking the frying pan off the fire when Sam walked out of the fringes of darkness and into camp. His hair was damp and he was dressed in clean clothes. He looked extremely handsome, with a little smile and twinkle in his eyes. To think this had been her husband—for a few minutes—at least. Cassie breathed a tiny sigh, telling herself to get her head out of the clouds and back to work. A towel was slung over his shoulder. The two white bags he'd gotten from the other miner were in his arms.

"You bathed," she said softly, standing up.

"Didn't want to come to supper covered in blood." He put the bags down on the makeshift table and held out his hands to her as if he were a youngster, turning them over for her to inspect. "I'll say, though, that river is dang cold. Pretty near froze my—" He stopped and gave her a funny look. "Well, I think you get my meaning."

"Perfectly, cowboy." She glanced at him mischievously. "How did you manage?"

"I'm just tough, I guess." He crossed his arms and ran his hands up and down his sides, to warm himself. "Supper done?"

"Almost. Do you want to go and see if Uncle Arvid is able to join us? I know it's late, but he must be hungry." She felt bad about asking Sam to do it, but after the accident earlier today she dreaded seeing her uncle. How was she going to get through the month?

"Reckon so."

When Sam walked off she dished up three plates of the same bacon and biscuits they'd had this morning and poured three cups of coffee.

Within moments, Sam was back. "He's hungry but said he wants to eat in his tent. You have his plate ready? I'll take it to him."

"Yes," she said, handing him Arvid's dinner and cup. "Is he feeling any better? Will he be able to eat this on his own?" She forced the questions out past her apprehension. Even if he hated her forever, she needed to see that he was well cared for.

Sam held plate and cup. "He looks pretty good, besides needing some attention to his, er, toiletries. Said he'll be able to eat on his own."

"If he'd let me I could warm some water and help him shave and clean up after he's finished."

"I'll ask him."

Cassie watched Sam leave. What on earth would she do without his help?

Without *him*, her conscience corrected. Yes, he was the thing she would miss most when the competition for the claim was over and they parted ways.

Sam ambled back into camp and went straight to where his plate sat on the troublemaking log. "Looks great."

"It's the exact same thing you ate this morning."

"Food is food. Besides, I thought it was good then, too."

Cassie hid her smile behind her coffee cup. You'd think he was eating a chocolate truffle by the look of pleasure on his face. "What did Uncle say?" She hoped he was ready to make up and forgive her.

"He said maybe in the mornin' he'd feel like getting cleaned up. But not tonight. Said he was tired now, and that as soon as he'd eaten he was going to sleep. I sure don't know how one person can sleep so much, but then, I'm not the one with a hurt back."

Another strip of bacon disappeared into Sam's mouth and he continued chewing vigorously.

Cassie broke off a piece of her biscuit and put it in her mouth. It was dry, and without much flavor. She sipped her coffee and swallowed. "What's our plan?"

Sam wiped his mouth with his palm and took a sip from his cup. "Well, in the morning, I'll skin and butcher the deer and smoke most of the meat. I'll keep back a few steaks for the next two days or so, but not much more. Then, after some breakfast, we'll pan for gold a few hours before breaking for the noontime meal. After that, I'll take the carcass out into the woods and bury it so it won't attract any unwanted visitors. Then mine some more, then supper."

He looked over at her. "That pretty much covers it. Sound good?"

She nodded.

Sam stood, placed his plate in the dishpan, and drained his coffee cup. He opened one of the bags, rummaging around.

A smile creased his face as he pulled out a jug of something and poured a small amount into his cup. "Would you like a little?" He took a sip. "It's mighty good."

"What is it?"

"Apple brandy."

She just looked at him, trying to decide. "I've never tasted it before."

"Don't have to if you don't want," he said.

Cassie handed him her now empty cup, and Sam poured in a little splash. She brought it up to her nose, taking a whiff. It smelled spicy and warm. Her mouth watered, prompting her to try it. "It does taste like apples. It's good."

"Anyone still out there?" Arvid yelled from his tent. "Or have you run off and left me here to die? These dishes need picking up. And I need to use the facilities."

Cassie set her cup down, intending to go to his aid.

"I'll go," Sam said slowly. Cassie watched as a slight tic moved his strong jaw. "He's too heavy for you to help, Cassie. I don't mind—much."

Cassie settled in. A week came and went with the same routine. Uncle Arvid's unwillingness to even try to get up weighed unfavorably on her troubled heart.

Sam had helped her at every turn. Thank goodness his knowledge of camping far exceeded hers. He cared for the horses as well as hunted and kept watch. Cassie searched out a secluded spot on the river to bathe. A quick splash in, suds up, three dips for a rinse and out again in the moonlight. Even though it was breathtakingly cold, it was one of her favorite things to do each evening after chores were done.

The gold they'd found was minimal, but enough to buoy their spirits. The competition was close. Cassie could never really bring herself to talk about what would happen at the end of the month. Who would stay and who would leave. These days with Sam were proving to be wonderful, and she knew him now on a much deeper level. Every day it got a little harder to conjure up the blinding hurt she'd felt the night they'd married—and then had her heart ripped in two.

She remembered the day Arvid let her and Sam help him out into the sunshine to sit for a couple of hours where he could soak up the warmth. Cassie took the opportunity to pull out his rumpled bedding and let it air in the sunshine, too. Keeping him clean had been the most perplexing problem, but she washed his clothes and helped him shave as often as he'd let her.

"I was thinking we should make a sluice box," Sam said, his legs stretched out and back against a log. Supper dishes were washed and put away. The night sounds closed in around them. "It's a good way to get through a lot more earth without breaking our backs so much, like we've been doing. What do you think?"

"How would that work? With the competition, I mean? Would we each need our own?"

"I don't think we'd have enough wood for two from the broken down shack I found upstream, so we'd have to share. Switch off." He ran his hand over his whiskered face, swatted at a mosquito that had landed on his arm and looked at her.

"Cass?"

She looked up, surprised.

"Did you hear what I said? What're you thinking about?"

"Josephine. Just wondering how she is. What she's doing. If she's well and happy…"

Without warning, Cassie's voice caught. She looked away from Sam's face, up through the trees to the full strawberry moon that hung amid the enormous white clouds. Twinkling stars added to the beauty and mystery of the heavens. Golden rays beamed down, softly lighting their campsite.

"And if she misses you as much as you miss her?" he finished for her. "There's no doubt. I'd lay money she's keeping track until you ride back into Rosenthal, ticking off the days of the month somewhere on Grace's good dining room wall with a piece of charcoal." He laughed and Cassie did, too. "Or somewhere else she isn't supposed to be. I'm sure of it."

"She is special, isn't she, Sam?"

"Very. Just like her sister."

"Sam," Cassie responded, getting a glimpse of his smiling eyes in the soft light of the moon. He was feigning a look of innocence that made her face heat up. Without warning, her thoughts flew back to their kiss in Grace's home. His proposal. Their wedding—or sham wedding—or whatever it was. She found her thoughts straying often in that direction these days. His nearness and the remembered sensation of his lips on hers, a feeling that had been unbearably good, made the thoughts persist. Her gazed dropped to his tempting mouth and she wondered if he ever thought about those times, too.

"What?"

Cassie didn't answer.

He shrugged. Stretching out his legs, he crossed them at the ankle. He laced his fingers together behind his head, trying to get comfortable on the hard ground with his back against the fireside log. "Josephine told me once about your ma and pa. How kind and loving they were. It was good to hear, Cassie. I'm pleased your family was like that. It's not always so, you know. Times can be difficult when people are strapped. They do and say things they don't mean sometimes. And it's the youngest ones that suffer the most."

"Yes," she said, her stomach knotting up like a neglected ball of yarn. An owl they'd grown used to hearing every night hooted from somewhere up on the ridge, bringing a feeling of normalcy, soothing her nerves. "I know what you mean." She didn't like to think of the years she'd shielded her sister from the truth.

"Until then, I'd wondered some about it. Because of Arvid. Brothers are usually cut from the same cloth. But that doesn't seem to be the case at all with your father. I'm glad."

Chapter Forty-Five

"Come on." Sam stood and extended his hand to Cassie. "Let's take a walk. It's not often we get such a beautiful night. Besides, I'd like to stretch my legs before going to sleep on that blanket I call a bed. I think Arvid is sneaking out and putting rocks under it when I'm not looking. I don't know about you, but I'll be thankful to sleep on a real mattress again, when the time comes."

Cassie hesitated only a moment before putting her hand in his. He thought he'd get a reaction to his remark about her uncle, but she didn't take the bait. He pulled her up from where she sat on the log and started walking out into the meadow.

"Why so quiet?" he asked.

"Nothing, really," she said.

"Come on. I know something's bothering you. Out with it."

Cassie shrugged.

The horses grazing in the moonlight raised their heads and looked at them as they slowly approached. It was Split Ear's turn to be tied to the oak tree next to camp, and he was none too pleased about it. His nicker sounded a bit sad at being

269

deserted now even by the humans. Blu and Meadowlark started walking their way.

Sam brushed his thumb back and forth across the top of Cassie's warm hand. "They look pretty, don't they?"

"They do. I wonder what happened to the stallion. Did he give up so easily?"

Sam chuckled. "He's just biding his time, letting us get good and comfortable. Then, when we're least expecting it, he'll swoop in and make his move."

She looked up at him, the light back in her eyes. "You think?" She edged closer to his side and hugged his arm. "You almost make him sound like he was a human."

Sam wiggled his eyebrows up and down, getting her to giggle. "Are we really that much different? I'm just biding *my* time to swoo—"

"Sam! Be serious!"

"I don't want to be serious. I don't want to think about the claim, or what's going to happen next. I don't want to think about when one of us leaves, and the other stays. I only want to enjoy your company this evening. And, that's exactly what I intend to do."

They were in the middle of the meadow now with the horses gathered around them, looking for whatever treat they might have in their pockets. Arvid's horse was the only one to hang back, watching them suspiciously. Sam let go of Cassie's hand and ran it down Blu's neck, stopping at her withers. He scratched the area firmly, causing a puff of white hairs to flutter down. The mare stretched her neck out as far as she could, her upper lip extended in pleasure.

He laughed again, feeling good inside. "How are you, girl?" he said, as he continued scratching. "You've had a nice holiday for the last few days. You're getting fat and lazy."

Meadowlark inched forward until Sam could reach her withers too. "Jealous?" he said, now scratching Cassie's mare until her head bobbed as well. In the throes of her pleasure, Meadowlark reached over and started nibbling at Blu's belly, who quickly pinned her ears and squealed. Meadowlark trotted away.

"Well, there you have it. I guess you can't have the good without the bad. Just nature." Without asking, Sam reached for Cassie's hand again and started toward the river.

Once at its bank, he looked until he found a rock big enough to accommodate them both. He sat and pulled Cassie down beside him, and waited for her to get settled. She was being quiet tonight and he wondered at the reason. Was it Arvid? The man had been keeping himself scarce these past few days, even more than before. He'd either lie on his bedroll all day or sit on the log. There was something unusual about him that put Sam on edge, even more so now, but he couldn't quite put his finger on what. He'd be watching him closely.

"You never said if you thought the sluice box was a good idea. Anything sounds better than the way we've been doing it. What do you think?"

Cassie nodded. "I agree. I'm tired of the bending and shoveling too. I'm about broken in half and have little gold to show for it. Do you know how to make one? One that works?"

"Hey, hey, hey. What's that supposed to mean?" He nudged her with his shoulder and she pushed back at him.

She smiled. "I'm just teasing you. But, do you?"

"Yes. Our last night in Hangtown I went over to the mining supply store, the one the Chinese man was running. He showed me several ideas and we talked at length. It doesn't look like it would be too difficult of a job."

"In that case, why not try? I think it's a good idea. You said that there was a shack up river where we can get the boards. Can we do that tomorrow?"

"My thoughts exactly," Sam said. "We'll go first thing after breakfast after we have your uncle settled and comfortable. I'm surprised he isn't better by now. Has he said anything else to you?"

"No. Not really. He pretty much wants me to leave him alone."

"Mmmm." Sam let that thought percolate. That old man was getting stranger by the day. Still, Sam couldn't complain too much. Arvid's seclusion meant he had Cassie all to himself.

For the next few minutes, they sat in silence, watching the river. Cassie enjoyed the feel of Sam so close by her side, his warmth seeping into her jacket and heating her skin. She was also getting great pleasure from his amicable mood and this nice turn of events. Without looking up, she could see his profile in the moonlight as he looked across the river and into the nearby mountains.

Holding hands was risky. She didn't like to admit it to herself but it brought her great joy, along with a delicious feeling of closeness. Despite the fact that he'd lied to her from the beginning about the claim, her heart had already fallen for him, long and hard. She would miss him way too much when it was time to move on, but she wasn't ready to be practical yet. There was always time for that later.

"Your brooch," he said, bringing her out of her thoughts. "You don't wear it much anymore. How come?"

Shame for the lie that still hung between them stung and she wished he hadn't mentioned it. She liked this feeling she and Sam were sharing. It felt completely right. Another lie, on top of the last one she'd told about the brooch, was not a way to keep it alive. The truth will set you free, her mother had always told her. Lies keep you trapped, unable to go forward or back.

"I fibbed about the brooch, Sam. What I told you wasn't even close to the truth." She turned so she could see his face.

He was watching her intently. "How so?"

"I never had a beau named Charles. I made him up. I've never had a beau at all."

Cassie withdrew her hand from the cocoon of Sam's warm one and laced her fingers together. Night air, cooled by the water and light summer breeze, blanketed her, bringing a chill.

"Now, that surprises me." The timber of his voice was deep and soft, more so than ever before. He took her hand back into his own.

Butterflies fluttered inside. "What? That I lied to you?"

"No. That you've never had a beau. A girl as pretty as you should have so many beaus she can't remember the names of them all."

He waited a moment, perhaps to give her a chance to respond. When she didn't, he said, "You still haven't answered the question. So, how come you're not wearing it anymore?"

"I'm afraid it'll fall off in the water. It was my mother's and her mother's before that. It's the only thing I have, besides the Bible that was passed down. I feel close to my ma when I wear it. My mama said to touch it when I want my guardian angel's help. I did when Josephine was on the cliff and when the outlaws were in Rosenthal. Also, the first day I met you, when Klem came to pay us a visit. I'm going to give it to Josephine when she's older and responsible enough not to lose it."

Sam straightened and Cassie thought a teasing comment was coming any moment. She looked at him.

"Cassie, you don't think I stole the claim from your uncle, do you? Or that whole cockamamie story of his? Surely, you can't believe that anymore?"

She tried to look away, but his longing gaze wouldn't let her. "I don't know what to believe anymore, Sam. Sitting here and holding your hand, it seems inconceivable. Then I remember that you would go so far to marry me just to get it, well—"

Sam sat up straighter and looked over her head for a moment. "Shhh," he said, clasping his hand over her mouth.

Chapter Forty-Six

"What is it?" Cassie's eyes were huge as he took his hand away from her face.

"Stay here," he whispered close to her ear. A ripple of warmth shot through him as his lips accidently brushed her skin. "I heard something."

In the field one of the horses nickered, answered by Split Ear up in camp.

She grabbed his arm as he stood up. "It's just the horses."

"Cassie," he said bending close. "I need to go check this out. You stay here where I can find you. Where I know you're safe."

He strode up the path, but stopped when he heard her quick steps behind him. He turned to meet her.

"I'm coming with you!" she said, a determined tilt to her chin.

"All right, but be quiet."

Sam stopped suddenly at the meadow's edge and Cassie bumped into his backside.

"The moon is too bright for us to go back the way we came."

"You think it's a person you heard? That someone is here?"

"Don't know. But I have the feeling of being watched. If I'm right, and there is someone watching from the bluff, we'd be an easy target if we cross the meadow in the open. We'll walk the perimeter and stay under the trees and brush."

Sam took Cassie's hand and veered to the left, ducking beneath some low-hanging branches. It was slower going, and much darker under the foliage. He tripped on a rock, but righted himself before falling. He guided Cassie past.

They stopped. Sam parted the bush they were behind and peered out, looking to the top of the bluff where they'd sat on their horses the day they first arrived.

"There." He pointed.

Cassie strained to see what he was looking at. "What? I don't see anything."

"Don't look directly at the bluff, just a little to one side. It's easier to see that way. There's one person, maybe two."

One of the mares in the meadow nickered and an unfamiliar, deep call answered from across the river from where they had been sitting.

Sam felt Cassie stiffen.

"Could be the stallion," he said. "From over there, most likely is." He ran his hands down both sides of her arms to comfort her. "Don't be scared."

"What about Uncle Arvid? He's in the camp alone."

"I'll bet he's asleep. Can I trust you to stay here if I sneak up the north side of the bluff and see just who we are dealing with?"

"No. I'm either going with you or going back to camp to keep my uncle safe."

"We don't know that whoever it is means us harm, Cassie."

"I feel pretty sure they do, them sneaking up after dark. This doesn't feel good at all."

"Okay, then come with me," Sam said, thankful he had his gun strapped to his thigh. He bent over and continued on though the underbrush. "I want to get up there before they make their decision to leave or invade our camp."

"Oh, that makes me feel a lot better," Cassie mumbled as he pulled her along.

Her heart was about to burst. Cassie's wasn't sure if it was from fright, or from trying to keep up with Sam as he ascended the bluff. He was so far ahead of her now she could scarcely make out his outline in the moonlight. She paused for a moment to catch her breath, then resumed the upward climb.

She stopped next to Sam, who was barely breathing hard. "Did you get a look at them?"

"They're gone."

"Well, hell! Did you see him, or them, or anything before they left?"

Sam turned around and sat on the hill. Cassie could see the half smile on his face.

"When did you start cussing?" he asked, and then chuckled. "You must be picking up your uncle's bad habits."

"That wasn't a curse. Just frustration. Did you see anything or not?"

"Just the tail end of two horses. With riders, of course."

Exhausted and still panting, she turned around and plopped down next to Sam. She took a deep breath and held it. A few moments went by.

"Don't you dare pass out on me," Sam said. "I don't want to have to lug you all the way down this hill." He reached over and brushed at something on her cheek.

"Dirt." His gaze melded with hers and the smile on his face faded away.

Desire smoldered in his eyes, and something more, too. "Oh." It was the only word she could get past her lips.

He leaned in slowly, and then stopped, as if searching for something. She felt hidden in the darkness, the sky a blanket of stars above, the cold night air surrounding her. She glanced at his mouth.

"What do you think they wanted?" she asked, trying to be nonchalant with his face so close to hers. She slowly raised her eyes until she was looking into his. Even in the moonlight she could see the longing deep inside.

"Impossible to know," he answered softly. "They could be other miners just looking for their claim, or they could be robbers, planning a little visit later."

"Sam!"

"You asked." He was so close now his words came out on her lips.

She felt sure he was going to kiss her. She hoped he would. As in the hallway at Grace's house, when she'd melted in his arms. She could remember every delectable tingle. He pulled her close and nuzzled her face, his cheek brushing hers. He smelled good, like the sourball he'd been eating, broken grass, and the fresh earth under their feet. The darkness of the night coiled around, cocooning them protectively.

The owl hooted from down by the river. The sound was enough to break the spell.

Cassie sat up and straightened her clothes.

"I guess..." they said at the same time and stopped. He looked embarrassed.

"You go first," Sam said.

She was thankful to be back on a normal keel with him. "I guess we should start back down."

"Again, my thoughts exactly. Funny how we keep doing that."

A shrill sound split the air, bringing them both up short.

"What in the blazes?" Sam shouted. "Look!" He pointed down the steep, shale-covered hill, and across the meadow.

It was the stallion. He issued another blast, and then galloped into the river, sending up plumes of water spray, and charged up the other bank to the excited mares. He circled them several times before halting.

"Come on!" Sam shouted, grabbing Cassie's hand. They scrambled and slid down the steep hill, half on their bottoms, as their boots skidded and slipped. Dirt and rock gave way. Cassie's heel caught on a root and she pitched forward, but Sam held her tight and kept going. They stopped before they got completely to the bottom so he could use the advantage of the height of the hill to see what was happening in the meadow.

The stallion reared and struck out at the sky before taking off after Arvid's gelding. It didn't take him but a moment to catch the hobbled gelding and with lips pulled back from his menacing teeth, take hold of the smaller horse by the crest of his neck and shake him like a rag doll. The gelding squealed loudly, wild with fear. He kicked out in every direction, trying to free himself of the devil that had hold of him. Breaking loose, he turned but was once again headed off by the angry stud and struck in the head when his attacker reared, lashing out.

"Oh, damn," Sam said, surprised. He took off, leaving Cassie where she stood. He had to get to the meadow before the stallion badly injured or killed Arvid's horse. He stopped in camp long enough to scoop up his rope, then ran through the brush and Manzanita.

Sam reached his destination and stopped. All was quiet. Well, almost quiet. The sound of a mare being bred was easily recognizable. He grabbed Cassie's arm when she caught up to him, before she could dash around.

"Sam, let me go! I've got to help Meadowlark," she cried, still unaware of what was happening.

"There's no help for her now."

Cassie yanked her arm free and darted a few feet into the moonlit area and stopped short.

"See what I mean?" Sam said softly from behind her.

The stallion snorted once as his front hooves hit the grass. He shook his head, lowered it, and walked a full circle around Meadowlark, smelling the ground. Arvid's horse stood on the outer edge of the field, still trembling in fear.

Sam stepped next to Cassie as the stallion stared in her direction. He tossed his proud head defiantly as if to mock their efforts. His forelock fell into his eyes.

"Oh, my gosh, Sam. He's so magnificent!"

Sam's chest filled with emotion. Here was an animal meant for freedom. "My thoughts…"

"Exactly." The word was said low, in awe, by both of them.

"Do you think he's already gotten to your mare, too?" she asked.

"Only time will tell. If not, and she's in season, he'd be doing now what he does best."

Chapter Forty-Seven

"Cassie, stay here," Sam cautioned as she started toward Meadowlark.

The stallion, his chest glistening in sweat, sides heaving from exertion, bit Blu in the hindquarters in an effort to herd her toward the river. When she moved only a few feet because of her restraints, he trotted over to Meadowlark, snorting and pawing the ground. One nasty bite to her mare's shoulder and Cassie took off toward her horse.

"Hyaw! Hyaw!" she screamed. "You stop that!" She waved her hands over her head emphatically.

The moment the stallion took a step in Cassie's direction, Sam drew his gun and fired into the sky, shattering the quiet night. The mares flinched at the sudden noise and the big bay took off toward the river, splashing across with dramatic flourish.

Cassie bolted toward her horse through the thick grass, anguish building inside. Even from this distance she could see several marks on the mare's hide, left behind by the stallion. Sam caught her around the middle and tumbled her into the tall grass.

"Hold up! You can't just run up to her like that. Both those mares are agitated and half-crazy right now. You're going to get your brains kicked out."

"Let me go!" In the softness of the grass, she pushed on his chest but he had her caught securely under him, his elbows resting on either side of her shoulders, his hands stroking her hair.

"I can see she's hurt," she tried again. She struggled against him helplessly. Before she realized what he meant to do, his lips were softly touching hers.

"Sam," she whispered, less forcefully now, melting in a sea of desire. "Sam—stop." It wasn't much of a demand. He kissed her slowly, taking his time. His head turned, ever deepening the caress.

Just when she thought it couldn't get any sweeter, he stood and pulled her to her feet.

"If you want to do something now, go check on the gelding," he said as if nothing had happened between them. "He still looks traumatized and I'm sure he'd welcome your ministering. I'll go catch him up and bring him over here. By the time you look him over, the mares may be settled down."

Blu flipped her head several times and returned call for call with their dashing midnight marauder, who was watching them from the hills beyond the river. Meadowlark looked back and forth between the two, pinning her ears at Blu and doing her fair share of whinnying. She snorted several times and squealed when Blu came close.

"I take that back. From the looks of 'em, they may not settle down until mornin'," Sam said.

He was right. Again. She couldn't argue with his logic the way the horses looked. The mares out in the field showed little resemblance to the docile animals they'd been before.

"Okay, go get the poor horse and we'll see what he needs," Cassie said, her insides still wobbly from Sam's kiss. "I think he took a blow to the head."

"He did. I winced when it happened," Sam replied. "He must have a headache the size of Texas."

"Can horses have headaches?"

"Don't see why not. Why don't you go get some rags to clean him up with," Sam suggested, as he started for the frightened gelding, the rope draped across his shoulder.

***

The next morning, after seeing to the mares and tacking them up in preparation for the trip up stream to get the boards for the sluice box, Sam put on a pot of coffee to boil and headed for the river. The weather was mild so he stripped naked after pulling off his boots and socks, and waded out into the chilly water, past the shallows and rocks, up to his waist.

Tensing his muscles against the cold, he splashed his face and ran a bar of red clover soap over his chest and arms. He dunked down once completely, submerging his head and lathering up his hair. He tossed the soap to shore and scrubbed vigorously to rid himself of dirt and grime and also in an effort to stay warm.

His teeth were clattering by the time he was satisfied that he'd done all he could do and scraped the excess water from his hair with his hands. He started for the shore where his towel was laid across a boulder.

The rocks, slippery with patches of moss, formed a natural route back toward the river's edge. A few feet from land the water became shallow, barely ankle deep, but still treacherous from algae that grew abundantly so close to the sun. Spring air, pungent with the scent of fish and moss, gently stirred the leaves. The birds were waking with their songs and chatter.

Sam slipped. He caught himself with a nearby rock. When he glanced down he was drawn by a flash of light.

He stopped. Stared into the water, concentrating.

What had caught his eye? A brightly colored fish? No. It was something smaller, and much more intense. *Could it be...?* His heart thudded in his chest.

The cold water forgotten, he stood riveted, naked as a jay-bird, not wanting to lose the place where he'd seen the sparkle. The stallion had run right across this spot last night. Maybe his hooves had dredged up something that had been buried beneath the river bottom.

Dropping to his hands and knees, he scanned the area, his face just inches from the water. A moment passed and he heard Cassie call his name. He dared not look away for fear of losing the spot. Slowly, he searched the bottom, with its sand and pebbles and its...

Sam sucked in a huge draught of air.

He reached down and wrapped his fingers around something almost completely buried in the sand. Bringing it to the surface he blinked several times. It was a nugget and no mistake. Big, too. Approximately twice the size of his thumb!

Cassie called him again. He quickly stood. Her next move would be to look for him right in this spot.

What if he won the competition today? How long would it take Cassie and Arvid to pack up and go? That was the deal. One would stay and one would go. He'd been pondering this possibility for some days now, trying to figure out a way of keeping her here with him.

"There you are." Cassie said, coming around the bend in the path.

She spun around. "Sam!" She clapped her hands over her eyes.

Sam closed his palm over the nugget as it warmed to his touch. He couldn't help the smile that creased his face. Happiness burst within his chest. He felt like singing his news to the world. Instead he said, "Want to join me?"

When she didn't respond he laughed. "Guess that means no. Throw me that towel and I'll come out. Is breakfast ready?"

Without looking at him, Cassie tossed the towel over her head in his direction and he caught it, careful not to drop his prize. He fastened the thick piece of cloth around his middle and came out of the water. On shore Cassie waited for him to slip his shirt on, now that he'd dried pretty much by the breeze and early morning sunshine.

"Almost. That's why I was calling. Didn't you hear me?"

"Yep, I did. I was hurrying so you wouldn't catch me in my birthday suit, but I guess I was too slow."

Sam was having a hard time not jumping for joy as he sat, still draped in the towel and pulled his boots onto his naked feet. He'd done it! Secured his future and Cassie's too, if she'd quit being so darned stubborn and admit she loved him.

He picked up his pants and hitched his head. "Come on."

They walked up the path side by side. "Well, I got Uncle Arvid out to the bushes and into camp. He seems to be doing pretty good today. The bacon and biscuits are done, and I've packed us a lunch for later."

"Good. Good." He could hardly contain himself. Think of all the things he'd be able to buy for her and Josephine. It felt like the best Christmas day a person could ever dream of. "Did the coffee get done? I could sure use a cup."

"Yes. It did. Thank you for putting it on. It's wonderful to wake up to a nice hot pot of coffee—already brewed."

Clutching the gold in his left hand, which was the opposite side from Cassie, Sam ran his other through his still wet hair, and smiled down into her bright, doe-like eyes. Her face turned pink.

"What's the matter?" He couldn't help but tease her, he felt so good. He glanced at the towel hugging his middle and his legs sticking out of his worn, dilapidated boots, knowing the answer to his own question. His shirt hung loosely around his chest. "I'm sorry. Am I embarrassing you? I thought by now you'd be used to us cohabitating. Guess not, again."

They were almost back to camp and Arvid was watching them closely. He sat on the log, his eyes no bigger than slits as he tried to read what they were saying to each other.

"Sam, nothing is going on. We're not cohabitating. We're camping in close proximity. There's a difference, you know."

"There is?"

"You know there is. Now stop kidding me. Uncle Arvid is going to wonder what has gotten into you. I've never seen you smile like that before, myself."

"Let him wonder. Maybe it'll spur him on to get up and out of that tent and into the river to help you—where he belongs. My gosh, Cassie, you've done every ounce of work since we got here. He should be ashamed of himself."

"He's hurt!"

"Is he?"

Cassie stopped and took hold of his arm, forcing him to stop too. "Sam, he's an old man. And he fell hard. It's a wonder he wasn't hurt worse."

"If you want to keep telling yourself that, fine. But I say it's been plenty long enough that he should either be back up and working, or on his way to town in the back of some wagon. I think you just don't want to admit that I'm right and you're wrong."

She looked over to her uncle and back at Sam. "We're not going to talk about this right now."

He could tell that she had the same doubts that he did about Arvid. She was just too stubborn to admit it.

"Let's get breakfast so we can get going up river," she said sternly. "I have gold to find. It's not going to jump out of the river right into my hand."

Sam turned toward camp, hiding the smile he felt coming on as the nugget almost burned a hole in his palm. "You're right about that, Cassie. The sooner we get panning, the sooner we'll end this competition."

Chapter Forty-Eight

Sam worked by Cassie's side in the warm sun, dismantling the old shack, the rushing river just yards away. She turned the boards over, exposing the nails, so Sam could come along and yank them out, then put them in the saddle bag he had slung over his shoulder. As it grew warm, Cassie couldn't help but notice each time he paused and undid the next button on his shirt. Soon the garment was unbuttoned all the way and swung open loosely around his muscular body.

The half demolished shack listed treacherously to one side, a hazard to anyone standing close. It looked as if a sneeze from an ant would knock them over. With his hammer, Sam jerked the remaining nails from the gray, cracking wood with ease. She hauled them away from the building, stacking them in the grass.

Early on, Sam had insisted she wear a pair of gloves he'd taken from his saddlebag. Surprisingly they fit her perfectly. He'd said they were his, but since they were too small for him, she should keep them. It seemed highly unlikely to her that he'd waste his money on something so blatantly wrong for him in the first place. Still, after several wicked looking slivers jabbed painfully through the leather, she was grateful he'd had them for her to use.

When the sun was directly overhead, they broke for a noon meal. Cassie wiped the moisture from her face with her shirtsleeve as she fanned herself with her hat, and envied him the casual state of his dress.

"We're almost done," Sam said, as he chewed on a piece of venison jerky. He handed her a strip that looked as if it had come from a week-old carcass. "Can you make it?"

Cassie nodded, staring at the venison.

"Don't you turn your nose up at that. It's good meat. You'll be hungry later if you do."

"So much of the wood is rotten," she said, putting the meat strip into her mouth before she could examine it further. "Will you have enough for a sluice box?"

"Plenty. We actually have enough now. Soon as we're finished eating I'm going to use my lariat to tie the boards together and we'll drag them with my horse. It'll be slow going on the way back, but we can do it."

He peered at her, and waved a hand in front of her face. "Cassie? Are you listening?"

"I was thinking how to get Uncle Arvid down to the river for a bath. The weather is pleasant and after seeing you there today, I think it's just what he needs."

"If I weren't such a nice guy I'd take offense at that remark. Seeing me in the river made you think of your uncle!"

Cassie couldn't resist laughing at his twinkling eyes and teasing smile.

"Actually, that's a good idea," Sam continued. "It's rejuvenating. And after all this time he is getting rather...*strong*."

"Sam." Cassie responded, trying to keep the laughter from her voice, "there's no reason to be mean. You know what he's been through."

"In my opinion, he's a conniving trickster as well as an ol' coyote, and now he even smells like one, too."

"I like it better when we don't talk about my uncle." Cassie tried to be mad at Sam, to keep her thoughts about him in line, but he was in such a wonderful mood it was impossible. He'd been humming the whole time he was working—that was, when he wasn't making some sort of silly joke. Talkative on the way over and was now smiling at her like a goofy boy.

She held his gaze as she dropped down onto her elbow, closer to the newly sprouted green grass and looked at him in earnest. It felt good. Her blood heated pleasantly as it raced through her veins. Her gaze roamed over his half-exposed chest, and when she realized where she was looking she felt her face flush.

He laughed, a deep, rich sound that was impossible not to love. His eyes were glistening with happiness as he chewed on his lunch. "What're you staring at?"

She jerked her gaze away.

"You thinkin' about that kiss, too?"

"What has gotten into you today? She demanded, exasperated. "Tell me this instant. I've never seen you so—"

"Do I have to have a reason to be enjoying your company?" He swung his arm wide. "Look. All this wild, undisturbed land. It's beautiful and unspoiled. I'll bet nary a white man has even ever seen it."

Cassie took a bite of biscuit she'd unwrapped from a blue-checkered napkin. "Someone built that shack, Sam."

He shrugged. "Good point. But, you know what I mean."

"You're telling me this wonderful mood of yours is because of the countryside?"

"Yes! And we're almost halfway through our month and we're incredibly close in our findings. What do we have so far, about a half of a vial each? That's about forty dollars' worth. A good amount, but hardly a fortune."

"Maybe, but it proves there's color in the claim. You getting discouraged?"

Sam lay back in the grass with his fingers laced behind his head. She was sure he was exposing his chest to her on purpose. The curious set to his lips made her heart race and her mouth practically go dry. Turning his head, he looked at her again with that I-know-something-you-don't know expression that was so puzzling.

"Discouraged?" He winked. "Never. Pass an apple, please."

Sam cinched his lariat tightly around the stack of wood and went to Blu's side, looking over at Cassie. She gathered up the napkins and her canteen, preparing to leave. He'd been deciding just how to proceed with the nugget. If Cassie knew he'd discovered the good-sized chunk of gold, he risked losing her forever. She and her uncle would have to forfeit their dibs on the claim. She would leave with him—at least, he thought she would.

If that happened, his only true chance at happiness in this lifetime would be gone. He'd acknowledged to heaven, and to himself, that for him, it was Cassie Angel and no other. She was the one he lived for, the one who made his heart happy—even if she was stubborn as a mule.

On the other hand, if Cassie thought she found the nugget, her uncle wouldn't waste a moment claiming it, and would run him off and maybe even Cassie too. Cassie and Josephine would be left to Arvid's mercy, and Sam was the only one that seemed to know just how bad that could be.

She mounted up and sat facing him. "Ready?"

Sam made a quick decision. He'd give the nugget to Cassie, someway, somehow, if she wouldn't agree to marry him. He'd rather it be a wedding gift, but if not, he'd settle for it being a parting gift, unbeknownst to Arvid. That would give her plenty of funds to rely on for years. If that happened, he and Seth would find another way to buy their ranch. But that wasn't the way he saw this playing out. He was going to win her heart once and for all!

He nodded and swung onto Blu, wrapping the rope snugly around his saddle horn. He squeezed his legs and the mare walked forward until the rope was taut. She hesitated for a moment when she felt the drag, but dutifully went forward when Sam kept pressure with his calves.

The countryside was uneven and in some places quite overgrown. Cassie had to dismount and guide the boards through obstacles of rocks and ravines when they got stuck. She had absolutely refused to switch places with him, saying she'd rather do this than have the rope stretched across her leg. She'd worked up a sheen in her effort, and her cheeks were as red as the apple he'd eaten.

Sam stopped and removed his hat. He ran his sleeve across his brow to soak up the sweat. "You doing okay, Cassie? I didn't realize this would be quite this time-consuming and difficult. I can see you're plumb wore out. Let's take a break."

Cassie took the opportunity to get a drink from her canteen before remounting. "I'm fine. Just worried about Uncle Arvid. We've been gone a lot longer than I thought we would be. He'll be red hot by the time we get back."

"Well, if he is, it's not your fault." Sam glanced at her to see what effect his words were having on the worrywart. Her eyes were wide as she gaped at something behind him.

Chapter Forty-Nine

Twenty feet up the path, two men on horses blocked their way. Sam couldn't go for his Colt now without being blown to bits if they were so inclined.

"Howdy," he called out in a friendly voice.

They were rough and unkempt and Sam couldn't tell if they were outlaws or miners. He'd never forgive himself if anything happened to Cassie.

"Howdy," the older one returned with a nod of his head. They rode forward slowly. "We heard a commotion coming from this side of the draw and wanted to see what it was all about. What're you doing?"

Sam felt, more than saw, Cassie ride up to his left side and stop. As he prepared to answer the question, and without taking his eyes off the strangers, he slowly unwound the rope that tethered him to the boards at his saddle horn. He hoped Cassie had heeded his warning and had the Derringer in her pocket. "Collecting some old boards we need for our claim down river. Who're you?"

"Partners in the claim north of here. One section of river past this one. Just setting up camp."

"How many more claims are up your way?" Sam asked, more calmly than he felt.

"We're the last. Pretty desolate. Didn't think it would be quite so far out. I shoulda known."

"Well, we best get moving," Sam said, looking over at Cassie. "Ready, little brother?"

Cassie nodded.

Sam wondered if they were going to let him ride by. They weren't making any effort to move their horses.

"Let's go," Sam said, wrapping the rope back around his saddle horn and urging his horse forward.

"Hold up." The older man reached for his saddlebag and Sam drew his gun.

"Jack!" his younger companion called out sharply.

The older man eyed Sam. "What the hell?" he said angrily, holding a letter in his hand.

Sam took a moment to reply. "What's that?"

"A letter for Sam Ridgeway. I figured that must be you when you said yours is the next claim. The man at the claim office asked me to give it to you when I came out. I'm of good mind to put it right back in my saddlebag and tell you to go to the devil, you drawing on us like that."

Sam thought quickly. Only Clemen, the man who'd raised him and Seth, knew where he was. It had to be from him. He holstered his gun. "You understand as well as I do a man has to be prepared, especially out here. I apologize for drawing." The young one looked as mean as all get out. The older was harder to read, chewing on a stick he had hanging between his teeth.

"I don't know?" the older one, with the letter, drawled.

Fed up, Sam rode alongside the man and pulled the post from his fingers. "I thank you for delivering this. Come on, Cassidy."

Sam passed the men with a clatter of noise. Cassie followed, moving Meadowlark quickly ahead of Blu. The men turned their horses and sat watching until they were over the ridge.

"Who's it from, Sam?"

Sam had taken the beat-up letter, with its stains and crumpled corners, and put it in his pocket without opening it. He felt agitated. "A family friend."

"That's all you're going to tell me? After all we've been through? I can't believe it. And it's impolite."

"Until I read it that's all I know."

Cassie stepped her horse close to his and gazed into his face. He saw her concern and excitement, too. What could he tell her? Only that it was bad news. Something he didn't want to hear. Or think about. He could move on as many times as he could count on both hands but it seemed impossible to outrun the past. It caught him like a faithful dog, but unlike man's best friend, always ended up biting him spitefully.

All of Cassie's fears had been well founded. It was dark by the time they clattered slowly into camp, where Uncle Arvid was shouting irritably, as if they were ignoring him on purpose.

As they got closer, Cassie had wanted to ride ahead, get back faster, but Sam wouldn't let her. The letter had chased his good mood away, even though he hadn't taken the time to read it.

"Cassie, is that you, girl?"

Uncle Arvid's harsh tone sent a chill of warning up her spine. She dismounted and fumbled with her reins.

"I'll be right there, Uncle. I'm tying up Meadowlark ."

"You and Ridgeway been gone all day! What're you two scheming up? A plot to cut me out? Or are you getting all lovey dovey?"

Cassie looked from the cold fire to her uncle's tent. His ranting was grating on her nerves. *How dare you say such things! We've done everything in our power to make you comfortable, and still you…* Irritation gave way to fear as she got closer to the tent. "I'm here," she said through the flap. "What do you need?" Even from this side of the tarp she could smell whiskey mixed with the sharp scent of kerosene from his lamp.

"What do I need? Food! Get me some supper! My belly thinks my throat's been cut."

Cassie turned to go.

"And make it fast!"

"I'll have it as soon as I can, *Uncle.*"

"Did I hear a tone from you, girl? Did I! You ain't too big for me to—"

She whirled and ran straight into Sam, who gripped her arms to keep her from falling. "Slow down, Cassie. He'll live—that is, if I decide not to kill him myself. I have a small flame going and," he held up the bucket, "I'm on my way to the river."

Cassie had to look away. She blinked several times to rid her eyes of the tears filling them. "Thank you," she murmured past a walnut-sized lump in her throat.

He gave her a quick hug, then said softly, "Don't mention it."

She tried to smile at his teasing but his standing up for her meant everything at that moment.

Back at the fire, Cassie mixed and moved with speed. The oil was hot in minutes and she scooped batter to form three small hotcakes in the bottom of the skillet. Sam came back from the river and haphazardly tossed about a half cup of coffee grinds into the basket of the coffee pot and set it into the flames.

He sat back on his heels. "If you win the claim, are you staying out here with him?" He hitched his head toward Arvid's tent.

Cassie stared at the tiny bubbles popping up through the thin batter as the edges of the cakes turned a pretty brown. "I haven't decided. To be honest, I'm not sure what I want to do anymore. When it was just Josephine and me planning to come out, it seemed like a good idea even though now I realize that was an outlandish notion. Actually, it was the only option we had. Now, after all the hours I've spent in that cold river, I don't know. If Uncle wasn't hurt maybe he'd be a different person."

Sam was staring. "Maybe."

She lifted the corner of one hotcake with her spatula to check to see if it was done.

"And if you found a nugget, one that would support you and the start-up costs of your bakery, what would you do? Stay here to try to find more, or go back to civilization?"

"Sam, why all these questions? You know as well as I do that that's just a dream. One few miners ever realize. I'm not silly enough to think that's the way it's going to happen. Like you said, a fortune is built one flake at a time."

Chapter Fifty

Sam watched as Cassie flipped the cakes and patted them down several times.

"Just what if?" he persisted.

She looked up at him and had to smile. His tone was so earnest, his expression just as solemn. He was watching her and she knew he wouldn't drop the subject until she answered.

"If I found the means that would fund what Josephine and I needed to get started, I'd pack up and go tomorrow."

"And what about Arvid?"

"What about him? He's my uncle. The only family we have. If he wants to be a part of it, then that's how it'll be."

"You think that would be good for Josephine?" Sam asked. "Him bossing her around, cursing in front of her, drinking, and who knows what else?"

"Cassie!" Arvid bellowed at the top of his lungs. His temper hadn't abated in the least. "Get up here, girl!"

Cassie looked at Sam and tried to read what he was thinking. She was glad the dusky light hid her embarrassment. She took the spatula and flipped the three hotcakes onto a plate and set four leftover strips of bacon from their morning meal, which had been heating up by the fire, alongside.

Sam spooned more batter into the hot skillet. She couldn't miss the angry slant of his mouth and his clenched jaw.

When a string of obscenities from Arvid's tent filled the silence, Sam dropped the pan he was holding into the coals and bolted up, taking a step in Arvid's direction. "I think your uncle would like to take that bath *right now*! It'll cool him off considerably."

Cassie grasped his arm. "No, Sam. I'll take care of it. It's not your responsibility."

He shook her off and started for the tent. "It's just not right, Cassie. Don't know how you stand it. He'll learn to treat you with respect—one way or another."

She took a hold of the back of his belt with one hand, and balanced the plate in the other. She set her heels in the dirt. "Stop, Sam! He's my uncle!" *And I'm trapped, just like my mother had been. To a no good...* "That's the only thing that keeps me going. It's the only thing I can do."

Sam stopped. With force, he kicked a rock and watched it sail into the bushes. For a long moment he gazed at the spot where it landed. Finally, he turned to her and tipped her face up with a lightly placed finger under her chin. "You're right. Go on and I'll tend to our supper."

As hard as it was, Sam kept quiet about Arvid through their meal and poured himself the last of the coffee as Cassie straightened up. At the moment, the letter he'd gotten from their new neighbors was on his mind. He'd been pondering what it could be about. He lifted a lantern and started down to the river.

He settled himself on a rock and took the post from his pocket, carefully opening it. As he'd thought, it was from Clemen. After a few lines of pleasantries and news from home—couples who'd wed, babies that had been born and such—Clemen got to the heart of his message. Sam's father, Brewster Ridgeway, was being granted clemency for good behavior after sixteen years behind bars. He was coming home to Greenville in three months' time and wanted to reunite with his sons. Clemen said he hadn't responded to the letter yet, and he would wait until he'd heard from Sam.

Anger wrapped itself around Sam's heart and squeezed mightily. His sons? When had Brewster Ridgeway ever thought of Seth and him as his sons? That was almost laughable. The joke would be on him if he thought he could just waltz in and pick up a life, one he'd never even tried to have before, with them and be welcome.

The letter rested in Sam's lap, forgotten as he studied the river, unable to see the sprays as they went up and over the rocks in the darkness of night.

It was a pity his mother, who'd come from a good family in Boston, hadn't seen through Brewster's lies for what they were before she accepted his proposal. How different her life could have been. She knew nothing of her husband's real past and so Sam and Seth had grown up with no knowledge of grandparents, except for the two on her side. The Ridgeway family line was a mystery.

"Sam?"

He turned and found Cassie standing behind him. He hadn't heard her approach and wasn't sure he was ready for any company after the news he'd just gotten.

"What does it say?" Her eyes were dark and worried, searching his face. He looked away.

She persisted. "The letter. Who's it from?" There was a forced lightness to her voice. Airy.

"A friend."

She laughed softly. "Who?"

"Clemen." He knew the name would mean nothing to her and yet he offered no more.

"You sure know how to shut someone out," she said a little sadly. She scooted onto the rock next to him, much in the way he'd made her sit with him. She gave him a nudge with her shoulder. "Come on. You'll feel better if you share your burden."

What could it hurt? He'd been carrying it around so long on his own he was ready to pass it over. "Clemen is a man who took my brother and me in when our ma died. I was eight and Seth was five. He fed us and clothed us and sent us to school. He taught us to ride and instilled in us a love for horses. He owned the livery in town and did business accordingly. For all purposes, I think of him as our father even though he and my ma never married."

Cassie picked up his hand and laced her fingers through his. "So, what does this Clemen have to say that's put that worried look into your eyes?"

This was a bold move for Cassie and Sam was surprised. No doubt it gave him a jolt of pleasure but, more than that, it moved him that she saw that he was hurting deeply and wanted to make things better.

"My real father, the one I said I hadn't seen for a long time, is getting out of prison. His sentence was lightened for good behavior." Sam laughed. "He's sent a message to Clemen telling him he wants to see Seth and me." He looked down at his boots and shook his head. "I won't, though. To me he's dead."

Cassie was quiet for a long time. "Can I ask what he did?"

"Does it matter?" he answered gruffly.

This was harder than he'd thought it would be. Surely when Cassie heard that he was the son of an outlaw she'd think differently of him.

"Sam?"

"He was part of an outlaw gang," he offered more civilly.

"I see."

"You can't. Not really. Your family was what one is meant to be. Affectionate and supportive. Responsible. Josephine's told me several times how loving your parents were. I don't think it's possible you could understand how I'm feeling right now."

Cassie rolled a little pebble under her boot and looked away.

"We're supposed to forgive, as hard as it might be," she said quietly. "No matter what. Seventy times seven. We can't see what's in someone's heart. Things aren't always what they seem, Sam."

Wrapped in the darkness of night, everything seemed still except for the flowing river. "What's that supposed to mean?"

When she turned back to face him, there was a look in her eyes he'd never seen before. Despair. Pain. Heartbreak. She was close and if he'd wanted to he could lean in and kiss her. But he didn't. He needed to know what was behind that expression.

Her eyes searched his face as if she were deciding whether to say what was on the tip of her tongue. Then softly: "I didn't have a loving pa."

He was confused. "But, Josephine said…"

"I know what Josephine has told you because it's what I told her. I wanted to give her good memories, of a ma and pa who loved each other, and us. My mother was devoted to my father, but he was no better than my Uncle Arvid. In some ways, maybe even worse. It was my mother that kept us together. Only because she really loved him. And forgave him. But she never trusted him—she couldn't. She worked hard to provide for us when he didn't. Josephine was too young to remember how things were and I hope God will forgive me for lying to her. Actually, my pa was murdered by one of his companions after a night of drinking and gambling."

Chapter Fifty-One

Sam felt as if he'd been clubbed over the head. The reassuring picture in his mind's eye evaporated, replaced by one much more disturbing. He fought to control his anger. Another Arvid! As Cassie and Josephine's father! And now, Cassie was repeating that same nightmarish situation with her uncle. He was positive Arvid would stick around only as long as his nieces had something to offer. Food, shelter, money. The man had all the qualities of a cur, except loyalty. He'd mooch off them as long as he could, all the while being lazy and unproductive. The minute Cassie's resources were gone, Arvid would be, too.

Cassie looked away and took a deep breath.

"You should've told me, Cassie. I would've run Arvid off the moment he stepped foot into Grace's house. I wish I'd known."

"It doesn't make a difference. I'm called to forgive my uncle, the same as I forgave my father." *If I hadn't, I'd be eaten up with bitterness right now.* "I know it's hard to understand. But, I promise you, forgiveness will help you, Sam."

"Just like that? Arvid can do whatever he wants and it doesn't matter?"

Sam felt Cassie's nervousness. She let go of his hand and stood. "It matters. I don't approve of many of his actions, and I may not choose to associate with him at some point in my life, but I do forgive him."

Sam picked up a rock by his feet and flung it into the river as he struggled to understand her thought process. "I haven't forgiven the choices my father made throughout his sorry life. And I don't see it happening in the future. You're a bigger person than I am."

She smiled at him now. "I didn't tell you about me and Josephine to get you riled. I told you so you'd know that I can understand how you're feeling. Sam, what if your father has changed? What if after all these years he's come to know right from wrong? What if he's sorry for all the pain and hardship he's created?"

"Knowing him the way I do, it's more like he's fed up with being locked away and realizes the only way out is to act contrite."

"Maybe that's so, about your father, I mean, but, then, maybe it's not. People *do* change and it would be such a blessing if your father had, and wanted to make amends with you and Seth. Maybe he's become the father you always wished you had. If you don't talk with him how will you ever know?"

She was trying so hard to be helpful and Sam appreciated it. "It may be as you say, but if my ma had a nickel every time she thought the same thing, we'd all be rich right now." He stood as well. "A dog can't change his spots."

The days came and went faster than Cassie believed possible. Sam built the sluice box as promised, and they took turns every other day using it to wash away mounds of clay and dirt leaving behind soil that they would carefully scoop out and pan, all for the hope of a few flakes of gold. It was much easier and Cassie was grateful Sam had come up with the idea in the first place. The hours spent in the freezing river were dangerously long, sapping away her vigor and leaving her feeling like a rag doll at the end of the day.

Sam kept badgering her to take a day off, but she wouldn't hear of it. The competition would be over in a week and she was doing exceptionally well. After the sluice box had been built her production surprisingly doubled what Sam was pulling from the river, and if she kept going at this pace, the claim would belong to the Angels.

Her heart constricted painfully. It felt as if it were her and Sam's claim now. They were the ones working it day in and day out. But a deal was a deal. If she won, then Sam would have to pack up and go. Leave her life forever. Ride out as fast as he'd ridden in. That had been the arrangement from the beginning. Now, as the day approached where daydream would turn into reality, the dream took on a tarnished aura of sadness and doubt.

Cassie hefted a shovelful of dirt from the side of the riverbank and carried it through the frigid water to the sluice box, nestled securely between two big rocks. The terrain formed a natural funnel. Her arms shook from the weight of the earth and rock, as she hurried to dump it between the two gray boards. The splash drenched her from the knees down, but she was too tired even to think about the cold. With a deep sigh, she watched the water wash away the reddish-brown cloud with ease, leaving a clear window to the bottom of the box.

The sun was low in the west and cast a slice of warmth under the brim of her hat. Between the cold water and the heat of the sun, her body didn't know how to regulate.

She turned to find Sam watching her. "Sure is hot for this late in the day."

"I'll bet it's almost a hundred degrees," he replied slowly. He was sitting on a rock, taking a break. "Mighty hot for this early in the season." He hitched his head toward a tree on the bank. "Want to take a breather in the shade?"

She shook her head. "No. Actually, the sun feels good. Besides, it's almost quitting time. Uncle will want his dinner on time tonight. Sam, I'm getting really worried. Is he ever going to get better?"

"Why should he?"

She stiffened. This was a sticking point with Sam. It was his favorite topic of discussion.

"He's old." It was her usual response, but by now she was more than suspicious herself. Fed up with his demanding ways, too. Uncle Arvid enjoyed lazing away day and night, moaning mainly when she offered to help him take a little walk. It seemed unbelievable that he could languish for so long. She was gradually coming to believe he must be faking it. Forgiving him was one thing, but she'd not get stuck in her mother's rut. No! The next time he started his business, then, she'd let him know things were about to change.

Sam stood and walked over to the sluice box and looked inside. He took hold of one side and rocked gently, as if to check on its stability. "He's not *that* old, Cassie. Go on and say it. You're as suspicious as I am. Mule-headed is what you are."

She shot him a look. He smiled to punctuate the joke. "Would you mind grabbing my canteen for me?"

When Cassie turned her back and started up the river's edge, Sam took out a vial he'd kept hidden in his pocket and carefully poured out the contents into the box, giving Cassie nine or ten flakes of gold he'd found that morning. He'd been salting the dirt she panned for more than a week, keeping less than half of what he panned for his own cache. After much thought, he'd come up with an idea for outing Arvid as the skunk he was, but it would take a little help from Cassie and he wasn't sure yet she'd go along willingly. For the time being, he had to act concerned at the prospect of losing the claim.

She was back with his canteen. He uncapped it and took a long drink. "Thirsty?" he asked, holding it out to her.

She shook her head.

Sam held up his vial, the one with the "S" scratched into the tin lid. "Hmm, a little under three quarters full. Can I see yours?"

Her face clouded. "Sure, but it's on the shore with my things."

Sam went over and picked it up. He held both between his thumb and forefinger, side by side in the sunshine. He looked for a long time, until he was sure he had her undivided attention. "You're winning by quite a bit now. I need to step up the heat."

Sam didn't miss her furrowed brow, or how she chewed her bottom lip. He was almost tempted to expose the plan to her right then and there. Almost. Much of the scheme's success depended on Arvid, and his reaction to the news of Cassie's steady, growing lead. The old coot asked about it every single night. Sam needed him to believe in Cassie's lead, so that when he learned it had been usurped, and that Sam was going to win the rights to the claim, it would come as a most unpleasant shock.

It was a gamble—but one he hoped would pay off handsomely in the end. If it did, Cassie would know beyond question that he'd been telling her the truth about the claim from the beginning and that her uncle was a lying crook. For Cassie's sake he hated to have to do it, but not enough to hold back from exposing Arvid for the wretchedly deceitful person he was. Sam was convinced Cassie and Josephine would be much better off without Arvid Angel complicating their lives.

"There's still a week left, Sam. Anything could happen."

"That's so. But it would take a whole lot of color to make up the difference." He shook his head as if discouraged. "I'm pretty sure I won't be the winner."

"You're not giving up!" She planted her hands on her hips as she gazed at him. "Are you?"

"No. Not yet. I'm still holding out for a miracle." He gestured to the sluice box. "It's getting dark. You want me to help you with these last few pans before we quit? Of course, any gold I find will be yours."

She looked up to the campsite, her brows drawn down in worry. Sam's familiar anger at Arvid, and his desire to throttle the man, fueled his blood.

"You sure you don't mind?" she asked.

"Nope." Sam picked up the small cradle and scraped some of the dirt from the bottom onto Cassie's gold pan. He did the same with his own.

They crouched side-by-side in amicable silence.

Minutes crawled by.

"Here—look." Cassie pointed at five little gold flakes in the black dirt. "This was a good one."

Practiced now, she pushed the slivers onto the rim of the dark gray pan with her fingernail, away from the rest of the dirt. One by one, she pressed them onto her little finger and scraped them into her container.

Sam looked into the bottom of his pan. "Hey, here're two more."

She was just putting the cap onto her vial. "You take those, Sam."

"I couldn't. They came from your dirt."

"I don't care. I mean it. They're yours!"

Sam hid his smile. "Only if you're absolutely sure."

"Of course I'm sure. You panned them. And, you were the one who thought of the sluice box in the first place. That was such a smart idea."

She was shivering like a newborn calf in a snowstorm, a sight Sam saw all too often of late but would never get used to. She stuck her vial into her pocket and moved toward the bank.

For the second time that day, Sam fished out the two slivers of gold from the dark earth at the bottom of his gold pan, but this time he put them into his vial marked with an "S" in the cap. He looked at Cassie. It was time to play his hand, and let the cards fall where they may.

Chapter Fifty-Two

"It's clear, even to a blind man, that you're going to win this competition, Cassie," Sam said, tipping the brim of his hat up so he could see into her face clearly. "I'm resigned to the fact. Let me be the first one to congratulate you."

Her head jerked up. She was standing on a grassy knoll waiting for him, her gold pan in one hand and canteen in the other. "That's *not* a fact." Her hair was pulled back but wisps had escaped, and her pants were soaked up to her knees.

"Well, maybe if I kept mining and you stopped, but with the daily growth on both ends good sense tells me you're the legitimate victor." He trudged up the side of the riverbank and was at her side. "I have something I want to ask you."

First, Sam picked up the jacket he'd brought with him this morning and draped it over her small frame. He patted her shoulders firmly and rubbed his hands up and down her arms several times. She smiled her thanks and looked to him expectantly.

He collected his thoughts. This was his only chance to clear up this crazy misconception. "Is there any possibility you think your uncle might be lying about how he got the claim before he put it in your drawer in Broken Branch?"

She glanced away from his face, a sequence of emotions crossing her face. She hesitated.

"I thought as much," Sam said, relief bolstering his confidence. "You do have doubts about his story. In that case, I have something else I want to ask and it's going to sound like a crazy request. But, hear me out. And keep an open mind." He took a step toward camp. "Come on. We can talk while we walk."

Clearly, Cassie was hesitant. A wall of distrust sprouted right before his eyes and began to grow up around her. But, fortunately for him, she hadn't out-and-out insisted her uncle's story was fact. There was still a chance his idea might work. He had at least to try. "I want to switch vials with you."

Cassie stopped and stared, wide eyed. They were at the halfway point to camp. She took a deep breath. "Why?"

"I have something I want to prove to you, and this may be the only way. At least the only way I can think of. All we'll do is switch the lids so the vial with the most gold, yours, will have the S for Sam. I'll keep it and you'll keep mine. We'll tell Arvid that today I made a killing."

She was listening to him intently.

"We'll both know that the vial I'll be holding, the one with the most gold and the 'S' on it, really belongs to you. During the day, when we're panning, we'll switch back to our real containers so our gold won't get mixed up. As soon as the week is over and we're heading for the assessor's office in town, we'll change them back. I promise not a flake of your gold will be lost or taken. But the net result is your uncle will think I'm winning."

Cassie stuck her hand in her pocket and closed her hand around the vial that held her and Josephine's future. Right now there was enough gold inside to lease a small Main Street building somewhere, and have lots of money left over for supplies and all the baking utensils her heart desired. It wasn't a fortune, but plenty to get her business up and running. Another week of the same good fortune and she wouldn't have to worry about paying the bills, or feeding Josephine, for a good long time.

"Cassie, say something." His voice was laced with uncertainty.

Stalling, she looked up to camp. She didn't see her uncle anywhere. He hadn't made it out of his tent again today. She brought her attention back to Sam, standing in front of her with a worried expression knitting his brow. What in the world was he planning?

"Cassie?"

"Sam, I don't know what to say. I can't see any reason whatsoever to do this silly thing you're requesting." She felt her mother's warning deep in her heart. It screamed for her to give him a flat-out no! *He was the one who'd lied to her and Josephine for days. No. She couldn't do it. Regardless that he'd helped her pan and do all the chores.*

Warmth came up in her face and she was thankful Sam couldn't know what she was thinking about him.

He held out his hand to her. His eyes were dark, mysterious. "Trust me."

She looked down at his hand for a long moment, thinking. Her heart and her head were battling for her attention, demanding she listen. Her mind screamed out every warning her mother had ever told her, accentuating all the examples she'd given her. But, her heart was full of Sam: his smiles; his hurts; all the things he'd done here to help make her days easier, better; all the times he'd taken her side. He'd thought of her every inch of the way. He'd been her advocate more times than she could count. She thought of the kiss.

For one instant she closed out the world and shut her eyes. *What should I do?* She held her breath, hoping for a reply.

Trust in him as you trust in Me.

The voice. The one that had told her to open her eyes to the mountain lion and to hide from the outlaws. She looked up into Sam's face and reached for his hand.

"You can trust me, Cassie," he said, as his fingers closed over hers. "I'm not trying to cheat you."

"I know." They were the only two words she could muster. She stepped closer when he gave a gentle tug, and he wrapped her in his arms.

***

Something, something was going on between those two, Arvid thought as he peeked out from the confines of his tent. They were cooking up a plan down there on the trail and he'd give his first born and then all the rest, if he'd had any, to know what it was. The competition would be over and done within a week and he was glad. He didn't know how much longer he could stay cooped up in this stinkin' tent. Thank goodness Cassie was the scrapper he'd always thought she was. She was beating that stupid cowboy by a country mile. Who'd have ever thought it would be so easy when that busybody old man suggested this contest?

One more week. He could make it. Arvid patted his stomach, thinking how soft he'd gotten while lying around. The food offerings had been monotonous, with a few exceptions, but soon he'd be plenty rich to enjoy eating at any restaurant, in any town he wanted. After the trip to measure the gold at the assayer's office, and get the claim papers notarized in his name, he'd take a couple of days off to enjoy the comforts of town, and sample all the things he'd missed most. Then he and Cassie would head back out here to get down to some real work—knowing that every last flake of gold from this claim would forever be his.

He wiped his hand over the beard that had grown during the past three weeks. There was a possibility Cassie might decide she didn't want to come back out to the claim with him. If she'd had enough of the cold and mud she might try to run off. He'd have to come up with some way to threaten her with Josephine. At this point, leaving Josephine with that woman in Rosenthal had been a boon. Probably, after some time, she would want to keep her and raise her as her own. He'd let her think that. When Josephine was a few years older and capable of work, he'd make the trip out and collect her. Two more hands would just mean all the more gold pulled from this river.

Arvid snickered and laid back on his blankets. This was working out much better than he'd ever dreamed it could.

Sam could hardly wait to see Arvid's face tonight when he asked about the gold. Oh, it was going to be worth all the aggravation the old man had caused him over the past few months. He glanced up the path where Cassie was bringing Arvid slowly from his tent.

He hunkered down by the fire and poked the burning logs with a stick. It gave several loud pops and sparks floated into the air. He snapped the stick in two, adding it to the flames, and then stirred the venison soup that bubbled softly. He watched the little explosions with amusement, imagining each was a pop of surprise on Arvid's face. Satisfaction spread throughout his core. He stood when he heard them coming into the clearing.

"Arvid," he offered in greeting, a smug happiness spreading in his chest.

"Ridgeway."

Sam glanced at Cassie's steady expression as her uncle clung to her arm. Arvid dragged his right foot a little too noticeably for Sam not to sneer inwardly. The man was insufferable.

"This is hot, Cassie. Shall I dish it up?"

"Thank you, Sam. That'd be a help."

"Thank you, Sam," Arvid mimicked with a snicker. "You two are just so damn refined. Blue-blooded thoroughbreds, the both of you. Ha!" His face twisted in scorn.

Sam reined in his temper with effort as he ladled up the soup. Cassie pretended not to hear the slur, but Sam knew differently. He handed her a steaming bowl and she passed it on to her uncle, whom she'd helped to sit on the log. Then she accepted one for herself. Dishing a third, Sam took a seat.

They ate in silence for a good ten minutes. Sam was the first to finish. He placed his bowl in the wash bucket and went over to where they kept the jug of apple brandy.

"Almost gone," he said, pouring a little into his cup. "Want some?" Cassie shook her head. Arvid didn't respond.

Sam took a little sip and settled onto the far end of the log. Taking his gold vial from his pocket, he held it up to look at it.

Arvid belched and wiped his mouth with his sleeve. "How bad she beating you now?"

Sam took a sip, savoring the tangy richness, and held it in his mouth. His eyes met Cassie's as he swallowed. "The tide has turned," he said evenly. "I'm in the lead."

The older man sat up so fast Sam knew he couldn't be in any pain. Arvid practically spit the coffee from his mouth when he said, "What're you talking about? Yesterday, and every other day before, Cassie has beaten the pants off you. Now all of a sudden you're winnin'?" Cassie's eyes narrowed as she looked at her uncle, intently.

Sam took another sip, making Arvid wait on his answer. This was too good to rush. "Found a little pocket today. Had so much color my eyes were sparkling." Sam laughed with gusto, putting on the best show he could. It did feel good after all this time.

"Lemme see," Arvid demanded.

"You have your vial handy, Cassie?" Sam asked.

"I'll get it." Cassie headed toward her tent. Sam hoped she could play along enough not to give his plan away. Most times, she wore her heart on her sleeve, her emotions transparent and readable as those of a puppy. A lie like this might be hard for her to pull off.

Cassie returned and handed her gold to her uncle. He looked at it closely, and then held his hand out to Sam. " Now lemme see yours, Ridgeway."

Sam shook his head. "I don't think I want to let you hold my findings. It just might slip from your fingers. You know how fragile this glass can be."

He walked over and held the vial in his hand up next to the one Arvid thought was Cassie's so the man could see the quarter-inch difference in the golden flakes. Sam almost laughed as Arvid's eyes bugged out hideously from his face.

Chapter Fifty-Three

"What were you doing today, girl! Napping? I knew you had a lazy bone."

Sam stepped closer to Arvid, his hand closing tightly around the vial he held in his hand to form a white-knuckled fist. "Don't talk that way to Cassie. She's working harder than five grown men put together. If you want to win this claim you better get your own backside up, and get to work."

Arvid slumped down quickly. "You know I can't!"

"Well, maybe not. But that only means in a week this place will be mine." He glanced again at Cassie, winking surreptitiously as he turned his attention to the fire. He held up his vial and gazed at it lovingly in the amber glow of the flames.

After a moment, he stole a glance at Arvid. The man's jaw clenched and Sam knew he wanted to give Cassie a tongue lashing to end all others, but was too afraid of what Sam would do to him if he did. The older man's face was pasty white and he looked about to lose his supper.

"There's still time. You two may beat me yet," Sam said, wanting to keep the conversation going. Rubbing salt into the wound was a temptation just too appealing. "It's possible, you know. Maybe there's another pocket where Cassie is working."

"I'm feeling weak again, Cassie girl. Help me back to my tent?" Arvid gazed at the ground where his bare feet made prints in the dirt. A little sigh escaped his lips.

Sam stepped over and grasped his arm. "She's just on her way to switch out the horses for the night, Arvid. But, I'll be happy to give you a hand."

Three days came and went without incident. Sam's odd request pertaining to the gold—and her uncle—weighed heavy on Cassie. Her uncle still hadn't gotten up to help her, and that was what Sam was trying to show her, she was sure. He remained sullenly in his tent, now not even coming out for meals. She would be glad when this whole affair was over and she was back with Josephine. Gold claim or not, she had enough money now, even if it was split with her uncle, to start her and Josephine's bakery and become self-sufficient.

She glanced over at Sam, who was using the sluice box. His expression indicated he was deep in thought. He dropped handfuls of dirt into the water from the bucket he'd hauled over from the bank. They'd been working for hours and he was getting quite a bit of color.

Cassie shivered. Moments before, the sun had disappeared behind one of the black clouds filling the sky, making the water feel even colder today than normal. Sam looked up, his face handsome in its contemplation.

"Will it rain?" she called to him, pressing two gold flakes onto her little finger and slipping them into her vial.

He looked over and smiled. He was about five feet away and the rushing of the river made it hard to hear. "It may.

Those clouds look pretty heavy, and the wind is picking up. Storms in the high county aren't unusual this time of year. Spring showers bring May flowers, or some such thing I heard said."

She smiled back. What was Sam up to—really? What if her uncle didn't ever get up and help her? What if he were crippled for life? That must be what Sam was trying to prove to her. They'd have to make a travois and drag him all the way back to town. That would be hard on her uncle, no doubt.

A gigantic raindrop plopped down on the side of Cassie's gold pan and splashed her face as she was peering into the black dirt at the bottom. Two more hit her hat and she looked up from her work. Sam stepped toward her.

He touched her elbow. "I think we should quit for the day. It's almost evening, anyway." His pant legs were rolled to mid-calf and his boots were soaked. "It'll give us a little extra time for supper. If it starts to rain in earnest we won't have a fire tonight. I don't know about you but I want something hot to fill my belly. Sound good?"

She turned with him and started for camp. "Yes. I'm about frozen through today. Some days I can't seem to shake the cold."

"I know what you mean," Sam agreed. "I'll be glad to get back to civilization. As monetarily successful as this month has been, there's a huge price to pay for it. I wouldn't want to be a miner forever."

Cassie tucked her gold pan under her arm and cupped her chapped red hands together. She put them to her mouth and blew into them in an attempt to gain back some feeling into her fingertips. When she could, she wore the gloves Sam had given her, but the thick leather made it impossible to fish out the gold flakes that had been abundant these last two weeks.

"Oh, I agree with you wholeheartedly," she answered. "For me, mining is just a means to an end. A fast end," she added with a laugh. "I can't wait to get away from here." She stopped and looked back to the river. "I won't miss it, that's for sure. Not like I miss—"

"Josephine," Sam said quickly, finishing her sentence. "I know what you mean." He was looking wistfully across the meadow to the rolling hills and beyond, to the mountains. "That little scrapper has been on my mind a lot lately too. It'll be good to get back to Rosenthal."

"Is that what you'll do if Uncle Arvid and I win the claim? Go back to Rosenthal and become sheriff?" As they walked through the ankle-high grass, Cassie noticed the horses looked a little skittish. Instead of grazing they were restive, and her mare nickered when she saw Cassie approaching. Her mane lifted in the strong breeze.

"I'll stop in Rosenthal and visit."

Cassie was surprised, and saddened. It sounded as if Sam was planning to move on.

"Just visit?"

"I didn't mention to you that in the letter Clemen sent was also a note about my brother Seth. He's found some good horse property northwest of here. On the coast. Above the booming city they call San Francisco. I'm sure you've heard of it."

She nodded, then grasped at her hat to keep the wind from whisking it off her head.

"It's a couple weeks' ride and the government is almost giving the land away to get people to settle the area. Seth wants me to meet him there. His money combined with mine should be enough to make our ranch a reality." He glanced down into her face. "It's exciting."

Cassie almost missed a step. *He's really going*! For some reason it just seemed he'd always be by her side. Protecting her. Making her laugh. Reaching inside her soul with but a glance.

"I'm happy for you, Sam," she said, managing to keep her emotions in check. But her heart thudded in her chest. And she knew then, if she hadn't before, that when Sam rode away it would be the worst moment of her life.

***

Sam reached up and poked the top of his tent, causing water to gush down both sides. He was restless. Unable to sleep. The rain had started a few hours ago and had been coming down steadily ever since. The trees swayed with the wind, moaning like a hurt animal.

A flash of light lit the sky. Though the lightning was miles away, the cramped interior of his tent brightened for an instant. A mighty *boom* followed a few moments later. So far the storm wasn't too threatening. It wasn't the storm itself, but the amount of rainfall that had Sam worried. He listened carefully.

Another flash of light, and then a reverberating crack rent the air again and rumbled on for several long seconds. Cassie must be awake. If not from the rain, surely from that last round of thunder and lightning. Sam wondered if she was frightened.

Water seeped in on two sides now and it wouldn't be long until everything inside his tent would be soaked. As Sam attempted to dam off a small rivulet, trying to come straight through his bedding, something made him pause. He stopped. Held his breath.

The storm had changed. The sky literally opened up and the downpour was deafening. His tent buckled and he reached up to catch it. His heart lurched as he heard Arvid's horse, tethered to the tree for the night, scream with fright. A mystifying rumbling, low and long, rolled menacingly down from the heart of the mountains.

Chapter Fifty-Four

Sam yanked on his boots and ran out into the rain unprotected. He crossed the few yards to Cassie's tent and pulled back the flap, diving inside. She was sitting with her blankets wrapped around her shoulders, her eyes wide with fear.

"Get your boots!" Sam yelled over the pounding deluge.

"What?"

Sam grabbed her boots and pushed them at her. Cassie struggled to pull them on as Sam yanked her up and dragged her from the tent. He reached inside and snatched up her blanket, stuffing it into her arms. They ran through camp hand in hand. He stopped only once to grab his saddle by the horn and to holler toward Arvid's tent. "Arvid! Wake up! Get your boots on. I'll be back to help you."

"We can't leave him!" Cassie screamed.

Sam didn't waste time arguing. "I'll come back for him. As soon as you're safe."

"Safe?"

"Flash flood coming."

She pulled on his arm and dug her heels into the mud, slipping and sliding. He'd anticipated her refusal to leave her

327

uncle behind and tightened his grip on her wrist, dragging her into a run. "Don't fight me, Cassie! It won't be long before this whole hillside will be swept clean."

Sam scrambled up the side of the mountain, pulling Cassie with one arm and balancing his saddle on his shoulder with the other. He forged ahead even though he heard Cassie gasp for air. He stumbled in the mud as rain, bushes, and brambles battered his face and body.

A good ways up, Sam stopped and looked around. They were halfway up the hill, and probably safe, but Sam felt reluctant to leave.

"Please, go get Uncle Arvid!" Cassie cried.

"I will." But still he hesitated, uncertain this terrain was out of harm's way. Then, suddenly, he picked Cassie up and boosted her onto the lowest branch of a nearby tree. "Climb up!"

Another rumble sounded through the canyon. "Sam, the horses?"

"Climb up!"

He blinked though the rain, looking up into her eyes. "Now would be a good time for a prayer." He wedged his saddle between two strong branches over his head. Turning, he heard Cassie gasp. "What is it?" he asked.

"My Bible. It's in my pack."

"I'll try to get it."

"No, don't! It's too dangerous. It's not worth risking your life."

Sam tossed Cassie's blanket up to her, then turned and began sliding back down the mud-slicked trail.

It took several minutes for Sam to get back into camp. The river was much higher and rising quickly. A torrent of water could come from the mountains at any second, moving so fast he wouldn't have a chance to get away.

He ran to Arvid's tent and jerked back the flap. Stunned, he stared for a moment at the empty bedroll. Cupping his hands around his mouth, Sam shouted several times through the storm, calling at the top of his lungs. He stopped and listened, but the violent river was all he could hear.

With the back of his hand, Sam swiped the water from his face and ran back to where Cassie's tent was now collapsed and floating in mud. He yanked up the canvas and tossed it to the side. In the dark he felt around for her pack.

A deep rumble sounded from up-river. The earth shook. In the next split second he saw the pack, snatched it up and bolted to free Arvid's horse from the tree. The chestnut gelding was gone. Shocked, he stood staring. How did the animal get free? Instantly, realization dawned on him. Arvid had ridden out.

A terrifying sound, louder than anything Cassie had ever heard in her life, came from the river. She whimpered and hugged the tree, not knowing what to expect. Rain beat down on her head. As if called up from the devil himself, a flash of lightning lit the area, illuminating a wall of water so horrifying she cried out as if in pain. The water crashed down and exploded over the river's bank, sweeping up into the horses' meadow. Small trees were ripped up and tossed around. The sight was so horrific she wanted to close her eyes but couldn't, so desperate was she to catch some sign of Sam.

"Oh, God," she gasped. She'd climbed a few feet higher, clutching the trunk. Prickly patches of bark pressed into her cheek painfully and she felt she might fall at any moment. Tears burned as they mixed with rain. "Save Sam! Please, God, save him!"

Cassie wanted to let go of the tree trunk and touch the spot above her heart, even though she knew full well her angel cameo wasn't there. She longed to, but didn't dare. It was in the small leather pouch with her vial of gold, in the pack with her Bible, all now washed away.

Quickly, and with a stab of guilt, she remembered her uncle was somewhere down in the watery ruin. "And save Uncle Arvid, too—please."

The water was still rising, inching closer and closer to the tree she was perched in. "Sam is okay. He's safe somewhere, waiting out the worst of it. Just like me. Just like me." A sob escaped from her throat.

Sunrise was just around the corner. Cassie glanced down to the water's edge. A bear careened down-river with the rushing water, his giant paws slapping the muddy torrent in an effort to stay afloat. It reached out and grasped a sapling that, up to this point, had withstood the force of the beating water. He pulled himself out and lumbered up onto solid ground. It opened its massive jaws and let loose an angry spine-chilling roar. Taking a step uphill, it approached the tree Cassie was precariously perched in. She held her breath and prayed.

She cocked her head and peered down carefully, not wanting to draw attention to herself. The animal must have been wounded for it gimped along slowly, dragging a hind leg. What if it smelled Sam's saddle hanging in the lower branches? Would it then spot her and climb up for a meal? Right when it was about to pass her tree by, it flopped down on its side.

What else could possibly happen? If Sam was in the water he was already miles away. Her heart constricted painfully at the thought. *Oh, Sam...Sam*. Time passed. Her arms hurt from the harshness of the bark digging into her soft skin. Every muscle in her body screamed for release.

But the ache of losing Sam overwhelmed all other senses. What was physical pain, compared to that? What was even the gold and all it represented worth to her now? Her Bible, or cameo, *or anything*—what did it matter—without him? She'd learned a hard lesson with so much time to reflect. It was Sam that God had sent to her. *He was her gold mine. He was her treasure. He was her life*! How foolish she'd been to throw all that away.

The sky to the east now bore the tiniest hint of pink amidst the dark clouds and Cassie willed daybreak to hurry up and come. Was the bear still there? She couldn't tell since she'd stopped staring at him and lost the spot in the dark underbrush where he slept. She'd just have to wait a little longer for sunrise.

Chapter Fifty-Five

A cold wind whipped Sam's drenched hair and pieced his clothes, driving a chill to his core. The rain had stopped, but still he shivered as he stared, mesmerized, at the swirling water beneath his feet. How long would it take for the muddy sludge to recede enough for him to escape the tree he was perched in? It was the same oak Arvid's horse had been tied to when the wave had come crashing toward him hours before. The thick branch really wouldn't be such a bad oasis but for the angry raccoon that had scrambled up before him and now resided above his head. Every few minutes the good-sized animal snarled viciously in his direction.

Sam's only thought was for Cassie. Had she stayed put in the tree where he'd left her, safely out of harm's way? And what of Arvid? What had happened to him? Whatever the outcome in his case, all Sam could think was *good riddance.*

Sunrise revealed the extent of the devastation. The meadow where the horses had grazed was submerged in murky water, and the camp below, gone. Much of the smaller vegetation, washed away. The sky, still dark after the storm, was a foreboding mass of gray clouds.

His insides rumbled. It wasn't far from his perch to the bank, but the water between the tree and where he wanted to go had been a ravine before the flood and still flowed swiftly, too dangerous to try to swim out. It would be some time until he'd be able to get to dry ground. In the meantime, his empty stomach felt as if it were on fire.

A menacing growl came from above Sam's head, followed by frantic scratching. Sam glanced up. The raccoon glowered as he ran his claws down the tree trunk, shredding the tender bark into thin curls. Sam laughed at the animal's obvious ploy to intimidate. "Oh, pipe down. I don't like this anymore than you do."

Cassie's saddle pack was draped over a branch at his side. Was there any food stashed inside? He scooted closer to take a look.

To his disappointment, he found no food, but her Bible caught his curiosity. Taking the book from the pack he opened it, and something—a dried flower, perhaps?—fell into the water and floated away.

Too late. He hoped it wasn't an important keepsake. He flipped slowly through the pages.

A noise below drew Sam's attention and he glanced down to see Cassie on the shore. He watched in dismay as her small form collapsed on the sodden ground after she determined there was nothing left of their camp. He could barely hear her over the noisy water, but she was weeping like a small child who'd lost absolutely everything she held dear. The sight of her tore at him and his urgent need to comfort her was like a shock to the core of his being.

"Cassie!" he shouted, stuffing the book back into the pack. "Up here! I saved your Bible. It's safe."

Her head snapped up. She looked around wildly. "Sam? Sam! Where are you?"

"Here. Up here. In the tree."

She scrambled to her feet, looking around quickly. Her clothes were ripped and encrusted with mud, her hair a windblown mess. A bedraggled field mouse came to mind. He smiled. Still, she was alive—and the most beautiful sight he'd ever seen.

He pulled himself carefully to his feet, finding his balance on the branch. He held her saddle pack out in front of him so she could see. "Look!" No sooner had the word left his mouth than there was a tremendous cracking sound.

With horror, Cassie watched Sam fall fifteen feet and splash into the water. Collecting her wits, she ran along the shore, trying to keep pace with him as he bobbed and churned down the swollen river. Another moment and she'd lose sight. "There's a big rock coming," she screamed. "Try to grab it!"

There was no telling if he'd heard her. Every few feet his head would disappear and then a moment later he'd resurface. Cassie jumped a log in her path, but then tripped and fell face down with a grunt of pain. Steeling herself, she struggled to her feet. "Sam!" she screamed between cupped hands. "Sam! Grab! The! Rock! Here it comes! Three, two, one...now!"

He did. She held her breath, fearful he wouldn't have the strength to hang on. Jumping up, she ran along the bank, her gaze darting between the stony terrain under her feet and Sam clinging to the rock. It seemed like an eternity until she reached him, scrabbling over rocks and debris. Dropping to her knees, she took hold of his arm, and with the strength of an agitated mama bear, heaved back onto her heels, dragging him out of the water. She collapsed onto him, and hugged him tightly. After a moment she pulled back and helped him to roll over.

"That was cold!" Incredibly, he laughed and tried to pull her close.

"Sam, you made it! You're alive! I was sure you were dead, washed away in that horrible flash flood. Then I saw you were safe, and I felt such relief. And then this!"

"Well, honey, I guess every dog has his day. I was blame lucky." His brows, sparkling with droplets, arched disarmingly as he gazed into her eyes. If she'd thought him handsome before, this morning he was entrancing. She couldn't look away.

"And in any event, you're not getting rid of me that easily—ever," he added so softly she had to watch his lips to know what he was saying.

His smile faded and he cupped her cold face in his hands. "Cassie. I…"

Sam pulled her toward him until their lips melded. Tingles blossomed everywhere. His mouth took hers hungrily, and she couldn't stop a little sound from escaping her throat. Heat pooled in her belly, despite the chill of the wind and wet clothes. Something powerful passed between them.

"How did you survive?" she whispered against his lips, not willing yet to end the pleasure of the moment. She still couldn't believe he was here, alive, kissing her and making her thoughts race in all manner of exciting, shiver-inducing directions. "When the water crashed through the valley there was so much. How did you do it?"

He pushed up on his elbow. "You saw me. I had only an instant to climb that tree, but up I went. I've been perched up there ever since."

A moment passed and then Sam startled. "Hey." He quickly looked around. "Your pack. With your Bible. Where is it?"

He looked panicked, and Cassie was alarmed. *Had he hit his head when he fell? Or during his wild ride in the water? It was possible.* The only thing she'd seen was Sam, falling like a rock into the mucky river. "Did you have it?"

He turned around to look upriver to the tree, which still held the scolding raccoon. Cassie's saddlebag was looped over the bottom branch a few feet above the water, slowly swinging back and forth.

***

The sight of Cassie huddled by the roaring flames of a campfire pleased Sam. The wood crackled aggressively, sending sparks dancing into the noontime sky. Without matches, it had taken him well over an hour to produce even the smallest spark, but now that it was warming his frozen hands, and Cassie's face all but glowed in its light, the payoff was worth every annoying moment.

He'd made a cursory look for the horses when he'd gone to retrieve his saddle, but had come up empty handed. But they couldn't be that far away. He'd whistled several times knowing that if Blu was within hearing distance, she'd make her way back to him. With luck, Meadowlark and Split Ear would follow. Arvid's horse was still a mystery. *Or maybe not,* he thought darkly.

It would be a few more hours before the water receded enough to fetch Cassie's saddlebag. It taunted them from the limb, swinging with every gust of wind, causing Cassie to bite her lip and furrow her brow. She'd been overjoyed he'd actually saved it from the flood, and he'd received many heartfelt kisses for that bit of work. He wished there was a way he could tell her all over again—and collect the same reward.

Unfortunately, the raccoon had spotted the new, interesting object. Whenever he started toward it, Cassie would let go a barrage of rocks, scaring him back up into the higher branches. She'd only now abandoned the pile of ammunition she'd gathered together on the bank to take a moment to warm herself by the fire. He could see she was brooding over something.

"We'll get it, Cassie," Sam assured her.

"I know we will." She exhaled in a long sigh. "I just can't believe Uncle Arvid is dead. Drowned. What a horrible way to die. I'll admit I was pretty fed up with his actions and the things he said, and did, but I never wished for anything like this. I feel awful when I think about the tongue lashing I was planning to give him the next time he was nasty. I was going to tell him that when this month was over I never wanted to see him again, and that he wasn't welcome in my or Josephine's life any longer. In other words, dead to us." She looked at her feet. "And now he is."

Sam tried to keep his suspicions to himself, but when a single tear slipped down Cassie's cheek, he'd had enough. When would that man be out of her life and stop hurting her? "I wouldn't be so quick to think he's dead."

Her head came up and she looked at him, her eyes unreadable. "What are you saying?"

337

He kicked at a dirt clod. He could be wrong. He certainly didn't want to spoil this change between the two of them. And talking about her uncle was the surest way of getting them into a fight. "Nothin'."

"Sam! Tell me."

There was nothing for it. "After I found Arvid's tent empty, I ran to where his horse was tied to set it free. But both he *and* the horse were gone. I think he jumped on his back and rode off."

He could see Cassie wasn't happy with his accusation. Her expression hardened and her eyes narrowed. "When are you going to admit that Uncle Arvid was hurt? That he didn't get up to help me when he thought you were winning the claim—because he couldn't." Her chin tilted stiffly. "He died waiting for you to return."

"He wasn't in his tent," Sam responded, more calmly than he felt.

"Well, maybe he crawled off into the bushes in an effort to get away from the water."

"You'd rather believe he drowned?"

She huffed and looked away. "I'll not speak ill of the dead."

"I checked his horse last night before going to bed, to make sure he was tied good and tight with the oncoming storm. I assure you, that animal didn't get untied on his own." Sam stared at her rigid back. "You're just angry because you don't want to face the truth."

He could reason with her from here to eternity and it wasn't going to do any good. For some reason she was determined to believe Arvid and not him. Something inside was stopping her. Made her turn a blind eye to all the man's shenanigans. Maybe it was because her mother had done the same with her father for all those years when Cassie was a little girl, trying to keep her family together.

Well, he couldn't figure it out, and he was tired of trying. He'd have to accept Cassie the way she was, because he wasn't going to change her. She'd not see the light. Clemen called that a blind trust. Certainly not a good thing in this case. Or, maybe she didn't really believe what she said, not really, not in her gut—maybe it was more a case of *wanting* to. Whatever she craved, Arvid wasn't going to give it to her, that was for sure. And yet nothing he said seemed to make a difference. A niggle of foreboding crept down Sam's spine as he watched her climb to her feet and go to the river's edge and shut him out. This was something she'd have to figure out on her own.

Chapter Fifty-Six

By evening the water around the tree was only ankle deep, and according to Sam, safe enough to get her saddle-pack. Cassie sloshed out, holding onto Sam's hand, and they both took the bag from the limb, carefully making sure it didn't fall into the murky mess. Cassie couldn't conceal her joy, and laughed happily.

Everything would be all right now. By a miracle, Sam had saved her mother's Bible, and she was grateful. The raccoon, perched in the higher branches, snarled several times but didn't move. Cassie thought he looked hungry and felt a little sorry for him because she knew exactly what he was going through. How she wished they had the two white bags of supplies. Heck, she'd settle for a sourball.

Back on shore, she ran over to the fire and dropped to her knees. Sam followed. She unbuckled the keeps and cautiously pulled the old book out and held it to her chest. She was too happy for words. She closed her eyes and sent up a prayer of thanks.

When she opened them, Sam was watching her.

"Thank you for saving this." Her throat was so tight she could barely get the words out.

His mouth tipped up at the corners, into an expression she'd come to know so well. "Don't mention it," he said softly, settling down next to her.

The longing in his face was evident and she reached over and stroked his whisker-covered cheek. His eyes softened. She scooted closer and snuggled under his arm. It was then she remembered the other important belongings inside. "Oh."

"What is it?"

Cassie handed the Bible to Sam so it wouldn't get dirty and reached for her pack. She opened the other side and brought out a small pouch tied with a narrow strip of leather.

She smiled into Sam's face. "My angel cameo," she said. She untied the knot and produced the pin. She handed it to Sam. "And…" She felt around. Hesitated. Felt again. It was as if she'd been punched in the stomach. The pouch was empty.

"What?" Sam asked in alarm.

"My vial of gold. It's gone!" She stared at her saddlebag as she fought to control her swirling emotions. Her mind raced back to the night before. As always, she'd placed the vial inside, next to her cameo, and made sure the leather strip was firmly tied with two distinct knots. The same routine she completed every evening after supper.

She looked up at Sam with disbelief clouding her eyes. "The pouch," she said slowly, as she searched his face. "It wasn't double knotted just now when I went to open it. I didn't notice at first, but now…"

Cassie stared at the things in her hands, barely able to keep the bile from rising in her throat. *How could I have been so blind*? Every time Sam had implicated her uncle, she'd foolishly defended Arvid. She'd known his temperament before, the trouble he'd caused her family, yet still she'd closed her eyes to it. Even after all Sam had done for her, and his shielding of her, she'd resisted his reasoning at every turn. In a flash of inspiration everything became clear causing her heart to lurch painfully. She'd wanted, no, *needed* affection so desperately, a deep seated love of the type that is all-encompassing and completely unconditional. She wanted to belong. Wanted Arvid to be her family. So much so that she'd closed her eyes to the truth about him. Worse, she'd closed her heart to the genuine love, the honest love that sat next to her right now. The love whose expression was one of utter devastation.

Sam ached inside. Cassie didn't have to verbalize what she was thinking. Her wounded, disbelieving expression said it all. She thought he'd stolen her vial! Taken it when he went back for her uncle.

How could she! A blast of anger ripped through him, making his jaw clench so tightly it felt as if his teeth would crack. It was difficult for him to accept, especially after all they'd been through this last month, hell—these last few hours.

"Go ahead and say it! You think I took it!" He flung her belongings onto her leather pouch, and stood, striding down to the water's edge. It was impossible to mask his anger any longer. What did it matter anyway?

She bolted to her feet and ran to catch up. "What are you saying? You're putting words into my mouth."

"You're so sure your uncle can't walk. Surely you don't think he pranced into your tent and filched your gold. No! You think I did!"

"I *don't* think that!"

"That's horse pucky, and you know it!" He looked away, trying to rein in his temper. *Just like good ol' Pa! Always thinking the worst of me!*

"Sam, calm down so I can explain—"

"Well, Cassie Angel—guess what?" he shouted, pointing a finger in her face. "If I did that then I'd only be stealing my own gold. It's my vial that's missing, not yours. If you cared to think about it." Before she could stop him, he strode back to his saddle and produced the other vial, then stomped back to her side. "*This* is yours!" he said, shoving it into her hands.

Cassie jerked back and the vial fell onto a rock, bursting into a hundred pieces. The fragments quickly swirled away in the murky water.

Cassie stared. A month's worth of toil, but more, her and Josephine's future, gone in an instant. When she looked up into Sam's face it was dark, a thundercloud rolling within.

"I don't think you took the vial, Sam. You'd never do anything like that. As much as it pains me to admit it, I will. Arvid was everything you'd said. Believing that he could actually do all those awful things, fake being hurt and all, and to me, his niece…it was just too painful. And it gets even better—he stole from me and left me to die."

Actually, losing the gold didn't mean a thing. Coming to see Uncle Arvid for who he really was, meant nothing to her either. Only Sam mattered. Losing him now would break her heart —forever. He was the only thing she cared about. She had to make him listen. He was so quiet she couldn't imagine what he was thinking.

"Did you hear what I said?" she asked softly. "I believe you're honest and good. I don't care a whit about the gold. I only care about you." She tried to touch his cheek, but he pulled away. "I've come to realize that our lives are only what we make them. Nothing more." She didn't dare push him too hard. She'd never seen him like this. Still, she couldn't stop from adding, "I love you."

Sam turned and gazed over the water, and the tree with the raccoon who was watching them. She laid her hand on his back, aching to ease his pain. "What is it? There's something more."

"I," he began in a gruff voice, still looking away, "I never thought I could love anyone, not after how my father treated us. But then you came along in your baggy clothes and a chip on your shoulder as wide as a barn door." Slowly he turned back to her, but his arms remained hanging loosely at his side. "You reminded me of myself. Struggling to make sense of each day, make it matter, and mean something. You touched me and my beliefs changed."

"Sam," she whispered, moved deeply by his words, his admission of love. She inched closer. Ragged sorrow clouded his eyes.

"There is just something in you, Cassie, that won't let you feel my love. No matter what I do, you can't see it. You won't believe it." He reached forward and swept a lock of her hair behind her ear.

His words wounded as she recalled the countless things, large and small, he'd done for her. His generosity, his thoughtfulness. "Let me make it up to you." Her eyes stung with tears. "I want to try." She ran her hands up his chest and looped them around his neck. She loved the feel of his body melding with hers. "I *can't* live without you, Sam." She went up on tiptoe and pressed her lips to his. "I can't."

At first he didn't respond and fear gripped Cassie's heart. Had she pushed him too far? Would he ever forgive her? "I love you," she said again softly against his mouth. She could see something was holding him back. "God help me, I do."

Suddenly, as if something inside had burst free, Sam wrapped her forcefully into his arms. She felt his strength, his anger, his love as her knees buckled and they dropped together to the sand. He took her face between his hands and looked deeply into her eyes. "I hope you mean that."

It was said so softly Cassie wasn't sure if it was Sam or the wind playing tricks on her.

"I do. And as long as we're together there isn't anything that can hurt you ever again. I'll make sure of it. It doesn't matter about gold or money or…or anything."

Grasping her face in his hands, he kissed her, and all thoughts flew from Cassie's mind. "I love you," Sam whispered. "I'll always love you."

Only Sam remained. His mouth moving over hers. Branding her as his own. He was her world. Her whole universe boiled down to him and their new life together. Her fervor matched his on the lonely, windswept shore.

Several minutes passed before she felt him loosen his hold and lean back so she could see into his face. His smile gladdened her heart.

"I have something I'd like to show you," he said. "That is, if you're not *too* angry with me about breaking your vial. And losing all your gold."

"Sam, I meant what I said. You're all I'll ever want or need. Nothing can ever change that, not ever! Not even a-a—" She tried to think of something that would show him how serious she was—"a gigantic gold nugget."

There it was again, that knowing expression she'd come to adore.

"That's good to hear," he said, kissing the tip of her nose. "Now close your eyes and open your hand."

***

It took a week of hard travel to reach Rosenthal. The town looked the same to Sam, but he knew he was no longer the man that had ridden out of here a month before. Several people recognized them, waving and following their horses toward Grace's house.

Cassie slipped out of her saddle and hurried toward the door. "Wait for me," Sam called as he tied their horses to the hitching post.

She was nearly frantic with excitement. "Hurry!"

Josephine must have been watching out the window because the door flew open with a bang and she rushed down the steps with Buddy hot on her heels, barking his own excitement. She flung herself into Cassie's arms. "Sissy, you're home! You're finally here!"

Her hair, now long enough to swish around a little, looked pretty. She wore a soft blue dress with a white crocheted collar. Snippets of white tights underneath could be seen as the two girls jumped about in a sisterly embrace so close Sam couldn't tell where one began and the other left off.

"Said I'd be back in a month, didn't I?" Cassie's voice was thick with emotion as she spread kisses across her sister's forehead. She pulled back a little so she could see into Josephine's face. "I couldn't break my promise, could I?"

Exceptionally wise for her years, Josephine shook her head slowly. "No, you'd *never* do that. I'm so glad. I love you."

"And I love you."

Sam had to blink unmanly tears from his eyes before they slipped free, but he succeeded. He grinned, glad for his part in making this reunion come to pass.

Grace appeared with a wooden spoon in one hand and a smudge of flour over her forehead. "I came to see what was going on," she said. "Hush now, Buddy!" Her smile was broad as she looked the three of them over. Didn't take her but half a second to spot the little band on Cassie's finger. "Well, I'll be. You two went and tied the knot. Again."

"Yes," Sam said. "We stopped in Hangtown on our way here, where we registered the claim in both our names." *And took the nugget to the assayer's office.* He smiled at the memory of Cassie when she learned its worth was a little over a thousand dollars. Plenty to start their ranch with money left to boot. "After that, we went and found a preacher."

"Actually, you didn't have to. My father totally forgot to file the necessary papers after you'd left, and you've been married all along. Congratulations!"

Cassie set Josephine back and embraced Grace. "Thank you for taking such good care of Josephine. You were right about the river not being a place for a little girl. It was extremely dangerous." Her glance to Sam said *flashflood*, but only briefly. Sam marveled as her eyes warmed and she smiled just that certain way, conveying without a single sound how much she loved him. It was special. A look reserved only for him.

"It's me who should be thanking you," Grace replied. "Josephine was a real pleasure to have, and this month has been one of the happiest I've ever known. That is, up until Arvid showed up looking to take her away."

"What?" Cassie blanched. She hurried to Sam's side and wrapped her arms around his middle, something he was getting mighty used to. "Uncle Arvid was *here*?"

Grace handed Josephine the batter-covered wooden spoon and wiped her hands on her apron. "Sweetie, would you run this into the kitchen for me, please?" Josephine hesitated for a moment, her eyes narrowing. Then, she nodded and obediently walked away.

"Yes. He showed up about five nights ago riding bareback and looked like he'd been through a twister. Jonathan saw him coming into town alone and felt there might be trouble. He took Josephine over to a neighbor's house where Arvid wouldn't find her. Your uncle was *very* angry, as you can imagine. He knew we were keeping her from him. I hope we did the right thing."

"We're indebted to you," Sam assured her. "Thank God for your fast thinking." He could feel Cassie shaking at the thought of her little sister with Arvid.

The other town-folk were now crowding around. Jonathan and Annabelle arrived hand in hand. The news had spread. "Come on inside everyone," Grace called. "We'll see how things ended up at the claim."

Cassie laid her head against Sam's chest and he looked down to see her eyes were closed. He couldn't wait to see Seth and introduce his new family to his brother. How fast life could change. How wonderfully fulfilling it could be. He kissed the top of her head.

"Come on, sweetheart," he said at last. "We don't want to keep our friends waiting."

Epilogue

Mendocino, California. Eleven months later.

Josephine's shriek brought Cassie from her upstairs room just in time to see the younger girl bolt through the door and send Ashes scampering outside for cover. The cat had journeyed with them from Broken Branch to Rosenthal and on to their new home in Mendocino, riding the whole way in Josephine's saddlebag. She was also present at the auction where Sam, Cassie and Seth had purchased over seven hundred acres of prime property.

The two brothers went right to work constructing a ranch house, followed by a barn and fencing. When that was done, they painstakingly renovated a small building on Main Street, less than a ten-minute buggy ride from home, where Cassie and Josephine—when the youngster wasn't in school or studying—could spend hour after hour baking their little hearts out. Angels' Sweets was a huge success from the first day it opened. Now Cassie had an employee watching over it for a couple of months.

"What's all this noise?" Cassie called from the second-story landing.

"Come quick! Meadowlark is foaling. Sam wants you to see it." Josephine was back out the door, running toward the barn.

Cassie placed the needlework she'd been stitching on her dresser and hurried down the stairs as best she could given her cumbersome size. As she approached the entryway, she glanced briefly at the still unopened letter on the mahogany sideboard. It was from Brewster Ridgeway. Sam and Seth had been corresponding with their father, and she felt it was only a matter of time before Sam would allow the senior Ridgeway a visit. At least Sam had a relative to forgive—she'd seen or heard nothing from Uncle Arvid. Not that she'd be too quick about warming up to him. He owed her an apology—a big one.

When she arrived at the barn, the brothers were in Meadowlark's stall, quietly watching so as not to make the mare nervous.

Sam smiled his greeting and Seth nodded. Her brother-in-law was closer to her own age than Sam's, but his resemblance to Sam was striking. On arrival he'd been shocked to find Sam married, but he had taken an obvious, instant shine to her and Josephine. Cassie now wondered what their lives had been like without his mischievous humor and handsome face.

"How is she?" Cassie asked quietly.

"Doing fine," Sam responded. "Thought you'd like to see the birth of Triple R's first foal." His brows arched knowingly. "I'll never be able to thank that stallion enough for his efforts."

When he smiled at her, like he was doing now, an overwhelming joy filled her soul. So much so she had to look away, knowing he was thinking about the baby she carried and the love that had created it. As hard as she tried, she couldn't dredge up what it felt like when she'd been suspicious of him. All that was dear to her he held safely in his hands. And that was just as she wanted it.

"You were right," she answered, swiftly switching her thoughts from her fine-looking husband to her laboring mare.

Seth laughed. "My gosh, Cass. When are you going to get over all that blushing? I've never seen anything quite like it."

A lopsided grin crept up Sam's face. "As far as I'm concerned, she can blush to her heart's content."

"I guess you're right, big brother," Seth agreed. "As long as she keeps bringing me more of those wonderful 'Aingel' doughnuts,"—he drew her name out for comic effect—"and cookies." He closed his eyes and smacked his lips, pretending to swoon.

Blu, stabled in the stall across the breezeway, snuffled, drawing everyone's attention. Cassie's eyes went wide. "And how is your mare doing today? Will there be two foals born?"

"Her bag's dropped and is waxing. I believe it won't be long for her, either. Maybe two, three days," Sam answered, glancing into the rafters at the dozen gray kittens playing there. Dust and straw filtered down onto them all and he shook his head in defeat. Ashes, free of her six kittens, rubbed affectionately back and forth on Josephine as the girl knelt in the straw. Josephine inched forward slowly and touched Meadowlark's neck, stroking her gently. "Poor girl."

Sam's gaze snagged Cassie's. The love she saw made her heart swell with emotion. She couldn't believe how God had blessed her with Sam, and his brother, and this wonderful life she found herself in. Every day was an adventure, and soon there would be another little person to add to their happiness.

"Look," Josephine whispered, barely containing her excitement. She was shaking. "It's coming."

About the Author

Caroline Fyffe grew up in the little town of El Dorado, CA, the youngest of five girls and whose main interest was the family's horses. An equine photographer for over twenty years now, she has worked throughout the United States and Germany. Long days in the arenas present plenty of opportunity to dream up all sorts of stories. Her love of horses and the Old West is the inspiration behind her books. Her debut book, *WHERE THE WIND BLOWS,* was the recipient of the prestigious Romance Writers of America's Golden Heart Award and also the Wisconsin RWA's Write Touch Readers' Award. Married for many years, Caroline's most cherished achievements are her two grown sons.

Other works: *MONTANA DAWN,* Book One of the McCutcheon Family Series; *TEXAS TWILIGHT*, Book Two of the McCutcheon Family Series; and *WHERE THE WIND BLOWS*.

Visit Caroline at www.carolinefyffe.com
See her photographs at www.carolinefyffephoto.com
Write to her at caroline@carolinefyffe.com.
She loves hearing from readers!

CPSIA information can be obtained at www.ICGtesting.com
Printed in the USA
LVOW041534191012

303632LV00001B/70/P

9 781475 051414